RED INK

RED INK

JULIE MAYHEW

CANDLEWICK PRESS

Copyright © 2015 by Julie Mayhew

First U.S. edition 2016

Library of Congress Catalog Card Number 2014957107
ISBN 978-0-7636-7731-2

15 16 17 18 19 20 BVG 10 9 8 7 6 5 4 3 2 1

Printed in Berryville, VA, U.S.A.

This book was typeset in Berling and Cochin.

Candlewick Press
99 Dover Street
Somerville, Massachusetts 02144

visit us at www.candlewick.com

For Will and Ollie

History repeats itself. Historians repeat each other.
—Philip Guedalla, 1920
(repeating Dr. Max Beerbohm, repeating Quintilian)

This is the recipe.

Take five pounds of hulled whole wheat. Hold it in your arms. Feel that it weighs nothing compared to the load that lies heavy on your heart. Wash the wheat; let your tears join in. Strike a match, strike up faith, light the gas. Watch the wheat bubble and boil. See steam rising like hope. Take the pot from the heat and pour the wheat through a sieve. Lay the grain on a sheet overnight to dry. Rest your head on your own sheets. Dream of a flower dying, shedding its seeds, allowing another flower to grow.

In the morning, on the day of remembrance, put the wheat in a bowl with walnuts, almonds, and parsley. Add a message of devotion, a wish for the future, your gratitude to God. Sprinkle in cinnamon, not guilt. Throw in sesame seeds; throw away your fear. Turn out your mixture and create a mound—a monument to love. Brown some flour and sift. Add a layer of sugar. Press flat. Finally, crush the skin of a pomegranate with the remains of your fury, and spread the seeds with love, in the shape of a cross.

Maria did not dream of a flower dying. The night before her mother's funeral, she did not sleep at all. She pressed one of Mama's cardigans close to her face, letting it transport her back to a farm where cistus shrubs turn the air bittersweet. She listened to Melon's snuffling breaths, envying the way her daughter remained untouched by grief. She thought of the day ahead, the day she would return her mother to the earth. She was not ready to let her go.

Auntie Eleni had outlined the ceremony and recommended a plot. She had also pressed into Maria's hands the pamphlet containing the recipe for the traditional *kollyva*—the boiled wheat.

"But I can't cook," said Maria, scanning the recipe. "I can't do it."

"You will find it within yourself," Eleni insisted.

And so she had.

Part One

17 DAYS SINCE

"You okay in there?"

I locked myself in the bathroom two hours ago.

"Yeah." One syllable is all he can have; otherwise he'll think we're friends.

"You're very quiet."

"I'm fine." Two syllables. He should think himself lucky.

My name is Melon Fouraki. Let's get that out of the way, straight off. Some kids get their parents' jewelry or record collections as hand-me-downs. Mum gave me this name. It is one of her memories—she was brought up on a melon farm in Crete. I'd rather she'd given me her old CDs. She also gave me Paul. Living with him is like wearing clothes made of sandpaper. Every move I make, I'm on edge. He watches so much, it hurts.

The bathroom is the only place to get away. I can hear him fidgeting on the hall landing outside, pretending not to be there. I can hear him creaking the floorboards. He's listening through the door for the sound of a fifteen-year-old trying to slit her wrists. I am not going to slit my wrists. Paul is a social worker, so he thinks everyone my age runs away from their foster home, sleeps on the streets, turns to crime, gets taken back into care, and then tries to kill themselves. He can't get his head around the fact that I am well balanced. They worked with each other, Paul and my mum, only they ended up shagging. He would say they were partners. "Partners." Idiot. He thinks they were proper boyfriend and girlfriend, but he's deluding himself. Mum only hooked up with him because she thought it would freak out the rest of Social Services if the Greek woman and the black man got it on. It's not as if they were living together or anything. Now Paul has moved in to look after me. How ironic. How tragic.

My mum is dead. Seventeen days ago it happened. Paul thinks I need sympathy and care and time and asking every five minutes how I am. I don't. Just because your mum is dead, that doesn't define you or anything. I am my own person.

Paul is still outside the door. I can't concentrate on writing in my book with him there.

"You'll turn into a prune if you stay in much longer." He is trying to sound casual and funny, as if me being locked in the bathroom is the most hilarious thing in the world and not a total crisis. He is picturing me collapsed in a bath of pink water, a razor on the edge of the tub, my eyes rolled back in their sockets. I'm not even in the bath. I just ran the water so Paul would hear and not question what I'm doing.

"Yes. All right," I yell back. Three syllables. Dammit.

I double-check the bathroom lock, make sure I fastened it, just in case Paul wigs out and decides to burst in on some kind of rescue mission. Mum fitted that hook-and-eye lock. That's why it's wonky and why the screws haven't

4

been pushed in all the way. If you lean on the door, it opens up a crack, like our front door with the chain on. If Mum was ever outside the bathroom wanting to know what I was doing, she would shoulder the door and stick her nose through the gap. Paul won't do this, not unless he gets a real panic on. As far as he's concerned, I'm naked in here, and he's a middle-aged social worker who's dead cautious about doing anything that might seem suspicious.

I was at Chick's house when the police came knocking. Chick's real name is Kathleen, but everyone calls her Chick because she's little and scrawny and kind of sweet at the same time. No one calls her Kathleen to her face, except for grown-ups. Kathleen's a geek's name. Mum was always moaning that I spent far too much time at Chick's. She never liked Chick's mum, Mrs. Lacey. She thought she acted all superior just because she has a part-time job making up the names for wall paint. You know, Pistachio Dream, Cerise Sunset, Arsehole Brown, that kind of thing. Mum said it was a pointless job, but I thought it was kind of cool to be paid to do something so, well, pointless. Anyway, I was at Chick's house when the police came looking for me, and I wonder whether Mum subconsciously did it on purpose, chose to get knocked over that evening just so she could prove her case about me spending too much time around Mrs. Lacey. That's the sort of thing she would do.

Once when we were in Crete visiting Granbabas, one August when it was so hot you couldn't breathe without cracking a full-on sweat, she made me sit with her in the ATM lobby of a bank in Hania, just because it had amazing

5

air-conditioning. We looked like such losers, sitting in those beach chairs we'd brought with us, the kind that make your knees touch your chin when you sit down. The locals came and went, swiping into the lobby with their ATM cards, getting their money, giving us weird looks, wondering if we were the bank manager's crazy relatives keeping an eye on things for him. Mum sat with her legs stretched out, her head tipped back, like she was sunbathing indoors. She kept sighing these big, long God-it's-so-hot sighs even though it got quite chilly in there after about half an hour. I would have given anything for a pushy bank clerk to have moved us on, but it was Sunday. No staff. We stayed there for three hours. Mum fell asleep, though because she'd kept her sunglasses on, I never noticed her eyes were shut.

Paul still won't shift from the door. "Well, I wouldn't mind a bath later, so . . ."

"So?"

"So, don't use up all the hot water, please, Melon."

He's still there, waiting. I get up from the floor, kneel over the bath, and swish my arm in the water. I hope the noise will prove that I'm still breathing and all my main arteries are intact. I listen for Paul's feet on the landing. There is a creak or two, a pause. He's thinking about saying something else; I can feel it. Nothing. Then the *crunch, crunch, crunch* of the loose boards under the stair carpet. He's gone. At last. I sit on the mat with my back up against the bath. The side of the bath is carpeted. Old mauve shag pile. The bathroom set is green, and there is a lime-scale stain from the bath taps down to the plughole, like tea running down the side of a mug. Mrs. Lacey's bathroom is beige with a sandstone mosaic.

6

Now that Paul has gone, I can write things down. That's why I'm in here. I don't want Paul to see what I am doing. He will think that it's a "positive step." He will think it shows I'm "coming to terms with everything." He will think I am close to embracing him in a big old do-gooding hug. Basically, he wants me to cry. I do not want to cry. I don't need to cry. "It hasn't hit you yet," he'll say. And I'll make some joke like, "No, maybe not, but it's definitely hit Mum, though, hasn't it?" Ha-ha-ha-ha. And he'll make a face and look like he is trying not to blub. This is mean of me, I know, but I just want to be left alone. If Paul can't understand that, he'll have to face the consequences. If only Mum had waited one more year, I'd have been sixteen and allowed to look after myself.

I can hear the scrape of a saucepan bottom against the stove burner coming from the kitchen downstairs. Paul is a noisy cook. A show-off. He has been cooking all evening, in between his panic attacks outside the bathroom door. He is always cooking for me. He thinks he's filling the gap left by Mum, but she never used to cook much. Frozen stuff, pasta sauces, lots of things on toast, that's what I'm used to. Tonight it is homemade soup. I don't want to have these meals with Paul. He tricks me into them. He'll ask, all casual, "Do you like soup?" (or risotto or bolognese or whatever), and I can hardly say no; otherwise, I'll never get to eat that particular food in front of him again. So I go, "Yes," and he goes, "Good, because that's what we're having for dinner tonight," and that's it. I'm stuck with it.

"Ten minutes until dinner, Melon." He always gives me these countdowns. We did this book in English a while back about what the world would be like after a nuclear war, so I've given some thought to what I might do if we got a real ten-minute warning. I wouldn't eat soup.

I push my sleeve up and put my arm underwater to pull out the bath plug. The water has gone cold. I ran hot water so that the boiler would make the right chugging noises for a proper bath. I am excellent at pretending. I even put in some of Mum's bubble bath to make the right smell. It reminded me of her getting ready to go out somewhere. There was this one time, she went to the Social Services Christmas Ball with Paul (which did not sound like the biggest night of fun on earth), and we had a massive argument just before she left the house. We didn't speak for a week. Or rather, I didn't speak to Mum for a week. She was useless at holding grudges. I am an expert.

I rake a wet hand through my hair to make it look like I've been in the bath. I can't get used to my hair being short. I grab for the ponytail at the back sometimes and forget that it's gone. I admit the haircut might have been a mistake. The fuss it caused was great, but the haircut itself sucks. The front section gets frizzy if I sit in a steamy room, and I get this fluffy halo around my face. Mind you, that used to happen even when my hair was long. Nothing stops it. Chick got her hair permed once—she actually chose to have curly hair—which I thought was total madness. I have big Greek curls. I have a big nose, big thighs, a big backside, and big boobs. The boobs are an especially great thing to have when your name is Melon. Mum always said she was the real Greek but I was the one with the "Greek woman's body." This is a polite way of

8

saying I'm a bit fat. I'm not fat—I know that really. I'm not like Freya Nightingale, who believes she's an elephant and always goes to the bathroom to puke after lunch. I just take up more room in this world. Mum was skinny all over, except in the right places. Real boobs that looked fake. She was a dinky person who looked like she would fit in your pocket. I look like I would split the seams.

I might look Greek, but I don't feel it. It's a costume I can't take off. Mum took me to Crete every year, but the threads that joined me to that place have been snipped, or they were never there in the first place. Mum tried to fix her threads loads of times, but I don't think she succeeded. The family didn't forgive her, not really. She never got that into her head. Now there's hardly any family left to visit. It's because of the curse. All the Fourakis family dies young.

My dad still lives there, though—Mum said. I've never actually met the man. She never delivered a living, breathing dad to me. I have a name; that's all. According to The Story, his name is Christos Drakakis. I say it to myself sometimes, test it out. *My dad is Christos Drakakis, and my name is Melon Drakaki. How do you do?* Except I hope I wouldn't have been called Melon if Christos had stuck around. He would have stopped Mum from being so stupid, and I would have been given a proper name with a saint's day, just like every other good Greek girl. I would have been named Sophia or Alexandra, something normal like that.

"Five minutes, Melon."

There are five minutes until the nuclear holocaust: What do I do? Find the epicenter and run toward it. I don't want

9

to survive with all the destruction and deformity and radiation sickness.

The stink of soup hits me when I step out of the bathroom. Cooking smells have a set path through this house—up the stairs, a swirl in one corner of the landing, and then on to collect in my bedroom. It must be the way the drafts work in this place. Mum's room never gets rid of that woody vanilla smell.

I go downstairs, stepping around Kojak, who has taken to sleeping in the middle of the staircase. He hasn't been the same since Mum died; he's gone mute. Before, he would be meowing around my ankles and following me into the kitchen. Now he stays put—a big gray ball with one eye on the front door, as if he's expecting Mum to walk in any minute.

I stop on the stairs and lift him up into a hug, but he freaks out. He bends his spine backward and twists out of my grip. He can't scamper upstairs fast enough. His claws pop and splutter against the stair carpet. He doesn't want attention from me. He goes to Mum's room.

Kojak's really old now. Maybe the heartache of it all will finish him off.

In the kitchen, Paul is listening to Jazz FM and wearing Mum's apron with the big purple flowers. Paul likes elevator music and doesn't seem to care about looking like a girl.

"Sweet potato and pea," he says, turning from the stove to look me up and down. He's checking for wrist cuts or signs of an overdose, no doubt. "Sit down."

He has set two places at the kitchen table, opposite each other. I sit down at one of the four chairs that doesn't have a place set. I don't want to eat with Paul *and* have to look at his face. Paul comes over with a full bowl of soup. He doesn't react to my choice of seat, just slides a place mat over to me and sets down the bowl. The smell is strong, spicy. He has put a dollop of something white on top that looks like bird poo. Paul ladles himself a bowl, adds the bird poo, and then comes to sit down. There is a basket of bread with dead-fly olives running through the middle.

"Nice?" he asks. Paul is always fishing for compliments.

"Not tried yet."

I reach for the bread, start tearing strips off and putting them in my mouth one by one, chewing thoughtfully, trying to delay the tasting of the soup. He'll have to wait for the next ice age before I tell him he's a great cook.

"You know, Melon, you don't have to lock yourself in the bathroom."

I look down at the steam rising off my soup, watch the edges of the bird poo spread.

"You can have your own space."

I reach for more bread, tear off a crust.

"What were you doing in there, anyway?"

"Mind your own business."

He shuts up, starts shoveling soup into his mouth, three big mouthfuls straight after one another, like he hasn't eaten all week. Only after the third mouthful does he go, "Ooh, hot." Idiot.

I put my spoon into the soup. I can't really put it off any longer. I can feel him watching me while I blow on it, then slurp. My skin aches from all the watching I get. He waits for a comment. I continue spooning. He nods, smiles.

11

He has taken my continued eating as a compliment, which it is not. I'm so angry I could tip the steaming lot all over his head. But I'm also bloody hungry.

"How was the session on Tuesday? You still haven't told me how it went."

This is the fifth time he has asked me this. I am counting.

"Was it helpful?"

"S'okay."

"Did you talk about the argument?"

This is a new one.

"What argument?" The lingering smell of the bath bubbles kicks me back to the night of the Christmas Ball again, the argument we had that night.

"Did you talk about the argument you had with your mum?"

"Which one?" I keep eating to prove I don't care what he knows.

"The one just before she died."

Hot soup clags up my throat. I turn cold.

"I just thought that it may be troubling you and that it would help to talk to someone about it."

"How do you know about that?" I say. I don't look at him. I keep my voice level so he understands that it's definitely not an issue.

"We used to talk, you know," he says. "Your mum and me."

15 DAYS SINCE

I don't talk about the argument at the session. Why would I? That's not what the session is about.

I was expecting an old man, gray, in a suit. Leather furniture. A desk. A couch for me to lie on. I get none of this. I get Amanda. Everything about her is nice. Which is unfair because I really want to hate her. I get a plastic chair in an upstairs room with white walls and a sandy-colored carpet. I suppose it's all meant to be calming. I just want to scream.

Amanda sits on the only other piece of furniture in the room, another plastic chair, smooths down the sides of her hair (a pointless thing to do; she is as frizzy as me), then switches on her very best sympathetic voice.

"Hello . . . Melon."

There is a pause between the greeting and the name. I am used to that pause. Amanda pulls her face into an exclamation mark and double-checks her notes.

"I think Social Services has misspelled . . ."

"No, it's Melon."

"Oh." She hides behind her folder.

"My mum named me Melon."

There. I cross my arms as an end to it.

Mum.

Amanda stiffens at the word, like an actor who's been given the wrong line and is forced to jump ahead in the script. I stare at her, working my chewing gum, realizing this is what it feels like to be cocky.

"Melon. Gosh! How lovely!"

My chewing gum squeaks on my teeth.

"I'm Amanda." She thrusts her name badge at me and holds it there, on the end of its lanyard, waiting for me to say something. What can I say about her "Amanda-ness"?

I nod.

"And I've got here as your surname, Fu . . . Fu . . ."

"Fouraki."

"Is that . . . ?"

"Greek? Yes."

"How lovely!"

I wince.

"So!"

Amanda draws in a big, meaningful breath to begin, then stops. Her faces changes, as if she's just remembered something awful. Has she left the iron on back at home, the gas burner blazing? No. It's tissues. She's forgotten tissues. She gets up and grabs a box from the windowsill. Then there's a horrible moment where she can't decide where to put them because there's no table and it seems a bit weird to put them on the floor. After faffing around for a bit, she decides to plonk the box on my lap. I want to die. If I don't sob like a baby now, I'll be in for it. So I do this little laugh.

Amanda cocks her head at me, switches the concerned face back on.

"So, how are you feeling today?"

"All right."

"Your social worker explained why you've come to see me?"

"Poppy, yeah."

"Poppy?"

"I mean, Barbara."

"You called her Poppy."

"That's what she calls herself. Barbara Popplewell. Poppy for short."

Amanda looks all sorts of confused. "Oh, I see. Lovely." But she's thinking it's unprofessional, Barbara using another name—I can tell.

"Because it's been"—Amanda goes back to her notes— "just over two weeks now." She doesn't add a "since" and finish the sentence. Am I supposed to do it for her, like some twisted version of *Family Feud? We asked 100 people the question, "It's been just over two weeks since what?" Our survey says the most popular answer iiiiis . . . "Your mother got whacked by a bus and was turned into asphalt."* Round of applause. The set of matching suitcases is yours.

"Yeah," I say. "Fifteen days. Not that I'm counting or anything."

Amanda tilts her head again, sends me a silent *poor you.* I ignore it, look out the window behind her. In the distance, two school teams are playing soccer in fluttering bibs. Small cries and a faint whistle come through the glass.

"So what feelings have come up for you since then?"

The correct answer here I presume is sad, lost, suicidal, fetch me a noose. Something along those lines. *Our survey says the most popular emotion in the wake of your mother's death iiiiis . . .*

"I'm a bit pissed off."

"Mmm, mmm." Amanda is nodding like crazy. In TV dramas when the counselor does this, the other person finds they can't help but keep on talking. Before they know it, they've confessed everything. I don't want to spill my guts, not here in this old house that was probably, long ago, someone's stately home. It seems wrong that a building like this is where the sad and the mad hang out. I am in the wrong place.

"Mmm, mmm." Amanda is still a nodding dog.

What feelings are coming up for you? I can't think of anything to say. Should I literally do what the question asks, stick two fingers down my throat and vomit up the strange, dark monster that has made its home inside of me? We could interrogate this creature instead.

Amanda keeps at it. "And what do you think is making you feel, as you say, 'pissed off'?"

You, I want to say, and Paul and Chick and Mrs. Lacey and everyone else who can't get over the fact that my mum is dead and it's no big deal. I don't say this. I raise my eyebrows.

"Sorry, that was a . . . I mean, obviously we know what's making you 'pissed off.' Obviously we both know that." Amanda drops behind her hair to think up some new questions. "I mean, I just want you to explain a bit more about why it's that particular feeling for you. Let's look at where these feelings are coming from within you. How are they making you behave?"

I go back to watching the school soccer game.

When I was thirteen, our whole class had individual sessions with a community school nurse in the medical room at the back of the sports center. Everyone lined up alongside the building and waited their turn for what our teachers were calling a "Year Nine Health Check." We'd all expected some routine head-lice examination, but rumors came down the line as each person came out. We were going to have to talk about our problems—even the boys, and boys, as everyone knows, don't have problems, apart from the fact they're boys, of course. The school nurse had decided she was going to weed out the drinkers, the drug-gies, the vomiters and the starvers, the arm slicers, and the sluts. Each of us girls was questioned to cringing point on all areas of "female troubles." Elaine Wilkie was not thrilled to be told she could get a yeast infection if she kept on wearing those thick tights of hers every day.

But that session was different from this. The school nurse hadn't been very good at prodding. She'd tried to get me to talk about something private; I'd squirmed and she'd backed off. I felt embarrassed that I didn't have anything sleazy to keep hidden. Not like Kayleigh Barnes. She'd been trading blow jobs for weed with her brother's friends since Year Seven.

In comparison to the school nurse, Amanda's heavy-duty compassion is like drowning in jam.

"That's it, really," I say. "I just feel pissed off."

"Can you explain exactly how that feels for you?"

"I just feel pissed off."

"Why is it *that* particular feeling that is coming up for you?"

"Don't know. Just is."

"Okay, well, let's, um, let's break it down, Melon."

Why do adults always use your name when it isn't necessary? There is no one else in the room. Of course she is talking to me. They do it all the time, adults, name-check each other. They do it to prove they haven't gone senile yet, to show that they still have enough of their brain left to remind someone what their name is. It's pathetic. It just sounds patronizing.

"I'm not really upset enough for you, am I?"

Amanda looks taken aback, and I'm just about to notch up a point for myself when I notice the spark in her eye. I've been tricked into saying something she wants to hear—I can sense it.

"I mean," I jump in, "I mean, I feel, I feel . . . But I'm just . . . I think people think that . . ."

Amanda's frantic nodding returns, as if what I'm saying makes absolute grammatical sense.

"I mean"—I raise my voice, try to stop Amanda's head from coming loose—"*you* think I should be more upset."

"How do *you* think you should be behaving?" Amanda shoots back, triumphant.

Ten points to the counselor.

Exasperation is fizzing on my tongue. Amanda reminds me of Mum: that self-satisfied face. I feel like I'm listening to *her* again, talking about the troubled kids at her job, boasting about her work as if it's curing cancer or something.

"Giving them easy ways out? No—this is not my job," Mum would go, lecturing me, as if I had started the discussion, as if I cared. "No. I find ways for teenagers to make the sensible decisions."

"What if I said, 'Fuck it. I'm going to keep selling drugs on the street; it keeps me in nice sneakers'?" I'd say back.

"Well, what I am asking you is this: How else can you make this 'sneaker money'? How else can you do it and not go to jail?"

"And what if I said, 'But this is simple'?"

"I would say, 'Now is the time! Now! Now is the time to rewrite your history. You plan to do this all of your life?'"

"'Yeah, why the fuck not? Got a problem with that?'"

"Melon, do not say this f-word."

"That's what it's like on the streets, Mum."

And so on it went.

Amanda waits for an answer, wearing her last successful piece of strategy like a blue ribbon. I go back a couple of moves.

"You think I should be crying."

"There are no 'shoulds,' Melon, just 'is.'"

"Right."

"The idea of us getting together is so we can work through the issues that are troubling you at this moment in time."

"Right."

"So we only have half an hour today for an initial assessment, but I think I should perhaps book you in for some more regular sessions with me."

I want to run out of the room.

"Or one of our other therapists here?"

19

I can't look at her.

"And you could try writing it all down. Your teachers tell me you're a really bright girl."

I wonder if my teachers would have said that if Mum hadn't died.

"Putting it down on paper is one way of getting it out." Amanda has slipped on her best kindergarten voice. "The tears you talk about are just another way of releasing the grief."

I try to torture Amanda with a weighted silence. Then I say, "What would I write?"

"Whatever you want."

There is that spark in Amanda's eyes again. She is going to ask me what I feel like writing.

"What do you feel like writing?"

"Dunno. What would you write?"

"That's irrelevant. We all experience grief differently. This is about you and what you feel."

I roll my eyes, look at the carpet, grip the edge of my seat. I have an urge to hit Amanda in the face, hard, to stop all this stupid talk, to make her understand. How will writing some kind of school essay get rid of the brick lodged in my ribs? I concentrate on holding on to the chair, reining myself in, stopping it from all coming out. Amanda doesn't get it. The something inside of me isn't grief, isn't loneliness, isn't anything that Amanda can stick a label onto. I snap.

"It's all right for you, dishing out the advice." The voice I'm using doesn't sound like mine. It's vicious. "You're not the one with the dead mum, are you?"

I wait for Amanda to pounce on my words, but she is still and calm. She closes her eyes, blinking away what I just said. She's not going to retaliate. She smiles a painful smile.

"No," she says, rising above it all. "You're right."

Amanda has a dead mum.

Amanda has a dead mum.

She looks beaten, soft at the edges, like another human being all of a sudden. My grip on the chair loosens. I shrink back. I feel something like guilt creeping up inside. I want to say sorry, but the word won't come out.

"Right," I say instead. I start nodding. "I'll do that. I'll write it down."

THE STORY

1

On an island far, far from here, where the sea is woven from strings of sapphire blue and where the sunshine throbs like a heartbeat, there once was a farm.

At first glance it was like any other small piece of land on the Akrotiri Peninsula. There was a tiny stone cottage, its uneven walls washed white. There was a tidy yard with a wire fence, where a goat held court to an army of chickens. And beyond the cistus bushes that oozed their lemon scent into the breezy air were endless slopes of turned, brown earth—soil given over to the growing of fruit. But this was no ordinary farm—it was a magical place. Here was where five-year-old Maria Fouraki fell in love for the very first time.

Maria's *babas* worked hard for his crop. Bow-backed, a crucifix of sweat across his shoulders, he deposited seeds in carefully tilled holes. Babas was a large, round man, and the years of toiling in the relentless sun were written dark on his skin and silver in his hair.

"Just a week is all it takes," Babas explained to his daughter, his only child—a precious gift. *"Agapoula mou,"* he called her, *"peristeraki mou." My little love, my little dove.* "Just a week," Babas told Maria, "and the growing will begin."

Maria listened, her brown eyes wide, to Babas's stories of germination and natural selection. *Only the strongest seed will survive.* She could not look away from the dark soil at her feet. She wanted the miracle to happen that minute. Babas, meanwhile, tilted his face to the sky, checking for subtle hints of the weather to come.

"If God be good and the summer fine, we shall soon have a new family of watermelons right here."

During the days that followed, Maria thought of nothing but the seeds. Why could she not see them growing?

"Be patient," said Babas. "It's all going on under the surface."

Maria imagined that the seeds were sleeping. Maria's mama would watch from the kitchen window as her daughter went to each of the hills of earth in turn, put her cheek to the soil, and whispered, "Wake up, wake up," in a voice no seed could refuse. When the strongest seedlings eventually burst free of their muddy blankets, Maria believed her soft words had made it happen. The melons would be her babies, and she must look after them.

The vines started creeping, spreading, and Maria helped Babas check each morning for darkling beetles, melon aphids, and yellow-striped armyworms. After a rainfall she would prune away overhanging leaves to make sure no mildew set in. She ran down the gullies between the crops, continuing her bright words of encouragement. She placed small hands on the rounding balls of green melon flesh, feeling the warmth that they had soaked up from the insistent

Greek sun. She imagined the fruits breathing, in and out, in and out. She tenderly instructed them to grow, to take up more space in this world.

One morning Maria was helping Mama feed the chickens when she heard a curious noise. She looked up to see Babas working his way along the highest slope, reaching under the melon plants and creating a sound.

Thud, thud.

The noise echoed around the yard. Maria felt her heart join in.

Thud, thud.

She raced up the hill to where Babas was down on his knees in the soil. "What's wrong?" she panted.

"Listen carefully, *agapoula mou.*" He knocked soundly on the skin of one of the green fruits that rested, bloated, on the soil.

Maria creased her forehead, the same way Babas did and the way his *babas* had done before that. A pinched "w" of skin—the Fourakis look of concern.

"That sound," said Babas with a smile. "You hear? That is just right."

"Just right?"

"*Ta karpouzia ine etima,*" announced Babas, expecting Maria to share in his delight. "The watermelons, they're ready."

"Ready for what?" Maria asked, her tiny hands clasped together as if in prayer.

The melons were piled in a perfect pyramid on the back of Babas's truck with no net or tarpaulin to hold them in place. Babas drove away at a snail's pace and would maintain that steady crawl all the way to Hania. Maria trailed the truck to the first junction, her eyes prickling with tears. She whispered more words of encouragement, this time urging one of her green children to topple from the truck. But Babas had done this journey many times before and was wise to the bumps in the road. The melons did not listen to Maria. The impossible structure of fruit stayed strong.

Maria stood on that dusty path and watched the truck disappear. She felt the ground fall away from her perfect summer. She was only five years old, but already, here it was, her first lesson in how to love and lose—a toughening-up for the future. A horrible something took hold of Maria's heart and gave it a painful twist. Her only thought: *How will I love anything more than I loved those melons?*

7 DAYS SINCE

"Car's here, Melon," Paul is yelling from downstairs.

I go into Mum's room, close the door behind me, and open up her Victorian relic of a wardrobe. Inside, the clothes are jammed together so tightly that none of them can breathe. A few dead cardigans lie on the bottom of the wardrobe, strangled by belts and shoelaces.

I'm looking for the burgundy dress.

Anything with a zipper wouldn't fit me. The burgundy dress is stretchy. It'll cling to the wrong bits, and my underwear seams will show, but I don't need to look sexy. I need to look like the grieving daughter. Everything in my closet makes me look too happy or too sad (both meanings of the word *sad*). I just want to wear my denim skirt and a T-shirt. Mum wouldn't have cared less, but today is all about Paul and what his bloody social worker friends think.

I take the dress off the hanger. It smells of those green plastic balls that keep the moths from eating your sweaters. After a bit of Impulse spray, it'll be fine.

I pull off my black sweater and drop my skirt to the floor. I put the dress on over my head, wriggle the thing into place. I thought the arms would be too small, but they go all the way to my wrists just fine. I tug the seams into the right places, then shut the wardrobe so I can see myself in the mirror on the door. Something squeezes my throat. It's like seeing a ghost. I look over my shoulder, expecting someone else to be there. There's Mum's empty bed, pillows made neat by Paul.

I go back to the reflection. There are differences—the way the dress stretches more than it ever had to over Mum's chest, the way my arms look like party balloons, the way my belly creates a little mound—but still . . .

Mum's stomach was the only thing about her body that was flawed. It was chopping-board flat, but she had these stretch marks, little silver lines worming their way around her belly button. It looked like a road map—Piccadilly Circus. There was a straight red line drawn underneath it all, just above where her skimpy pants stopped. These lines and scar never went brown like the rest of her skin, even after a whole day's sunbathing in Crete. I pointed them out once when we were on Tersanas Beach, and she waved me away as if I were a stupid fly.

"Oh, I am not caring about those," she'd said. Then she'd slowly rolled herself over. The local boys on the patch of sand next to us had watched, drooling, as if my mum were a supermarket rotisserie chicken. They were closer to my age than hers.

Mum propped herself up on her elbows and added, "Actually, I am liking them, the lines. They remind me that I give birth to you." She had smiled—pleased with that. She could never be like everyone else and have at least one little hang-up.

The more I look in the mirror, the more I see our

27

differences and the less I see that first thing—that ghost. It's gone. I've scared it off.

"Car's here, Melon," Paul yells again.

I heard him the first time. I know he's twitching by the front door, desperate for nothing to go wrong, as if us being five minutes late would be a bigger disaster than Mum dying in the first place.

Before I go, I find the bottle of vanilla perfume on Mum's yard-sale dressing table and give myself a good squirting. I leave my sweater and skirt on the floor. Mum was never one to stress about mess.

Paul is waiting downstairs in the hallway in a black suit. His mum, Irene, is flapping around him like an overweight butterfly. They've been crying. They have matching gluey streaks on powder-brown cheeks. Irene fixes Paul's tie and picks imaginary fluff off his jacket. Her dress is all vibrant reds and golds and purples. It's in-your-face cheerful. She's a giant weeping Red Admiral butterfly in a house of gloom. Irene is staying at the house when we go so she can sort out the food for afterward. It feels totally wrong that everyone will be chewing on Jamaican chicken drumsticks and lumps of fried plantain after a big "Greek" funeral. Paul said it's what Mum would have wanted. I said it was slap-dash. He argued that it would be "multicultural," so I reminded him what he had originally said—that the whole thing had to be Greek. "Make your mind up," I told him. That got him running back to his reference books. If it had been up to Mum, there would be more of an after-show party—a laser light show, drag queens in G-strings, that kind of thing.

I'm halfway down the stairs, stepping carefully over Kojak, when I realize Paul is staring at me with this stricken face.

"What?" I go.

He is looking me up and down in horror, as if I've come downstairs smeared in mud rather than dressed all smart.

"I bought that dress for your mum," he croaks.

"Did you?" I go. I give Kojak a rub behind the ears—he must be feeling it even worse today. I do the rest of the stairs and then unhook my coat off the end of the banister. I need to get my bag from the living room. "She still in there?"

Paul's Adam's apple is doing a dance. "They've carried her into the car."

"Good."

I go into the living room. Everything is like it was, except the air seems different. Museum air. The coffin has gone. There is a bowl of apple, quince, and pomegranate on the coffee table. Paul has done loads of research on all the right Greek rituals—found some really weird ones, dragged out from the Dark Ages. He was talking about putting a coin under Mum's tongue to pay Charon, the miser who will ferry her body across the river Styx. Loopy stuff. People who exaggerate their Irish roots are called Plastic Paddies, I heard once. Paul has become a Plastic Zorba. Just like Mum.

The one thing I know he is doing right is the *kollyva*. I got his mum, Irene, to make this massive dish of boiled wheat for the wake. Sounds gross, but it's what you're supposed to do. I know this because Mum talked about it in The Story. Paul thought I'd gotten it wrong, that you only make *kollyva* for the days when you remember the dead, not funerals—but I set him straight on that one. Irene put almonds and icing on top of the wheat. I told her it had to be decorated with a cross too, made out of pomegranate seeds.

Back in the hallway, Paul is holding the front door open, taking big breaths. The hand that's not on the door is trembling. I can't look at that hand. Something about it makes me feel sick.

"Let's go, then." Paul is pretending to be cheerful and efficient. I don't want to join in with this jolly chitchat, so I'm glad when Irene steps between us. She won't let me escape without giving her a hug. It's like being wrapped in a blanket.

"You be brave, now."

I'm almost disappointed when she lets me go, this woman I hardly know.

Once we're in the car, Paul pulls himself together.

"You're wearing your mum's perfume. That's nice," he goes.

He puts his hand on top of mine, gives it a pat. I go rigid. He moves his hand away.

"Bit strong, though," I say. "Gets in your throat."

I pull up the neck of the dress and give it a sniff. Paul looks away, starts craning his head around the driver's shoulder to check that the car carrying Mum is still there. I don't know where he thinks it's going to go—speeding off to do the pickup for some bank robbers? We crawl along the main street so passersby can have a good chance to see who's been unlucky. I try not to look at the car ahead. The cheesy wreaths spelling out MUM in pink carnations were Paul's idea. So was the big, flowery Greek flag. The little dove in white roses was my choice.

"I wish you'd had a look at her, spent some time with her, Melon."

I do a shudder to show him what I think about that. I drive my hands between my knees, look out the car window. It seems a shame it's not raining. Funerals should be rainy.

"She looked very peaceful. Very beautiful."

"Done her nice, had they?"

Cara Moran's mum works in a funeral parlor. Cara is always telling gory stories about how dead people's insides fall out if you don't block up all their holes. She says her mum sticks cotton balls in people's cheeks and makes them look like a chipmunk storing nuts before she gives them a makeover; otherwise, their faces sink in. She says you have to use special blush and lipstick to cover up all the blue skin. I'm pissed off with Paul that he let someone like Cara's mum loose on Mum and then stuck her in the living room for general display. Paul said it's the Greek way. I said it was twisted.

In Mum's will it said she wanted a Greek funeral. I think she meant a funeral in actual Greece, not a theme-park one over here. I'm so relieved Paul didn't figure that one out. We'd be sticking her coffin on easyJet now if he had. She also said she wanted her ashes scattered on the melon farm in Crete, which has caused Paul a massive headache

31

because the Greek Orthodox church won't let you get cremated. Shows how much Mum knew about it all. She probably just wrote that in her will to sound romantic. Or to play a joke on us.

So Paul has had to freestyle. The Orthodox churches won't have us, so we're using an English one instead and doing all the Greek stuff around the edges. The church he's chosen is huge, which is a massive waste. There'll only be me, Paul, and a couple of social workers rattling around inside. The Greek bunch isn't coming over to say their good-byes. Surprise, surprise.

It's ridiculous that we are doing it in a church at all. Mum was never really into God. She never went to church when she was alive. I was brought up godless, which means no one is looking over me and keeping me safe. I think of the want ad I'll have to put in the newspaper when I'm older and need some spiritual guidance:

WANTED: GOD

TO FILL THE HOLE LEFT BY DISINTERESTED MOTHER

I wonder where Mum's gone now. Heaven? Hell? A never-ending boat trip on the river Styx?

It takes no time to get to the church. The car was a waste too. We could have walked. The chauffeur holds the door open for me. I'm so embarrassed. The church towers over us, ready to swallow us up. Me and Paul walk up the path side by side. I have this horrible premonition of him giving me away at my wedding.

32

"Hello, Melon."

It's Mrs. Lacey. Mrs. Lacey is here. Why is Mrs. Lacey here?

Paul moves off to shake hands with some social worker friend by the church door.

There is only one reason Mrs. Lacey would come — Chick! Chick has pulled herself together! Chick has come to support me!

Mrs. Lacey takes hold of my elbow with a sympathetic crab claw.

"I'm very sorry for your loss," she says, like a robot, as if the last week never happened.

"Thanks," I say. Then, because she's caught me by surprise, I go, "You too."

Weirdly, she nods.

"I mean, it's okay," I correct myself. "It's not your fault."

She gives me that stare, the one that says she's locking her explosives away in a fireproof box.

"Kathleen is very sorry too."

"Is she?" I ask. I scan the churchyard over Mrs. Lacey's shoulder. "Where is Chick?"

"Ice-skating practice." She says this like Chick is doing missionary work in the Congo.

"Oh. Right. Nice."

"She's very stressed, finding it very difficult. She's practicing for the Autumn Ice Show auditions. She could be a wood nymph."

"That's really . . ." What? I can't find the words. I can imagine Chick as a wood nymph, those spidery legs.

"Yes, yes." Mrs. Lacey nods, her mind lost on Chick's current ordeal.

"Well, I'd better go in," I say. "Get a good seat."

"Yes, you'd better," Mrs. Lacey says, stern for no reason.

Paul beckons me over and we walk into the church, into its big stone insides.

And it is full.

Every seat is taken. Every pew is packed, black shoulder to black shoulder.

The place hums with the sound of people talking under their breath, but when I walk in, it hushes. Apart from Mum, I guess I'm the star attraction. I walk down the aisle, and it's like walking into the rib cage of a massive whale. Everyone turns and looks at me as I pass. I stare at all these unfamiliar faces one by one, and I think, *What are you all doing here?*

Afterward, at the reception, right in the middle of our living room, among all those social workers and neighbors and kids that Mum has helped out over the years, Mum's friend Poppy, who she used to work with, decided to do this speech.

"Maria used to tell me this story about when she was growing up in Crete," she went, "and . . ." Then she broke down in tears and couldn't continue.

It was the funniest thing. Like, funny ha-ha and funny weird all at the same time.

Poppy had started sobbing because she'd spotted a pottery ashtray on our mantelpiece, some wonky yellow-

and-red thing that Mum had made in an evening class. It wasn't anything important—Mum's interest in pottery making had fizzled out ages ago, and she was never any good at it. But Poppy went over to the mantelpiece and grabbed this thing like it was one of the Elgin Marbles and started wailing even harder, clutching the hideous thing to her chest. The hairpins and whatnot that Mum had been stashing inside of it fell all over the carpet. I was nearly pissing myself from laughing.

Then Poppy went, "Maria used to talk about this piece of thread," and suddenly I didn't feel like laughing anymore. "The piece of thread that connects her heart to mine." Poppy had ditched whatever Crete story Mum had spun for her and moved on to something else. My story . . .

"She said that when something happened to me . . ." Poppy started to hold it together now, but I just wished she would stop. "When I felt something tugging at my heart," Poppy went on, "Maria said she felt it too."

I couldn't believe it. Mum had used the same line on someone else—Poppy—just some woman from work.

Poppy got full of it then. She was loving the moment. "'I know, Maria, babe,' I told her, 'I feel it too.'"

When Mum had last talked to me about the piece of thread, I told her that it was a load of rubbish. I told her she never had any kind of clue what I was going through, that she never understood.

"Oh, don't you believe it," she'd gone. This angry little "w" of skin was creased into her forehead. "I know, I feel it. I have this piece of thread." She'd plucked angrily at the fabric of her T-shirt, at her heart. Her accent went strong. Her face looked in pain. I still didn't understand what she meant, though. I couldn't feel what she felt. It was only when Poppy did that speech at the reception that I experienced it for the first time—the thread, the tug.

THE DAY

People should be fitted with black-box recorders. You know, something that survives the crash, the disaster that gets them in the end. Pry open that box and inside you'd find out what they'd been thinking at the exact moment that it happened. Their last thought would probably be how annoyed they were with you, because of that thing you said or did. Or maybe death would make them realize that the bad things you'd done and said didn't really matter after all.

But what if you wrenched open that box and inside you heard that person thinking about how much they loved you? What if that was their last dying thought? What a guilt trip.

Me and Chick are watching weight lifting on TV at the exact moment it happens. When the bus hits Mum. 6:09 p.m. I find this out afterward. Don't ask me why we're watching weight lifting. I'm not into it or anything. I'm not that sad. It's just really funny. All those little midgety women so pumped up that they look like men. We are in hysterics. At the exact moment it happens, we are in hysterics.

I knock for Chick after the argument. Our house is one of loads of little, new buildings squashed together. Chick's house is big and fat and sits by itself. Chick answers, eyes still on the TV through the living-room doorway. She hops from socked foot to socked foot, bursting for an imaginary pee.

"Hi, Chick," I go.

Chick twitches for a lookout onto the street behind me, then she's turning toward the kitchen, watching for any movement from her mum, then she's back eyeing the TV. Chick acts like a deer in the headlights. She's always like that.

"Hey, Mel. Come in."

At last I get the Chick smile—barbed-wire teeth in a blond, dolly head.

"Mum's driving me mad," I say, which will be enough of an excuse for me to stay for dinner.

Chick's walking back to the TV without closing the door, so I do it. I follow her pink leggings, which have given up trying to get a grip on her chopstick thighs. They've surrendered in wrinkles around her ankles.

"Watching weight lifting," she singsongs. "On the sofa." Chick will watch everything and anything.

Mrs. Lacey's living room is painted Avarice Green with a sludge-gray carpet and cream sofas. There's an empty bag of Cheetos on the coffee table and orange crumbs on the sofa. Chick lives on Cheetos. I find a good spot on the sofa away from the cheese dust. I don't want Mrs. Lacey to blame it on me. I chuck my bag at the armchair.

On TV, a woman is grinning like a loony, groaning and shaking under a barbell. She looks like she's trying to do a poo.

Chick goes, "You can get these pills that kill fat in your body and keep you from getting lardy."

It sounds like it has nothing to do with anything, but I

38

can see why it came into Chick's head. We're like that. We've known each other eleven years, since primary school. The women on TV are squatty, chunky hulks, and Chick's got this thing about getting fat, even though she's built like a Twiglet. If she wasn't my best friend I'd hate her for the amount of Cheetos she can scoff.

The dumpy woman with the grin drops the barbell and roars. Both me and Chick yell, "Denied!" at exactly the same time. That means we have to do the jinx thing where you link little fingers and make a wish.

"Why did she yell like that?" Chick asks. "Did she drop it on her foot?" Chick can be a bit dippy. She doesn't do as well as me at school.

"No, it's just what they do to get rid of all that anger and energy and stuff."

"Oh." Chick is nodding like she knew this all along.

She sticks her thumb in her mouth and rubs her nose with a finger at the same time. The other hand gets hold of a chunk of hair and dabs her split ends against her cheek. I'm supposed to keep it a secret, the thumb-sucking.

"Do you think they're lesbians?" I say. The grinning woman is moody now. She lumbers off the stage and gets a towel wrapped over her shoulders by a coach. The coach looks scary tall next to this little bricky weight lifter.

"What, all of them? Lesbians?"

"Dunno."

Suddenly Chick pulls her thumb out and she's smiling. There is orange Cheetos gunk around the brackets of her braces. "Do you think those fat pills can make you grow taller than a four-foot dwarf?"

"Or make you look like a woman again?" I go.

I'm smiling too now because I know we're off on one. We'll keep going and going, saying stupider and stupider things until we can't breathe properly because we're laughing so hard and one of us begs for mercy. That is how we work.

"Or get rid of your . . ." Chick doubles over on the sofa, her words gobbled up by giggles. She laughs like a little kid doing an impression of a machine gun—*ak-ak-ak-ak*.

"What?" I squeal, tipping forward with her. I'm halfway to hysterics. I know the answer is going to be good.

"Get rid of her . . ." Chick is gone again. She's red now, hugging a cushion, doing those snorting things because she can't get the laugh out.

"Her what?" I go. "Her penis?"

Chick screams at the word. *Penis!* She's shaking her head. *No, not penis.* We're both crying a bit now, as well as laughing. We mouth the word "penis" at each other and clutch our spasming tummies.

"No, her . . ." She just can't get to the word.

"Say it, Chick, before I piss myself."

Chick sits up straight and tries to fan laughter away from her face. "I was going to say"—she takes a deep breath—"her mustache."

We both go under again, laughing with no sound because we can't get enough breath.

Then Mrs. Lacey walks into the room, wanting to know what we both want for dinner. Straightaway we can't remember what was so funny. Just like that.

Two and a half hours after the meal, the police turn up.

When it happens, it's like being sucked down the plughole. My skin and clothes are dry, but I'm spinning in the middle of the water. There is the color blue, then bright white, then blue again. There is a sun, really strong, flashing off the water, blinding me. For a minute, I'm lying on the deck of this boat I've never seen before. I can see the wooden floorboards and feel the sicky sway of the sea. Then that image is gone. The boat has gone. More falling. All the blood disappears from my head and goes to my feet. More water. This time a river. I'm trying to cross to the other bank on stepping stones that sink when I tread on them. They rise up again once I've stepped off. More falling. Then there is a firecracker bang in my head and a train track of spikes up the back of my neck. My hands go to my head and the blood finds its way there too. I'm coming up. I'm desperate for a mouthful of air. A final whoosh.

I can see two pairs of feet and feel carpet on my cheek. For a terrifying moment I have no idea where I am, who I am. Then the jigsaw puzzle starts fitting together in my head. I'm Melon Fouraki. I'm fifteen years old. I'm lying on my side, on the floor in Chick's hallway. I recognize Chick's boots on the shoe rack. My arms and legs are in this weird arrangement. The recovery position. We had a first-aid talk at school once and we had to lay each other out like this on the gym floor. Chin up to keep the airway open, mouth down to let any vomit out.

My ears echo like they're full of water, then I hear this woman's voice from down the bottom of the rabbit hole.

"Oh, God, she'll want to come and live with us." She becomes clearer by the end of the sentence. I'm tuning her in on an old radio.

"You're okay. Just stay put for a moment." This is a different woman's voice, closer to me, a northern accent that I don't recognize. Someone who smells of body spray and gasoline is crouched over me. Her coat scratches and rustles as she moves. She's got a firm hand on my shoulder, trying to stop me from floating to the ceiling.

I lift my head and I get fireworks against a black background.

"Don't try to shift just yet, Melon. You fainted, my love. Try to lie still and breathe deeply." The northern woman's voice is soft and chocolatey. It instantly makes you want to do what she says.

I lie still, looking at the black-shoed feet of a uniformed man, next to the hairy toes of Chick's dad. A walkie-talkie makes a phlegmy cough, and the black-shoed man mutters something into his handset. It gives another choking bark.

I don't understand how I ended up on the pastel-blue carpet of the Laceys' hallway.

Then more jigsaw pieces slot together in my head. I remember the policeman and policewoman making me sit down in the middle seat of the sofa in the living room. I was thinking about Cheetos crumbs. How stupid. The television had been switched off—a big honor in the Lacey house. The floor lamp with its shade like a fancy hat was the only light in the room. Mr. and Mrs. Lacey—Rowena and Victor, although I'm never allowed to call them that— stood at the edge of the room, defending the curtains. Chick

42

was hanging on to the door, not sure whether to come into the room, one of her pink-socked feet working up and down the door's inner edge.

Me and Chick had been upstairs, watching TV in Chick's room for the few hours since dinner. We'd been feeding raisins to Chick's hamsters. It was so embarrassing to be summoned into the living room. It became Mr. and Mrs. Lacey's turf in the evening. It felt like wandering into the teachers' lounge at school. Plain wrong. There were two glasses of wine half finished on the coffee table. I don't know why, but seeing that felt like getting a glimpse of Mr. and Mrs. Lacey naked. The room smelled different from when me and Chick kicked around in there after school.

The policewoman sat down next to me on the sofa. She was stocky, and when her backside hit the cushions, I almost tipped into her lap.

I'd laughed when she said it, when the policewoman said it. The two officers had probably decided before they walked in the house that news like that sounded better coming from a woman. Or maybe they'd argued in the car over who should do it. *It's your turn. No, I did the last one.* Something like that. So, I laughed. Not because it was funny but because it was a bit surreal, sitting in Chick's living room like that at 9:30 p.m. on a Monday night, and because I'd been bracing myself for something bad as I came down the stairs. No one ever comes by that late in the evening to say something good, do they? So the laugh was just the pressure to have a reaction, the right reaction, even though I had no clue what that right reaction was. If I was on a soap opera, I would stare wildly at the camera and say, *No, no, it can't be, it can't be,* then crumple up my face and sob because people think you're a really good actor if you can cry on the spot and make yourself look ugly. But I just laughed and went blank.

So the policewoman said, "I'll make some tea, shall I?"

And then I had this mad, panicky thought that the thing Mum used to say was turning out to be true, that all the Fourakis family dies young. And then I realized I might have to go to identify a body, and I knew I wouldn't be able to do that, so I said I had to go to the bathroom. I did need to pee; it was no lie. And then . . . I must have fainted before I got there.

My bladder feels like it's going to burst. Thank God. If I'd wet myself when I'd fainted, Mrs. Lacey would have freaked out about the carpet.

Mr. Lacey's hairy toes have walked off to the kitchen where Mrs. Lacey seems to be in a frenzy, despite having a dry carpet. She's sobbing out loud. I can hear the grippy bottoms of her big fur slippers pacing across the tiles. Mrs. Lacey didn't really know my mum. Only vaguely. Only enough to disapprove. They'd met briefly on doorsteps. They'd probably spoken on the phone once or twice, when they didn't know where me and Chick were. It's a bit weird that Mrs. Lacey is so upset.

"Oh, God, oh, God," Mrs. Lacey is repeating, demented.

"Calm down, Ro." Mr. Lacey must be used to this over-reacting.

"But we'll be the ones who have to take her in, Victor. Have you thought about that?"

"Will you be quiet? She can hear you."

Mrs. Lacey stops pacing. She sighs. "I'm going to be the next one fainting, I tell you."

The crouching policewoman shares a glance with the towering policeman.

All I'm thinking is, *Where's Chick?* I want her to burst into the hallway to tell me this is all a stupid dream. Any minute she'll do it. I know it. Right now, she's either in the kitchen, watching her mum and dad argue, or she's gone upstairs. No. I hear a game-show theme song. Chick's in the living room. She's switched the television back on.

THE STORY

2

Often boundaries solve problems and sometimes they create them. A line drawn in the earth can provide clarity—or start a war.

In ancient times, locals believed that one fatal eruption at Thíra might cause the Akrotiri Peninsula to crack along its boundary line and float away from Crete.

"Sounds improbable?" Babas said to Maria. He raised one silver eyebrow. "But this shuddering and shattering was exactly how God formed our islands long, long ago."

"When dinosaurs lived here?" Maria had asked, eight years old and goggle-eyed.

"Yes, *agapoula mou, peristeraki mou*, when dinosaurs roamed my melon patch."

From this explanation, Maria assumed that God and the dinosaurs had divided Babas's land from the Drakakis farm next door. There were no stone wall partitions, just a deep, natural crevice that ran along the back of Babas's northern field. However, where the Drakakis plot hugged the Fourakis farm to the east, only tradition held firm whose land was whose. And tradition is always open to interpretation.

"I keep my borders free of weeds, do I not?" Babas would storm into the kitchen, fiery and sweating mud.

"Yes," Mama would reply as she served up stewed cabbage and sausage.

"I would not let my land grow wild?"

"No," Mama would say, taking her seat and clasping her hands, ready for Babas to say grace.

"It is he who should be keeping those tangled vines in check," Babas would mutter, breaking the skin of a sausage with an angry bite. "I am not the one to blame."

"Yes" was always Mama's reply, and then she would bow her head and send some quiet words to the heavens herself.

Babas and Grigoris Drakakis's arguments were as omnipresent as the sea breeze from Kalathás Bay, as dependable as the melon harvest, as sure as a girl grows taller with every passing summer.

The Fourakis and Drakakis children did not join their parents' wars.

Christos, the youngest Drakakis son, was small and wiry—a boy in no way suited to the heave-ho of farmwork. Even the chickens ignored his timid commands. He preferred hiding out with Maria in the dinosaurs' gully that divided their farms, telling her of his dream to one day run away and become an artist. Where exactly a person ran away to in order to become an artist was still a mystery to Christos, but as soon as he found the answer, he would go there. Maria, in return, confessed her desire to stay in Crete and take over the growing of melons.

When Maria and Christos's limbs grew too long to hide away in their furrowed den, they took themselves to Tersanas

Beach. Secluded in the mouth of a cove, they did comic impressions of their blustering fathers. Nose to nose, barefoot in the sand, they deepened their voices, blew out their cheeks, speared their fingers in the air. They shouted until they could no longer keep up the act and fell on top of each other, giggling.

Christos told Maria a secret—he had spied on his older brother, Yiannis, as he led a girl behind the goat sheds late one night. Yiannis had kissed the girl against a wall, and the girl had arched her back and lifted her face to the moonlight. They had both made the most peculiar sounds. The next day Christos had asked Yiannis what he had been doing. He wanted to know why his older brother's face had knotted up into an expression somewhere between grief and surprise.

"He says it's called 'making beautiful music,'" Christos told Maria.

The idea that Yiannis's piggy grunts were in any way beautiful made Maria and Christos fall back in the hot sand with laughter.

But still, their curiosity was awoken.

Babas did not realize that while he concentrated his fury on unkempt weeds, he had neglected to see how lush and wild his fifteen-year-old daughter had grown. When you discover that your little girl, your melon prized above all others, is carrying the bastard grandchild of your enemy next door, it changes everything.

Forever.

To Babas, a line had been drawn in the earth, and Maria had stepped across it. He could not look her in the eye. His words and stories dried up.

Maria's mama, always in the background, stepped forward and became the industrious one. She would not allow shame to be brought upon her family. She would not watch her husband shun his only daughter. She decided they must leave the island to allow painful wounds to heal. So Mama, Maria, and Maria's unborn baby, at the time no bigger than a butter bean, made their way to London, where Mama's sister had gone to live some years before.

"They will be more understanding there," said Mama.

Babas took one last look at Maria, his little love, his little dove.

"Pah!" he said, instead of good-bye.

7 YEARS BEFORE

I'm eight and three-quarters years old.

There is a *bong* sound. Soft and comfy. The NO SMOKING light comes on above my head, and Mum says, "Tut." Sometimes Mum goes and smokes in the bathroom. This always makes the air hostesses cross and gets Mum a big telling-off.

Mum is click-clacking with her seat belt, making it complicated. Really, it's easy. Mine's buckled. Friendly hands around my waist. I'm already eating cherry drops to keep my ears from popping. Crack the hard shell and there's a fizz inside. I'm ready for liftoff.

The smell of meat and baby-food potatoes is filling up the aeroplane. The meal is the best part. You get a tray with four other smaller trays on top. One has a yogurt in it with a swollen-up top. You have to be careful when you open it. It could pop all over you, or over the seat in front, or on a stranger sitting nearby. If that happens, it's very funny, but you have to say sorry. Another little tray has a bread roll with a packet of butter and margarine. Butter *and* margarine; you get to choose. If you can't decide, you can have butter on one half of your bun and margarine on the other. Mum puts the salt and pepper from the packets on top to make salt-

and-pepper-flavored bread. Another tray has the hot stuff in it. When you take the foil off, the steam gets you with a sting. The last tray has a warm jam cake. Well, it's not always jam cake, but it is always dessert. If you think about it, with the yogurt, that makes two desserts, really.

I'd quite like to take the small trays home with me. The air hostesses probably just throw them out. You never see air hostesses washing up. Some of the trays are blue and some are yellow, and their edges are smooth and shiny. I'm not sure what I'd use mine for, but I'd find something. They're just nice to have, really. I ask Mum if I can keep the little trays, and she just says, "You are not eating your mashed potato, no? Melon?"

The hot stuff is too much food for me and too little for Mum. So when I'm halfway done, we take my big blue tray with the foil and swap it with Mum's. That way it looks like I've been good and eaten all mine, and Mum gets seconds. You shouldn't have seconds if you're fat, but Mum is skinny, so it's okay.

"If she turn to the side, she disappear" is what Auntie Aphrodite says. She says it really grumpily, so it must be a bad thing to disappear. Auntie Aphrodite has boobies that finish where her belt starts and arms like marshmallows. She is named after the goddess of love and the most beautiful woman ever. Mum says this is *very* funny.

"Flowers they are growing wherever she is walking; birds they are flocking wherever she is flying!" Mum says before doing a harrumph noise and laughing a lot. I have never seen Auntie Aphrodite's flowers or her birds, but I would like to.

When we get to Crete, Auntie Aphrodite will make all

the food and Mum won't eat much of it, probably because she's so full from all that aeroplane dinner.

We'll have Toblerone for dessert on the plane too. One of those big triangle ones in the boxes off the air hostess's cart. I always say how nice the pilot teddy bears are on the top of the cart, but teddy bears are just daylight robbery if you buy them on a plane. So I get a pen with a jumbo-jet cap instead, which is less money. I shouldn't expect it to last long, though, Mum says, and the air hostess hears her and gives her a moody look. Air hostesses are always cross, so you can't blame yourself for upsetting them. It's a really glamorous job, but Mum says the altitude gets to them.

Anyway, we have Toblerone, which is a special treat. If you think about it, after the yogurt and the jam cake, it's kind of like having a third dessert. Auntie Aphrodite always makes a dessert that sounds a bit like balaclava but it isn't that word, because that's one of those woolly hats with holes in it. Balaclava, or whatever it is, is a bit like a greasy sausage roll without any sausage in it. Mum feeds mine to the stray cats that come around the table legs, and we pretend I ate it all up. Lying like that is okay because it's so I don't hurt Auntie Aphrodite's feelings.

Auntie Aphrodite is my *granbabas*'s sister, so really she's my great-auntie Aphrodite, except I don't call her that. Although she's the oldest, Granbabas still gets to boss her around because he's in charge of the family. Mum loves Granbabas (except she just calls him Babas) but they don't cuddle or hold hands, like I do with Mum, because they're different. Mum and Granbabas say things in Greek to each other and I don't know what any of it means, because they say it too fast and the words are all different. So probably they say lots of nice things instead of holding hands.

Mum says to Granbabas, "Speak English in front of Melon."

Granbabas can speak English, but with parts missing—like Mum, but worse.

"If she grown up here, she know what I say."

Granbabas is kind of right, but if I had lived in Crete all the time, then I wouldn't speak any English, except a little bit to tourists, which would be just as bad as not knowing how to do Greek. Svetlana in my class has a dad that's from the Czech Republic and a mum from Barnet, so she can speak two languages at the same time. Mum could have talked in Greek to me in England but she didn't. Also I don't have a dad to do the English part, so that wouldn't really have worked.

The reason I don't have a dad is because when my mum came to England, she already had me in her tummy, so she didn't need to marry a man to get a baby. I was born when Mum was sixteen years old, which is a bit too young to be having babies, so we don't talk about that. We'll talk about it when I'm older. Auntie Aphrodite says it's shameful that Mum had me so young and she shakes her head, even though it was eight and three-quarter years ago, which is ages. When Auntie Aphrodite says "shameful" she looks at me. Mum puts her arm around me so I don't feel shameful on my own. She gives me a squeeze and calls me her *"agapoula mou, peristeraki mou."* This is Mum's name for me. It means I'm a lovely dove.

When we've had the balaclava, there is coffee, which I

don't have because it's too much like mud, and then some *tsikoudia*, which is not for children. Granbabas makes *tsikoudia* in the bath and then puts it in lemonade bottles. I'm not sure how he turns the bathwater into *tsikoudia*, but it smells like petrol so I don't have any. Mum has three of the little glasses straight after each other, and it makes her eyes watery. I ask her if it's crying, and she says, "No, it's just *tsikoudia*." So, if you think about it, there's no actual point to drinking it.

Tsikoudia makes Auntie Aphrodite giggly, and she gets Granbabas and my other auntie, Auntie Despina, and the other Greek ladies whose names I don't know to do Greek dancing. You have to stand in a circle and hold hands, but just fingers, and then move one way and then back the other. It doesn't look that hard, not as difficult as country dancing, but one year Mum tried to join in and Auntie Aphrodite told her to sit down because she wasn't doing it properly. If it had been me who wasn't allowed to join in with my friends, Mum would have used her hands-on-hips voice and told the others not to be so mean. She doesn't do it for herself, though.

This time, when Auntie Aphrodite started Greek dancing, we just watched, even though Mum practiced lots this year in the kitchen in our house with Greek tapes she got from the market. When the ladies dance in a circle, it looks like they're trying to screw themselves down into the ground. Auntie Aphrodite's boobies wobble lots. You must not smile when you do Greek dancing because it's a serious thing. I'm not sure why. It just is.

We only see Auntie Aphrodite and Granbabas for one

night because they're too busy to see us again. Even though Mum is Granbabas's only daughter and I'm his only granddaughter and we have come all this way just for a week, just for them. Granbabas's farm takes up all his time. I never knew melons could be so much trouble. Auntie Aphrodite has four children and eleven grandchildren that take up all her time, and they live in Crete, so that means they're more important. The rest of the week, me and Mum will do beach things together. Really, that's more fun than pretending to be happy.

Mum will try to do a big-hug thing when we say good-bye, and Granbabas will try to get out of it. Maybe he knows we'll be back next year, so he's not that upset about us going. Mum kisses Granbabas's brown and wrinkly cheek and tries not to cry, but he won't kiss her back. Granbabas doesn't ever look like he'll cry, because that's more of a girl thing. Auntie Aphrodite will just do a shooing thing with her hand and look embarrassed. I always wave properly.

On the beach I write a postcard to Chick with my new aeroplane pen, because I promised I would send her something and I am missing her like mad. The pen has four sliding buttons down the sides. One for blue ink, one for black, one for green, and one for red. I choose red and start writing.

"No!" Mum screams. She snatches the postcard off me in a way that really, really scares me. "This is what you are wishing for? You are wishing that Kathleen is dead?" She is ever so cross.

The frightening moment steals my voice. My eyes are

trying to cry, but I make them stop because it's silly to cry about a postcard. Mum is pointing a corner of the card at me. It has pictures of pretty Greek pots on it. They are called urns.

I manage to shake my head. No, I don't want Chick to die. She is my best friend in the whole universe.

"Then you do not use the red ink," Mum says. She strokes my hair flat, which means it's okay now; she's not angry anymore. She gives me back the postcard, which has a little crease on it now.

"You write to someone in the red ink, you wish them dead," Mum says.

So I click the red sliding button back up, even out the postcard's crease with my thumb, and choose the blue ink instead.

4 DAYS SINCE

When Chick's dad comes upstairs, I get the urge to recite the planets to him.

MERCURY, VENUS, EARTH, MARS, JUPITER, SATURN,
URANUS, NEPTUNE

I've been up in Chick's bedroom on my own for the last hour; I need to say something out loud. I've learned the planet order and don't need to look at my book anymore. I wonder if Mr. Lacey would be interested. I've got no idea what he's into. I don't think he actually has any interests. There are some bowling balls on the shelf in his study downstairs, but I've never heard Chick mention her dad actually using them. Who owns bowling balls but never goes bowling? Weirdos, that's who. Mr. Lacey revolves around Chick and Mrs. Lacey and forgets about being a real person himself. Trying to talk to him about the universe would be pointless.

There is no one I can talk to about the universe.

Mr. Lacey is peeking around Chick's bedroom door. His hair is thin on top with blond wisps around his ears. At this angle, with his head all separated from his body, he looks like a clown.

"Melon, could you come downstairs for a moment?" This is Mr. Lacey's serious voice. I imagine him with a big red nose and a flower that squirts water.

"Why?"

"There's someone here who needs to speak to you."

"The police?"

That was who it was the last time Mr. Lacey did this, poked his head around the door and told me to go downstairs. The police were waiting to tell me about Mum.

"Oh, no, no, Melon, sorry, no, someone else, if you could just . . ." Mr. Lacey wants to be hard-faced. He's not even close.

"Right." I carry on drawing circle planets with oval, dotted paths that lead nowhere, just back to where they started.

"Now, if you don't mind."

I'm expecting the men in white coats. Mrs. Lacey will have sent for them.

As I come down the stairs, I can hear Mrs. Lacey's serious news program on the radio in the kitchen. Long words leak into the hall. Through the banisters I can see Chick sitting at the kitchen table doing her homework while her mum cooks. She must have heard me on the stairs, but her head stays down. She's pretending to be engrossed in her French textbook. *Look up*, I think. *Look up and see me.* No. She's deaf, blind, and dumb. The air is prickly with garlic.

Before all this, Chick would have done anything to avoid her mum and the serious radio stuff. Now she can't be in the same room as me. Even with the TV on, the silence between us is like a big, screaming black hole. It doesn't feel as though something really awful has happened to me; it feels like I've done something terrible to Chick. I've made everything scary and miserable. I am a bad friend.

At the living-room door, Mr. Lacey does this ridiculous, twirly hand gesture to usher me in. He's not saying who's in there. I'm ready for the worst. Bring it on. Let it chew me up and turn me to dust.

It's Poppy. Mum's best friend from work.

She's here to tell me that this whole week has been one big joke. Poppy will take me to where Mum is hiding and she'll jump out and say, *"Boo!"* We'll have such a laugh, the three of us, about the fact that Mum's not really dead, about how the Laceys are such idiots. We'll laugh until we can't breathe.

When Poppy looks up, I know straightaway that this isn't going to happen. She is wearing the mask — the sorry mask, the death mask.

Poppy clocks my haircut and her face crumples. "It looks nice, Melon, your hair," she lies.

That's the first thing she says. Not "hello."

"You think?"

"Yeah, babe."

Poppy is sitting in the armchair by the TV, peeling off her rain poncho. She's wearing a skirt made from curtains that goes all the way down to the floor. I know Poppy smokes weed because I heard her talking to Mum about it once.

Mum went to her, "I could never. No. Would be very bad for me. And I worry for M-E-L-O-N." As if I couldn't spell my own stupid name.

I run my hand up the back of my hair, ruffle it up. I still can't get used to the way it feels, short tight curls that coil around your fingers.

"So what's the big deal, then?" I go. "About my hair, if it looks okay?"

Mr. Lacey does an "excuse me" cough.

"I don't think it's just about the hair, babe," goes Poppy. She seems to know the whole story. How can that be? How come they're talking to Poppy but not to me?

"No, no, that's not the point," Mr. Lacey blusters, getting ready to make a speech. He's shoving at his rolled-up sleeves—one of those baggy pastel shirts Mrs. Lacey buys for him because she thinks they make him look cool.

"Do you want to leave us alone for few minutes, Victor? Would you mind?"

Poppy is excellent at telling people to piss off in a nice way.

Mr. Lacey waits for a moment, trying to prove that he's still in charge and not being told what to do. Finally he shifts. Yeah, piss off, Mr. Shitty Shirt.

"I'll be in the kitchen with the girls," he says.

What he means is, he'll be in the kitchen stressing about leaving us alone with the contents of his living room.

Poppy does a flat smile.

"With the 'girls,' eh?" she says quietly once Mr. Lacey's gone.

"Dickhead," I say in agreement.

"You liking it here, yeah?"

"They hug a lot."

"That's nice, I suppose."

60

"Each other, not me."

"Oh." Poppy grins, a mean grin that I like. "Probably for the best, eh, babe?"

Poppy doesn't like her real name. Barbara is a granny name for ladies who push shopping carts and have too many cats. Poppy is older than Mum and is too old to have kids. Plus, she's single. That's why she pretends she's still twenty-one, so she doesn't have to face up to it all. The name Poppy doesn't suit her either. It's a little girl's name, for someone with pigtails and a pinafore dress.

I used to think Poppy was just some drip who came to sit in our kitchen and gossip, but here she is—she has actually bothered to come to visit and see how I am. The house feels different now that Poppy is in it. The stuffy cream sofa, that lamp stand with the hat—they all look embarrassed. Everything about Poppy is wonky and carefree, and everything about this house is up its own arse.

"Right," says Poppy. She's grinning like there's trouble ahead. Fun trouble.

She goes to her bag, a massive leather job like a doctor might carry, and pulls out a folder.

"Right," she says again, this time with less fun.

She's fumbling through the folder, pulling a pen out of the scarf that's holding up her bird's nest hair. She bites off the cap.

Then I realize.

"I hope you don't mind, Melon, me coming to do this initial assessment?"

Poppy is here because she's a social worker. Mr. and Mrs. Lacey have brought her in.

"I thought it would be good because we already know each other. It's one hurdle out of the way, isn't it?"

She is using her work voice now.

"I really should have sent someone else in my place, I know, someone more independent, someone from my team who doesn't know you, but I just felt I had to do this for your mother. I hope you understand and that you're happy with that. And anyway, this is just a short visit."

My *mother*? Why doesn't she just say "mum" or "Maria"?

"Sorry, you don't need to know this. What I mean is, we'll assign someone independent to do all your follow-ups so there's some clear blue water between us and whoever you end up living with. But you can always call on me if, well, if that feels more comfortable for you. How does that sound?"

She makes no sense at all. I nod.

"So we'll carry on, shall we?"

I can barely manage a shrug.

"So how are you holding up?"

"All right."

"Good, good. What I'm here to do today is find out if you've got any ideas of what you would like to do now, where you would like to live. I want to find out what would make you happy."

She is using the script in her head, the one she uses on all the other motherless kids.

"Mr. and Mrs. Lacey have been very generous and let you stay here for the last few days, but I'm afraid that can't go on much longer."

"Because of the haircut?"

"Yes. Well, no. Because of a number of reasons."

It's a teacher's voice, a telephone voice.

"Now, you have an aunt in Crete, isn't that right? Antigone, isn't it?"

"Aphrodite."

"Aphrodite." She writes it down. "Do you have a number for her?"

I nod.

"You let me have that and I'll try to get in contact with her for you, to let her know what has happened. Okay?"

I imagine Auntie Aphrodite getting the phone call from Poppy. She'll pretend she doesn't speak English. She'll huff and puff Poppy away.

"Your mother also mentioned an aunt in Kentish Town."

"Eleni?"

"Yes."

Mum and Eleni don't speak. "She's . . . dead."

"Oh, Melon. I'm sorry about that."

"S'okay. Happened ages ago."

"Is there anyone else?"

Christos Drakakis, I think to myself. *My dad is Christos Drakakis, and my name is Melon Drakaki. How do you do?*

"No, there's no one, really."

"Okay. Now, are you aware of the provision that your mother made for you in her will?"

Your mother. Is that what it says in her script? Poppy is talking like a robot.

I have no idea what's in Mum's will. I didn't even realize she had one. But I can't let Poppy know more about all this than me. That would make me look bad. That would make it seem like I didn't even know my own mother. Maybe Mum wants me bags-packed and on the next plane to Crete. Who knows.

"So what do you think about that?" Poppy goes. "About going back to your mum's house and having Paul care for you?"

I knew it.

I look at the TV squatting in the corner, even though it has nothing to say for itself.

No, really, I knew it. I knew about the will, about Paul. I was watching television when Mum told me she'd put that in her will. I remember now. I wasn't really paying attention when she told me. I didn't think it was important. I didn't think she would actually go and die one day. The whole idea was as far away as the other planets.

"What are you thinking, Melon?"

"Mercury, Venus, Earth, Mars," I say. "Jupiter, Saturn, Uranus, Neptune."

Poppy narrows her eyes at me, confused. "What's that, then?"

"The solar system, the planets."

"Oh, right, yeah. Didn't you forget Pluto?"

"No."

"Yeah, you did, babe. Pluto's a planet."

"It's a dwarf planet."

"When I was at school, it was a proper planet."

"Yeah, well, it's not now. Listen to me. It goes like this: Mercury, Venus, Earth, Mars, Jupiter, Saturn, Uranus, Neptune."

"All right, babe." Poppy bites her lip. "Things probably changed since I was at school, eh?"

She smiles. I look away.

"You like space and stuff, do you?" she asks.

"Science exam."

"Now, your exams." We're back on safe ground for Poppy. "No one expects you to take them, you know. What with everything that's happened. You could take another year if you like. I've spoken to your teachers."

As if I would want to be the kid at school who has to redo a whole extra year. As if I don't get picked on enough already. Besides, I've never studied so much in my life. There's been nothing else to do here while Chick and Mr. and Mrs. Lacey have their hug-ins in the kitchen, acting like some huge tragedy has happened to them and not someone else.

"No, I'm ready for the exams."

"Well, that's very impressive, babe, considering."

Considering what? No one will say it out loud. It's like saying "Macbeth" in the theater; it brings bad luck. Your mum died—jinx!—yours will die too now. Say it; say it out loud. The worst has already happened.

"Do you know about the big bang, then?" I say.

"Well, I . . ."

"Do you know about it or not?"

"Kind of, but I wouldn't . . ."

"Well, they think that's how the universe started, some big explosion, because they know all the other galaxies are racing away from us really fast."

65

"That right?"

"What else would make them run away from us like that? It would have to be something big, wouldn't it?"

Poppy searches the room, looking for something to say.

"Wouldn't it?"

"I expect so."

All this stuff is inside me, going around and around, going unsaid.

"I can see you've really been doing your homework," Poppy goes.

"Yeah."

"So, Paul . . . Your mum wanted Paul to look after you. Does that sound like a good idea?"

It sounds like an easy idea. The Laceys don't want me; Paul does.

Paul.

Mum and Poppy talked about him loads when they were gossiping in our kitchen, especially back when he and Mum had just started going out. She carried on like some love-struck, soppy cow.

One time, I came down the stairs and I heard Mum go, "And you know what it is they say about the black men's cocks, don't you?"

She said it all matter-of-fact, as if she was telling Poppy that frozen peas are on sale, two for one.

"This, it is all true, I am telling you this."

Poppy had squawked, really loud, acting like a virgin.

Then I walked in. "I heard that," I went.

I took my time getting a snack and pouring myself a

glass of juice, and the whole time Poppy tried really hard to be a grown-up and not to laugh.

Mum went, "Sorry, Poppy, my daughter is thinking I am big bad deviant racist."

This was apparently hilarious, because Poppy then gave up the adult act and laughed so hard I thought she would wet her pants.

The real joke is that from the little bit I've seen of him, Paul is the dullest, straightest person to ever walk the earth. He's no sex god. He is one million light-years away from being that.

"So?" Poppy is giving me a hopeful face. "What do you think about living with Paul?"

All I can think about is what a black man's cock might look like. I can't help it.

"Do you think Paul is the right person to help you through all this?"

I'm lost. I have no other cocks to compare it with.

"After all, you're going through the same thing. You've both lost someone you love and . . ."

Poppy's voice wobbles. A fat tear spills down her face.

"Sorry, Melon, not very professional of me, is it? I really shouldn't have come. Probably get into trouble for this. I do apologize."

"S'okay."

Poppy is trying to smile, but the harder she tries, the more the tears come. She gives up speaking and just sits there sniffing and sighing, little girl sighs, willing herself happy. There is laughter going on in the kitchen. I don't want to join in with the laughing or the crying.

"It could go two ways," I say eventually. "The universe."

"Oh, yeah?" Poppy wipes her eyes and tries to rustle up her business face.

"Either the other galaxies will keep running away from us forever and ever, into eternity. Or . . ."

Poppy blinks away more tears. "Or?"

"Or there will come this point when they can't run away any farther and they'll have to start running back, and then everything will contract in on itself."

"What happens then?"

"My book calls it the big crunch."

"Sounds painful."

"Yeah. Doesn't it?"

I wonder if this is enough to get me through an exam question on the creation of the universe. And a question about the end of it all.

"Have you managed to talk to someone about what's happened, Melon?"

"No one is really into talking about it."

"No, no. Paul may be good for that, but I think you need somebody independent."

I'm trying to remember—did I, at any point, say "yes" to living with Paul?

"I'm going to organize for you to go to see someone, Melon. Someone you can talk to about your feelings."

"Another social worker?"

"No, a bereavement counselor."

"Oh."

"Right, so, I'll get things moving, shall I?"

The door to the living room opens a crack and Mr. Lacey's

clown head appears. Our talk is over and we got nowhere. We followed a little oval dotted path, back to where we started.

"We're going to serve up dinner in a few minutes, so . . ."

So what? I think. *Go away, dickhead.*

"So, if you could wind things up."

Dinner will be something in a tomato-y garlic sauce. That's all Mrs. Lacey ever cooks. Peel back all the fancy lettuce and nuts that she chucks on top and that's all there is. Pasta in a tomato-y garlic sauce, chicken in a tomato-y garlic sauce, beef in a tomato-y garlic sauce. The same thing over and over. The smell of garlic is shouting at us from the hallway.

When Poppy goes home, I will have to sit at the kitchen table and we will all eat in silence. Either that or I'll listen to Mr. and Mrs. Lacey do their happy family show, which is so fake it's suffocating. Chick can't keep up the pretense of it all; she just "yeps" and "nopes" in roughly the right places. She hardly eats, won't look me in the eye. I can't bear it.

"We're just deciding whether Melon should return to her home, aren't we, Melon?"

"Yes," I say. "I want to go home."

I do. It is my decision. I'm leaving because I want to, not because Mr. and Mrs. Lacey want me to.

"I don't want to be here." I spit out the word "here" like bad milk. "I'd rather live with Paul."

I make it sound as though Paul is a better man than him.

"That's great," says Mr. Lacey, not hearing how angry I am. "That's great that you know what you want."

69

No, listen to me, I think. Listen to me. I'm saying, *Fuck you*. I'm saying, *Fuck you all*.

Mr. Lacey smiles a winner's smile.

Except I'm not saying it, am I? I'm not saying *fuck you*. Not out loud. Not for real. I'm as bad as them.

I'm trapped on my little oval dotted path back to my home.

MERCURY, VENUS, EARTH, MARS, JUPITER, SATURN,

URANUS, NEPTUNE . . . PAUL

Whatever I say, I will end up living with Paul. There is no one else left. I'm like the earth with its magnetic field that repels charged particles. The only charged particles that get through are called social workers. Everyone else is running away from me, as fast as they can.

16 DAYS SINCE

I have bought a new hardback notebook. I open it up on the dining-room table. Its spine cracks. A big noise in a quiet house. A clean, lined page looks back at me. Usually I love that—the buzz of new stationery. Going back to school in the fall is the worst thing ever, but having a chunky pad of fresh writing paper in your bag makes it all feel better. My favorite thing is a pristine, untouched school planner. By November it doesn't feel special anymore. The grimness of being at school takes over. But in September, at the beginning, that planner is the nicest thing.

This blank page is giving off no good vibes, though. I check the clock on the wall—a pottery sunshine face with hands coming out of the nose. Five p.m. I have an hour and a half to get writing before Paul comes home.

Paul went back to work at the end of last week. When you have a proper job, after two weeks of compassionate leave, you have to just get over yourself. School isn't being so pushy with me.

On his first day back, Paul came home looking haggard. I never knew black skin could look pale and pasty. It can.

"Going back to work was very challenging," he said to me. He stood there in the kitchen, looking down, nodding for a while. "Yes, very challenging," he muttered.

He didn't move, just stayed put, chewing his bottom lip, waiting, as if I was supposed to do something about it.

"What do you want?" I went, with a sort-of laugh. "A medal?"

That made him shift.

On his first day back, Paul cleaned out Mum's desk. I imagine that was "very challenging," since Mum was a nightmare hoarder and sneaky with it too. Paul brought home a box of junk, but I didn't take a look inside. All I saw was the framed picture of me on my first day at school sticking out of the top.

It was mean of everyone at Children's Services to make Paul do the clearing out, what with him being so soft. Did they leave her desk exactly as she'd left it on that Monday evening? Her coffee cups going moldy, urgent paperwork getting ignored, as if she was away on a trip and would be back any day soon to sort it out. Maybe it was kept as a shrine. You hear of those parents who can't bear to move a single object in their kid's bedroom after they've died. They leave clothes and magazines scattered everywhere. Maybe the people at Mum's work laid flowers on her desk, like people tie bouquets to lampposts where car accidents have happened. Paul did that. Where the bus hit Mum. Those flowers must have shriveled up by now, their plastic wrapping turned a sick yellow color in the sun. I don't know this for sure. I mean, why would I actually visit the spot where it happened? I'm not that morbid.

A blank page.

You could try writing it all down, Amanda said.

A blank page.

That's my head. Blank.

I used to visit Mum's office quite often. Before she died. I know her desk; I can picture it. It was near the wobbly table with the kettle and the tea bags and the miniature fridge. If I went to see Mum at work, there'd always be little groups of harsh-faced girls hanging around outside the revolving doors in the lobby. They'd be wearing too many hair accessories. They'd usually be smoking. If I walked past with Mum, she would say "hi" and pretend not to notice the smell of weed. They were her kids—the ones who had to report to her because they'd been in trouble with the police. She'd tell them how to sort out their lives, give them a target and a purpose. She'd help them find their groove.

"Is like when a stylus falls into place on a record," Mum told me. "Music begins to play."

She gave loads of time to those kids. I reckon she thought of them as her other children. She'd only had me and never met anyone else to have more babies, so the troubled kids filled the gap.

Chick's an only child too. That's one of our bonding things—the lack of brothers and sisters and the fact that everyone thinks you're a spoiled brat who doesn't know how to share. Or at least it was one of our bonding things. It means nothing now.

73

Chick says her mum chose to have just her because you don't do a proper job as a parent if you have several kids. I think Mum would have had more babies, though, if she'd met the right person. Someone else after Paul. She was still young enough.

One of Mum's troubled kids came up to talk to me at the funeral reception. Siobhan, her name was. I'd always thought that those kids hated Mum for sticking her nose into their lives, but Siobhan was head over heels for her.

"Your mum was amazing," she said. "She totally understood what I was going through."

The way Siobhan gushed made me feel uncomfortable. It felt like this girl had stolen something from me.

"She, like, totally got me. 'Cause she'd been there, yeah?"

Siobhan was wearing a thick black turtleneck, and because it was really hot in our living room and because she was getting so excited, her cheeks burst into horrible red blotches.

"Your mum saved my life. It was totally because of her that I got myself off drugs."

Siobhan was waving her hands around, slopping wine on the carpet. Mum obviously hadn't got Siobhan off the booze as well.

"I totally didn't know, like, who I was."

The way Siobhan talked about my mum was the way crazy people talk about finding God.

"Until I met your mum, I never knew what was special about me."

Siobhan never explained what her special thing was, the thing that Mum helped her to find. I really wanted to know that.

A blank page.

I sweep the side of my hand over the notebook, clearing away imaginary dust. Write something. Something special.

When I was little, I believed there was something special about me. It was my job in life to find out what it was. Mum said she gave me my name to make me special, but I was pretty sure that wasn't *the* special thing. It was something else. If I didn't find out what it was before I was old, before I was twenty-four, say, then I would have failed. That's what I believed. I still do believe that. My time is running out. I could get knocked over tomorrow, like Mum did, and never know. Although, more and more, I'm starting to think there is no special thing in me. Maybe not everyone gets one.

I unzip my pencil case—another scary-loud sound in a silent house—and pull out a pen without looking. A red one. My shoulders tense. Someone walks over my grave. The red pen feels hot in my fingers. I go to put it back in the pencil case, find a blue pen instead. Then I think, what does it matter now?

A blank page.

Amanda expects me to write about how sad I am. When we need to do an essay, Mrs. Castleman, our English teacher, tells us to put the subject in capital letters in the middle of the page—*SAD*—then brainstorm around it. *Spread your thoughts out*, she says, *and organize them afterward*. I would like to be back at school now, doing proper essay plans, getting ready for my exams, but Paul thinks this will be "very challenging." It will not be "very challenging"; it will be a relief. I never thought I would wish to be back at school, but this house, empty, with nothing to do except think . . . Kojak is terrible company.

SAD. I have no thoughts about that to be spreading about.

I need to write something more important, something that will make things okay. Amanda doesn't know what she's talking about. She might have a dead mum, but she doesn't have my dead mum.

A blank page.

What I write in this book will make a difference, because the things I do have huge consequences. That's what the dark thing is that's been living inside my ribs since the police came to call—my power. I understand it now. When I was walking home from the stationery shop after buying this notebook, I did something—I used that power. I went to the office shop on the main street, the one I've never been to before. It looks too boring, too businessy. I could have gone to one of the nice stationery shops in town, but since the haircut, I don't feel like going too far anymore. And anyway, this notebook that I found is perfect. It's got a purple cover made of velvet with fancy writing pressed into it, like the opposite of braille. Greek writing.

On my way home, heading back along Long Lane, there was a stocky man walking two miniature sausage dogs. He was in front of me, on the opposite side of the road. The man was butch looking—a bodybuilder type—but his dogs made him look so drippy. He'd dressed them in matching navy sweaters. Double drippy. One of the dogs, the littler one at the back, was struggling to keep up on its tiny, stumpy legs. It kept turning to look at me, which slowed it down even more. The man was yanking the leash, making the little dog skid across the sidewalk. The dog seemed scared of me, which was stupid because I wasn't going to do anything. But then I thought, what if I did do something? So I kept staring at the dog, feeling myself getting a hold over it somehow. Then when I thought it was really under my spell, I made this sudden turn to cross the road toward the dog. The thing nearly exploded with fright. It yelped and hopped, got into such a tizzy that it tangled itself in its leash. That was very funny.

And then the man kicked the dog. Really hard. A boot into its stomach.

"Stop it," he said, really gruff. The dog let out this horrible squeal, a sound that put the taste of metal in the back of my throat. That was my power. I did that. I kicked that dog. Me—who likes animals, who used to nurse injured garden birds in cardboard boxes as a kid, who stops in the street to sign those petitions against vivisection—I kicked that dog. I didn't mean to, but that's not the point. It was my fault. Just like I didn't mean to do the things I did the day Mum died. But I did them, without thinking, and look what happened. Imagine what I could achieve if I really put some thought into it.

A blank page.

Paul will be home soon and I've written nothing. If I concentrate hard enough, something will come. I *click-clack* the pen between my teeth. In English once, Mrs. Castleman gave us all a postcard and told us to use it as inspiration. *Just write,* she said, *anything that comes into your head.* My postcard was of a polar bear with its head turned over its shoulder. Its mouth was open, and it was panting like a puppy, laughing almost. I'd written a fairy tale about an ice palace guarded by friendly polar bears. Kids' stuff. The thing about polar bears is everyone thinks they're cute and beautiful, but really they're vicious.

On the top of the stereo in the corner there is a picture of Mum. When Paul moved in, he framed several photos of her and put one in every room. You can't go anywhere in the house and not be reminded. Except my room and the bathroom. But even there, you can't forget. She is everywhere. I get up and bring the photo over to the dining-room table. It's sealed in a heavy block of see-through plastic. I like the frame. It's something I'd never have imagined Paul choosing. I put the picture next to my note-book on the table and sit down.

In this picture, Mum is laughing. Her hair is falling forward. One of her bony hands (a flea-market ring on every finger) is pulling back a handful of curls on one side of her face. Her mouth is open; you can see two fillings. Mum's other hand is pushed into her lap, which makes her look shy. Something she definitely wasn't. On that hand, her left hand, there is a diamond ring. I don't remember that ring from when she was alive. The background is leafy.

78

She could be in the depths of a forest somewhere, but more likely she's in a London park. The overflowing trash can and the kids with the crack pipe are probably just out of shot.

I don't know where this picture was taken. I don't know where most of the other pictures around the house were taken either. I don't like that, Paul knowing this whole other person that I've never met.

I wonder where I was when Paul took this picture. It looks sunny. Maybe I spent that weekend sunbathing in Chick's backyard. Maybe Mum had told me that she had a day trip planned with Paul and I paid no attention. Maybe I just left the house before she had the chance to say, writing "Gone to Chick's" on the notepad in the kitchen before I went. Maybe she told me about it afterward, what a good time they'd had, but I didn't listen. I never listened.

A blank page.

I throw the pen across the room. It hits the wall, leaving a red scratch of ink. It drops behind the dusty fern plant on the cabinet. Through the dining-room window, I can see a mum trying to get her two kids to go up the path of one of the houses behind ours. I don't know who she is. I don't know any of our neighbors. If Mum was here, she'd tell you her name straightaway, know where she works, what she eats for breakfast, everything. I used to be close to Pamela, our old next-door neighbor, but she moved to Canada last year.

The mum-I-don't-know can't get the youngest of her

kids, a little girl, a toddler, to go into the house. The girl wants to crouch down in the gutter and pull something out of the edges of the drain. The mother goes back and yanks her up by one of her pink-jacketed arms. The girl squeals, and keeps squealing the whole way up the path. The mum opens the front door; they go inside. The door shuts behind them and I can't hear the girl crying anymore.

I didn't listen. I never listened.

A blank page.

I have a heading.
Yes. I have a heading.
A heading isn't much but it's something.
I find a blue pen in my pencil case, pull off the cap with my teeth. I am going to break the curse of the empty page. I write:

THE STORY

I get out my ruler and underline it, neatly, twice. Yes, this is what I have to write. I did listen. I know every word.

THE DAY

I am keeping a list in the back of my *Great Expectations* study guide—every possible way that my name can be twisted into something else.

MELON-CHOLY

MELON-OMA

SMELLY MELON

Some are names that I've had used on me before; some are bound to get used sooner or later.

MELON BELL-END

MELON THE FELON

BIG MELONS

Writing them down helps. If I get to know them, if I can guess what's coming, then the names won't bother me so much.

MELON HEAD

MELON TITS

MELON ARSE

They'll be like advertising slogans that people repeat over and over. They won't mean anything in the real world.

The trouble is, when I look at the list, I know the most ridiculous thing I've written down is the name at the top.

MELON.

My real name. There is no getting away from it: I have a stupid, stupid name.

Ian Grainger knows this. And I hate him. If me or Chick ever mention him, we always say, "God!" afterward. Guaranteed. He's just so immature. When he's acting amazed, he sucks in his cheeks and makes a noise like he's calling a cat. Idiot. And he has to keep flicking his hair out of his eyes. He thinks the flicking thing is cool. It's not. It just makes him look like he's got Tourette's. He also walks with a limp, all the time, even though there is nothing wrong with his leg. This is so we all think his bits are so huge they keep him from walking properly. He wishes. Lucy Bloss reckons he's got a massive dick, but has she ever really been there? She's all talk.

I'm in the lineup outside the science lab, at the front of the line with Chick. Ian's at the back. It's biology today. Reproduction. It's hard to look any of the boys in the eye after Mr. Spencer has put up that picture on the overhead projector — the one of a woman's pelvis cut in half so you can see all of her tubes. I prefer physics.

Mr. Spencer is late, so we're standing there, killing time. Chick is telling me about her summer vacation, which her mum and dad have just booked. The Laceys go to

Playa de las Américas in Tenerife every year. Which is bizarre. There is a whole world out there to visit, and the Laceys have no family abroad forcing them to go to the same place all the time. We still have to go to Crete every summer even though Granbabas is dead, and Auntie Aphrodite pretends to speak less and less English each time we visit.

Anyway, Chick tells me that they're going to a new place on vacation this year. This is big news in the Lacey household.

"It's in Italy and it has loads of towers," Chick goes. "S'called San Jimmy . . . San Jimmy . . . I don't know, San Jimmy something."

"Wow," I go.

It makes me think. If the Laceys can change the habit of a lifetime, maybe I could convince Mum to try somewhere new. The Crete pantomime with Auntie Aphrodite each year is painful.

"Mum read that it's *the* place to go right now," Chick goes. She doesn't realize it, but she's boasting. Then Chick drops the bombshell: "But it doesn't have a beach."

"No way!"

"Yes way! Nightmare."

At least me and Mum get plenty of beach time when we go to Crete.

Then I hear my name being yelled from the end of the line. Straightaway, I know that it's Ian Grainger.

Ian Grainger has called my name.

There's a little explosion in my chest. A part of me thinks maybe Ian Grainger really wants to talk to me about something. That would be okay. I admit, that would be quite a bonus. The other part of me thinks—not likely.

I look back along the line, and Ian's head is sticking out. He's waiting for me to answer. The explosion in my chest spreads. I feel it between my legs. I don't know why. It's a sensation so strong that everyone else must be able to see what's happening. I'm blushing too; my cheeks are burning, and I haven't even said anything yet. I am officially pathetic.

"Yeah?" I go at last, and it's a good "yeah," really bored and not interested.

"Not you!" Ian slams back.

The warm explosion turns into a knife stab. I duck back behind Chick.

Ian is doing one of those dumb boy laughs. He's yelling again. "Why do ya think everyone's always talking aboutcha, Melon?"

Ian's mates start spewing laughter. The whole class is looking at me now, most of them doing that face that says, *It's really bad to laugh.* They are doing that face while pissing themselves laughing.

Ian isn't letting me off yet. "We were just, like, you know, yelling out names of food and stuff. Bananas! Cake! Mickey D's!"

The laughing cranks up.

"Chicken fucking vindaloo!"

This is Dylan, who is puny and zitty and should thank his lucky stars he gets to hang around with Ian; otherwise, his head would be forever down a flushing toilet. The laughing dies down when he opens his mouth. He hasn't got the same influence.

The explosion inside me has gone. I'm cold. The only parts of me left on fire are my ears. Both of them. Mum says if your left ear burns, someone is talking lovingly about you. If it's the right, it's spite. So that means Ian loves me and hates me at the same time. He doesn't. He totally hates me.

I turn back to face the glass double doors of the science lab. I catch a glance at my reflection, make sure I don't look like I'm crying. I tip my head forward. Long, bushy hair is good for hiding behind. I keep threatening Mum that I'm going to hack it all off, but I only say that to upset her. Really I want to grow my hair long enough to sit on.

I can see Chick's face out of the corner of my eye, looking almost as shamed as me.

"Prick," I mutter quietly, so no one else can hear. I don't want a fight.

I pray Chick will start blabbering on about San Jimmy-wherever again and its hopeless lack of a beach, but she's gone dumb. The whole line has gone whispery quiet. Me and Chick stand there, hunched over, waiting for the firing squad.

Then it comes again, like I knew it would. "Meh-lon!" Chirpy like a doorbell. Ding-dong.

I focus on the white scuffs around the toes of my black ballet flats. I concentrate on not crying. Crying would not be cool.

"Hey, Melon! It's rude to ignore someone when they're talking to ya."

The shoes are really interesting, I tell myself. The shoes are really interesting.

"Melon! I'm fucking talking to ya. Where's ya fucking manners, man?"

85

"Turn around, Mel," Chick hisses. I can't look at her.

"Melllll-ohhhhhn!" Ian is squealing it now, like an opera singer.

I obey. I turn my body. Last thing I do is let my gaze meet his. His eyes are brown, too brown. They're black and sticky.

"Yes? Can we help you?" Ian does his snooty voice.

I try to stare him out.

He pouts at me, pretending to be a girl.

Nothing about this is even slightly funny, yet Lucy Bloss goes solo and bursts into shrieky laughter. Everyone looks at her for a minute, which is exactly what she wanted, so she milks it. She clamps a fingerless-gloved hand over her mouth and rolls her eyes at Emily Winters and Dionne Agu. Then she forces out a few giggly hiccups for extra effect. She is so fake. I mean, who wears fingerless gloves in the middle of March?

Ian smiles at Lucy. This means they are probably going together again. They make up and break up all the time, so it's hard to keep up. And anyway, who can be bothered to waste their time trying to keep up?

Ian is mouthing my name, feeling his chest, pretending he has boobs. *Mehhhh-lllonnn*, his lips go. His tongue makes a meal of it. *Mehhhh-lllonnn*.

I've lost count of the number of times I have asked Mum why she gave me such a stupid, stupid name. Every time I ask, I get The Story. I get whispering at seeds; I get yellow-striped armyworms, I get laying hands on warm fruit. I don't get answers.

Before I get The Story, Mum will usually go, "Why you ask about your name today, *peristeraki mou*? They make fun of your tits at school?"

I hate the way she says "tits"—it's so porn mag, so throwaway, as though nothing that worries me is important to her. My name is important. The size of my chest is important. The two of them work together to ruin my life.

The last time I asked Mum about my name, I was trying on bras. I have prayed every night since I was eleven that my boobs would stop growing. I've had to buy a larger bra every year since then. I thought if I asked Mum at the exact moment I was trying on some new, ridiculous cup size, she would realize what she'd done. She would immediately say sorry for naming me Melon, and our next stop would be the courthouse to change it. Some hope.

We were in the changing rooms. I was staring at my big woman's figure in the mirror. Mum was sitting on the leather stool in the corner of the cubicle, searching for cigarettes and a lighter in her massive shoulder bag. When I asked, she ignored me. Instead she said, "Smells in here, hey? Cheesy, no?"

"You can't smoke in here, Mum," I told her.

She ignored that too, and answered the original question.

"I want you to be different," she went, still ransacking her bag.

"I want to be like the other girls," I said back.

I really wanted her to hear that. I really wanted her to see me, standing there, the thick white elastic crisscrossing my boobs. A sturdy bra, a boring bra. I'm not allowed anything pretty. With my chest, it makes me look too grown-up, Mum says. Makes me look like a stripper, she means.

"When you older, you be grateful to be different." That's what she told me. I wasn't going to get my sorry. I took off the bra.

"Maria?" she goes, poofing air through her lips. "Everyone has this name!"

And then she was off. "On an island far, far from here, where the sea is woven from strings of sapphire blue . . ." Whispering at seeds, yellow-striped armyworms, warm fruit, *ta karpouzia ine etima!* Blah, blah, blah. By the time she'd gotten to the part about the truck driving away, she was halfway through a cigarette and I was back in my sweater. She stopped then, poked a finger at the bra on its hanger.

"What, you are not liking it?"

"It's fine, Mum," I said. "Let's just go."

Mum stubbed out her cigarette in the lid of the packet.

Outside the cubicle, a shop assistant was squirting air freshener and giving Mum a dirty look. Mum breezed away from the changing rooms, refusing to notice.

Ian is still mouthing my name. He licks the nipple of one of his huge, invisible breasts. Everyone is cracking up. Especially Lucy. Everyone in the line is waiting for me to say something. Or, even better, to run to the nearest bathroom to cry. If I bolt, Lucy will send Dionne Agu to follow me and report back.

I have no razor-sharp reply, no witty answer. I have . . . nothing.

So I laugh.

It's a horrible sound, really phony, but it does the job. Ian stops feeling himself up. He tosses out a chuckle. The laugh shows that I've got a better sense of humor than Lucy Bloss. After all, I'm the one getting picked on, not her. The laugh has let Ian off the hook. He turns away.

The ripples of giggling along the line die down. They're disappointed, I know it. They wanted me to crumble. That would have been something to talk about.

Ian has forgotten me already. He's kicking Dylan's backpack, pretending to start a fight. They're shouting about something else now.

"Phew-ee!" goes Chick, mouse-like.

I shrug, I smile, like it's nothing.

Inside, I am still searching for that killer line—something to plunge right down into Ian's soul, something to stop him dead, something to wound him. Make him choke. Something to make him . . . like me.

I feel sick. I hate myself for making it easy on Ian. I hate everyone in that line for laughing. But more than that, I hate Mum for giving me my stupid, stupid name.

When I get home, I will tell Mum this. I will tell her how she has made my life hell.

6 YEARS BEFORE

I am nine and a quarter years old and my bag is packed. I've got clean underwear and socks for three days, a nightie, my school uniform, a spare sweater, and a pair of jeans. I also have a house key so I can go back and get more clothes if I need them. Inside my wheelie suitcase there are also cherry drops and Arthur, my lion, so he won't be lonely on his own in my bedroom.

I'm going to stay with Pamela next door while Mum goes to Crete. Usually Mum and me go to Crete together. But that's only in the summer. Now it's winter. Granbabas has died. But we musn't feel sad. Mum says he's had a good life and he's lucky his heart held out this long and it is the fate of everyone in the Fourakis family to die young. So if we're not supposed to be sad about Granbabas dying, Mum must be doing all that crying for a different reason.

Pamela's house is the same as ours but the other way around. When you walk in our door, the stairs are in front of you and you turn right to go into the living room. In Pamela's house, you turn left. I'm worried that I'm going to get up in the night to pee and walk smack into the wall with the window instead of going the right way along the landing for Pamela's bathroom.

Pamela has short white hair that doesn't move. It stands up from her head in one big wave. I'm looking forward to finding out how she makes it do that. One of her front teeth is twisted and pops out of her lips when she smiles. She has lots of wrinkles on her neck, which get filled up by all the tiny gold chains she wears. Pamela's son and daughter are both grown up and have moved out; that's how come she has room for me to stay. The daughter is named Sophie and she lives in Canada. Pamela often shows us postcards from Sophie when she chats with Mum over the backyard fence. Pamela's son is named Brian. He still lives nearby and visits lots. When Mum bumps into him outside the house, she says, "Hi, Brian," and he just nods his head and does this weird little salute. I've never heard him speak. Brian does Pamela's outdoor jobs for her and sits around with a grumpy face drinking her tea. I wish it had been Brian who had moved to Canada rather than Sophie, but I suppose Pamela prefers it this way because her yard stays tidy.

In Pamela's house there is no wall between the kitchen and dining room. This is because she has "knocked through." I try to imagine Pamela with a sledgehammer bashing through the bricks and then decide that Brian must have done it for her. Mum sometimes says she would like to knock through our kitchen wall. I worry that I'll wake up one morning and come downstairs to find that she's done it in the night, just because she felt like it.

The other walls in Pamela's kitchen and dining room are covered in plates. There are kings and queens on them, flowers, ones that say MOTHER and SISTER and FRIEND, and ones with dogs. Pamela has a Westie named Ernie who yaps at Kojak through the wire fence that separates our yards. Kojak just ignores him. I wonder which of the plates Pamela will take down off the wall for us to eat on come dinnertime.

Once she's let us in, Pamela says, "Why don't you go and watch a bit of TV, lovie, while I have a chat with your mummy in the kitchen." So I turn left into the living room, and Mum and Pamela go straight on to the kitchen. Pamela's sofas have extra pink covers on the armrests and headrests. On top of her TV set there is a pottery milkmaid looking embarrassed while a pottery boy whispers in her ear.

Even with the sound up on the TV, I can hear bits of their conversation, because there is no wall between the dining room and the living room either, just an archway. I don't think this is because Pamela has knocked through. The living room and dining room are all one in our house too.

Pamela is asking Mum about her flight and whether she will be okay, and Mum is telling Pamela that Granbabas had a good life and was lucky that his heart lasted so long and it is the fate of everyone in the Fourakis family to die young, so we shouldn't be sad. Still, I can hear that Mum is crying a bit. I wonder if this is because she is leaving me behind. We've never been apart for a night my whole life, except for when I sleep over at Chick's house, but that doesn't count because I know Mum is only a few streets away. I said this to Mum when she was rushing around packing my case, and she said to me, "No, silly, we spend many weeks apart before this."

I don't remember that at all. So I asked, "When? When were we apart that long?"

Mum stopped folding clothes and stared at me for a moment like she was doing a sum in her head. Then she went, "No, you are right. This is first time."

Pamela is asking Mum what I would especially like for dinner, and Mum is telling her that I'll eat anything, which isn't really true. But Mum has already given me the talk about not being any trouble because it's very nice of Pamela to offer to look after me. I'm worried I'm going to get fish with the eye still in for dinner and I'll have to pretend to like it just to be no bother. On the TV there is a program where a woman is explaining to two little boys how boogies are made. She's mixing together dough and green food coloring and putting it in blobs on a baking tray.

In the kitchen, Pamela is telling Mum to get going now and to not worry about me. Mum is sniffing and sighing and saying something about not being sure that she can handle it all. Pamela is telling her she doesn't have to go if she doesn't want to, and Mum is saying no, no, she has to go. Then Mum tells Pamela a lie. I'm not listening to the TV at all when she says it. I hear it clearly. Mum says, "I have to go. I did not go home for my mother's funeral and this is very bad, very bad. I must make up for it." This isn't true.

Mum's mum, my *yia-yia*, whom I never knew, she died over here in England when I was a baby, not in Crete. Mum has told me The Story. I know all about the funeral. Mum organized the whole thing. She even cooked this big dish of special wheat that you're supposed to make—like a birthday

93

cake except it's for a dead person—and Mum never cooks anything like that unless she has to. The funeral sounded beautiful. I wish I could have been there.

The boogie woman on TV is demonstrating how germs get up your nose by kicking balls into a net while the two boys try to stop them. Mum comes into the room now and pretends she hasn't been crying. She gives me a big squeeze that stops me breathing for a moment and tells me I must be good. She uses her telling-off voice, so it feels like I've already been bad when I haven't even had the chance yet.

In the hallway, Pamela opens the front door for Mum and we both wave her off in a taxi.

"So," says Pamela once the taxi has gone, "let's have some fun, shall we?"

Staying at Pamela's is great. She cooks lasagne and fish and chips (no eye in the fish) and shepherd's pie all from scratch, not from a package, and she doesn't complain at all when I watch hours and hours of television. Ernie, her Westie, decides he really likes me, so he sleeps on the end of my bed at night. When we pop back to my house each day to feed Kojak, I feel very guilty for making friends with a dog.

Pamela tucks me in at night and tells me I mustn't worry about Mum. Until she talks about not being worried, I had forgotten I should be worried. I guess Mum will find it hard with Auntie Aphrodite being even grumpier than usual, so I think about not worrying about that. But then I remember something I am really worried about—that Granbabas will give his farm to Mum. When Chick's gran died, her old house got left to Mrs. Lacey. Chick's mum sold the house—that's how come Chick got new ice skates—but Mum won't do that with Granbabas's farm. She'll want us to go and live there because she loves Crete so much. When she was growing up, all Mum ever wanted to be was a melon farmer. I would hate it there. I'd have to leave Chick, I wouldn't understand the TV because I can't speak Greek, and I don't think they ever have snow.

While Mum is away, it snows in London. Not enough to keep us from going to school, but enough to build a snowman in Pamela's backyard. When we've used up all of her snow, we climb over the fence into our yard and build another snowman.

"Someone to guard your house and keep it safe," says Pamela. I like that. I want it to never melt.

When Mum gets back, she rushes into Pamela's living room, where I am watching TV, picks me up, and spins me around until I'm dizzy.

Pamela follows her in and asks her how it was.

"Cold," says Mum, and Pamela nods like this explains everything.

The "cold" makes me hopeful. "Did you have snow too?" I ask.

"No, no snow," says Mum. "Not yet." The "yet" also makes me hopeful.

Mum doesn't mention moving to the farm when we get home. I don't bring it up in case it's just something she's forgotten and I might remind her by talking about it. Mum has brought me back a present from Crete—a brown leather satchel with red and green flowers. The bits of the satchel with flowers painted on are sunken into the leather. When you run your fingertips over these dips and grooves, it feels nice. I really like the satchel, but when I take it to school a couple of the girls say it's stupid and cheap and looks like it came from a dollar store. So after that I hang it on the back of my bedroom door and tell Mum I don't want to take it to school anymore in case I spoil it.

After two weeks of not mentioning the farm, I'm bursting to know what is going on, so I cross my fingers behind my back for good luck and ask, "Are we going to have to move to the farm?"

Mum isn't looking at me. She is concentrating on stirring beans and putting toast in the toaster at the same time.

"What farm?"

"The melon farm. Now that you own it, are we going to have to move there?"

"I don't own any farm." The toast pops up and makes me jump. "Auntie Aphrodite is owning the farm."

"Why?"

"Eggs, fridge, please."

I do as I'm told and get two eggs out from under the flip-up bit in the fridge door. Without thinking, I pass them straight to her and she hisses at me to put them on the counter. With all the questions, I forgot. It's very, very bad luck to pass eggs straight to someone. Mum waits a few seconds, then picks up the eggs and cracks them into a frying pan.

"Why?" I try asking again. "Why does Auntie Aphrodite own the farm?"

"Because Granbabas say it so, that is why."

Mum is swearing at the beans for sticking to the pan.

"Why isn't it you who gets the farm?"

"Because it just isn't, okay, Melon? Now, you are washing hands and sitting up at table."

We eat dinner without saying much. Mum stabs at the beans like she's still angry with them for burning. I breathe a sigh of relief. Finding out that the farm belongs to Auntie Aphrodite is the best news. The beans taste good.

By the end of the meal, Mum has calmed down enough for me to ask another question.

"Why did you tell Pamela that you got into trouble for not going to Crete for your mum's funeral when it all happened here?"

Mum looks at me like she did when we were packing my suitcase—the "doing the sums" face.

"Because"—she picks toast crumbs off the table with the end of her thumb—"because sometimes it is the kind thing to say a lie rather than to tell the truth."

"Oh," I say. "Okay."

"Okay?" says Mum.

Then she lets me off doing the washing up.

THE STORY

3

In the early morning, London's streets are strangely subdued. Chaos has come and gone. Stop for a moment in one of the city's squares and you will hear murmurs of the night before, of the years before, of centuries ago. But London isn't a place for looking backward. History is only a promise that anything could happen in the future. In this place of possibilities, Mama and Maria made their new home.

They began by lodging with Auntie Eleni, Mama's sister who had left Crete ten years before with a small suitcase and a big dream. Eleni was a robust woman with a bighearted spirit, a woman whose hands were surprisingly soft considering she spent all her time dealing with the dampness of other people's laundry. With her husband, Vassilis, she owned the Laundromat on Kentish Town Road. Though her welcome was generous, space in Eleni's house near the train station was not. So Mama understood that as soon as Maria's baby arrived, they would need to move on.

Germination took on a whole new meaning for fifteen-year-old Maria as she started this new life away from the gullied melon patch. She rested her hands on her taut, expanding belly, feeling the warmth within, encouraging her baby to grow.

In the fluorescent light of the delivery room, hair glued to the red of her cheeks, Maria gave birth to a baby girl with frantic limbs—and the final slivers of her childhood slipped away.

Nothing that had happened before that day had really meant anything. Or rather, everything that had happened before that day had only been leading up to this. From now on, Maria decided, she would be like Babas—she would avoid the bumps in the road. And she would make sure only the strongest memories would survive.

Maria examined the creased, swollen features of the baby squirming in her arms, a mystery ready to solve, and no other name in the world seemed right. The round hopefulness of the fruits that blossomed back home and the bold-eyed girl before her were the same thing.

And that was how Melon got her name.

Mama, Maria, and Melon took their few belongings and rented a flat above the Taj Mahal Tandoori House, a few doors down from the Papadakis Washateria. The scent of chili, cumin, coriander, and fenugreek drifted from the kitchen below, infiltrated their bedrooms, and seduced their taste buds.

Maria took the double room and made Melon's first crib from the bottom drawer of a cabinet. Mama took the single room, where she did nothing more to make her mark than hang a crucifix above her bed. The living room and kitchen were all one, furnished with a well-loved three-piece furniture set, the fabric of the arms worn through.

The rent did not pay itself, so while Maria's days were spent deciphering a new alphabet at a school for English, her evenings were spent taking orders at the Mount Olympus restaurant across the street. The owner, a Londoner, was so pleased to hire an authentic Greek waitress that he decided to believe Maria's story that she was twenty-one years old and eligible for a decent wage.

Mama looked after Melon day and night. God had granted Mama just one opportunity to raise a child, but here was another gift from heaven. While Melon napped, Mama steamed through ironing work, sourced by her sister, and in the evening she sang Cretan lullabies until her granddaughter's nasal breaths became slow, slow whispers in the dark.

But Mama still missed home. She missed the patchwork quilt of flat, dry earth that spread out around their farm. She missed Maria's *babas*, her darling Manolis.

She wrote letters describing her anxiety as they had boarded the aeroplane at Hania, the strange, cold air when they landed. She told Manolis of Eleni's achievements—*my sister, a thriving businesswoman!*

And she tried to explain.

At first she could not find the words, but driven by the desperate feelings that possessed her at night, the sentences came. *We are two bricks that belong side by side, strong, building the walls of our family. I will come back to you, if you need me like I need you. I love you. Your devoted Chrysoula.*

Babas never replied. But Babas's interfering sister Aphrodite did. *You should have thought of all this*, read Aphrodite's scrawl, *before you deserted your husband.*

100

Maria, meanwhile, embraced all that London offered, good and bad—the bawdy banter of car horns, the tinny bass lines of other people's music, the way rain traveled down a window pane. She rode with Melon on red double-decker buses, paying no attention to numbers or destinations, each journey unveiling a new part of the city, a new crop of Gothic buildings with sooty faces, a new green space hidden in the maze of roads. When Maria heard Greek words being spoken on board the bus, above the fast talk of the English teenagers, she would immediately introduce herself.

This was how she came to meet Anastasios "Tassos" Georgakis from Agios Nikolaos in Crete. Their lives had begun on the same small island only to converge hundreds of miles away. He was a lean older gentleman with slender wrists and inviting eyes who wore an insubstantial tweed jacket whatever the weather. Tassos had come to the U.K. as a student many years ago and now worked for the Greek embassy. He said his work consisted solely of helping tourists replace lost passports, but Maria suspected there was more to it than that. She invited him to the flat for *biskota amigdalou* and a pot of English tea—and to meet her mama.

They were immediate friends—Mama and Tassos. They watched television together in the evenings, with Tassos translating. And when Maria came home from the restaurant at night, she would hear their laughter in the living room, the merry *click-clack* of their Greek tongues.

Maria turned her attention to Melon, who was growing strong and broad, a sign of Babas's Fourakis blood staking its claim above the genes of Christos Drakakis. Maria did not want her daughter seeking out conversation on the top decks of buses, so she found a playgroup for Melon, somewhere for her to pick up her accentless English.

But while Maria focused on her thriving daughter, she neglected to see how Tassos had only gone so far in healing Mama's homesickness. When land is left uncared for, weeds grow. When a sense of longing goes unanswered, an illness takes over.

"I have found a lump, in my breast."

Mama said the fated words one dark afternoon in November, and Maria could not speak. How could she have stayed blind to the pain in Mama's heart? Why hadn't she stopped? Why hadn't she listened?

"You musn't be sad," said Mama, who had already resigned herself to her destiny. "I knew this would happen when I married your father and took on his name—all the Fourakis family dies young."

3 DAYS SINCE

I have stolen Chick's credit card. She owes me. My mum is dead. Hers is still alive.

Although, you would think it was the other way around. Chick is the one acting like her arm has been chopped off. Yesterday I cracked a joke, a really funny one, about our math teacher, Miss Boniface, and that weird thing she does with her neck, and Chick just looked at me like I had murdered her hamsters. I've since thought about murdering Chick's hamsters, but I do want her to speak to me again, not hate me forever.

That's all I want. I want her to talk.

Chick thinks she's not allowed to smile. She's terrified that something is going to make her laugh and this will be disrespectful to my mum. Rubbish. Now that I'm stuck in the middle of it all, I see that there are no rules about how to behave around death. The Lacey household has made its own rules.

1. YOU MUST ACT SOLEMN AT ALL TIMES EVEN THOUGH YOU DIDN'T REALLY KNOW THE PERSON WHO DIED.

2. IF YOU WANDER INTO A ROOM WHERE THE DEAD PERSON'S DAUGHTER IS, YOU MUST EXIT, QUICK. YOU WILL HAVE NO CLUE HOW TO ACT OR WHAT TO SAY.

3. THIS IS THE LAW.

Every time she thinks I'm out of earshot, Mrs. Lacey says something like, "I don't know what to do with her. How should I know what to do with her?" Mr. Lacey will tell her, "Please keep your voice down, Rowena." Never anything constructive, always the same line: "Please keep your voice down, Rowena." I wish people would speak up. Yell a bit. That would be better than the crushing silence.

I'm waiting at the Tube station. It's good to be outside. Men in orange overalls are working on the tracks beyond the end of the platform. From this perspective, they look like midgets. Oompa Loompas. Chick played an Oompa Loompa in one of her Christmas ice-skating things. She had to wear hideous orange tights and paint her face with this stuff that made her skin break out. Two of the little orange men are carrying what looks like a stretcher with a body on top. Must be sandbags. Must be.

I've heard Mr. and Mrs. Lacey bad-mouthing Mum too. Mostly Mrs. Lacey. She'll huff and go, "Lord knows how she brought that girl up. Am I expected to right all the wrongs?" I don't like that. Only I am allowed to criticize Mum.

The least Chick can do is lend me her credit card. I haven't gotten near enough to Chick to ask her permission. She'd probably say "yes" if I did, anything to make me go away. No, actually, she wouldn't, because she knows her

104

mum would freak out. That would be great. To make Mrs. Lacey freak out. A reaction. Something real.

Four minutes until a train. An age. I want to get out of here. I feel like I'm skipping school and I'm going to get busted any minute. It's Thursday morning. A school day. I've never skipped school. Ever. Of course, I'm not really skipping now. "Compassionate leave." That's what they call it. I'm not sure what's more compassionate: making me stay at Chick's house with Mrs. Lacey, or sending me to school to get stared at by everyone. Mrs. Lacey is taking time off work to look after me. She's not doing much "looking after." She's done plenty of cleaning and read enough magazines. The best I get is a stiff, "Are you okay?" She looks terrified of what I might say back, so I don't dare to say, "No, actually." I just say, "Yeah, fine." Sometimes Mrs. Lacey goes, "You must miss her very much," or, "We must be thankful that she didn't suffer." They sound like sentences she found in a greeting card. She says them under her breath, without looking me in the eye. Mrs. Lacey has gone to the doctor this morning, and I took the chance to escape. I'd rather be at school, though it would be bad to carry on like nothing had happened. Plus, no one else at school has had a parent die. I am now officially even more of a freak than I ever was. Brilliant.

There's the sound of a Coke can being kicked down the stairs onto the platform, then the scuffle of shoes trying to get at it first. I look up.

Ian. Ian Grainger. The last thing I need right now.

I'm doing well holding things together, but if Ian starts on me, I don't know what will happen. I might cry, wail, faint, explode. Literally. Pieces of me flying everywhere.

I may not be skipping school, but Ian definitely is. Eleven thirty. He should be in English now. He's in his uniform, so I'm guessing he did math first thing, then decided to sack it for the day. Ian's with Murray Bulger, who is fat yet somehow manages to be worthy of Ian's friendship. Dylan is with them too. Puny, stupid Dylan.

Dylan kicks the can onto the gravel of the train tracks.

"Fuckhead," goes Ian. He gives the back of Dylan's head a proper whacking, then walks off ahead of the others. Limping. It's funny how the limp isn't there when he plays soccer.

Ian picks a spot by the yellow line at the edge of the platform and dumps down his bag. Dylan and Murray join him, do the same with their bags. All three of them put their hands into their coat pockets. Ian first, the other two following. Sheep. They stand poking their toes at the line, then scan along the platform for a train. They notice me. Murray swings his head back toward the other two, lowers his voice, says something I can't hear. They half nod, look at their feet, then pretend to find the massive poster for deodorant across the tracks really, really interesting.

They know.

One of two things must have happened. Either there was some cringe-worthy speech made by the headmaster at assembly Tuesday morning about why I wasn't there, or Chick has been spreading it around. Chick will earn some proper kudos at school for this—the juiciest bit of gossip since Pooja Varma got arrested for shoplifting. Or maybe this story is bigger. Someone actually died. And Chick has firsthand knowledge—details. When Pooja nicked those clothes, we had to make up most of the story just so we could keep talking about it.

However they found out, Ian, Murray, and Dylan know.

I brace myself. I'm ready for them to do the thing with my name.

But nothing.

I look back along the tracks: a train is nosing its way into the station. I look back at the boys. Still nothing. Their turtle heads have shrunk down into their jacket shells. They're pretending I'm not there.

The Tube train clatters into the station, shouting down the silence and whipping my hair across my face. The current of air makes the boys' hair do a wave. They're rooted to the spot, looking at their feet. The doors stop right in front of me, and the doors nearest to the boys will take them onto the same car. I expect them to move along to another part of the train, but that would mean acknowledging that they've seen me. Too embarrassing.

The doors open. We all get into an empty car.

"Mind the gap."

That's where I am right now, in the gap. *Please mind the gap between the death of your mother and the edge of normal.*

The doors close. I sit down. Only when the train hiccups into life do I dare check where they are. They're on the seats by the glass panel at the end of the car. They're looking at me now, but they're not saying anything. I'm in the middle of the train, another two glass panels of protection away. I won't need it, though. They're not going to do the thing with my name. I can feel the pity oozing off them, although they're grudging about it at the same time. Mum dying has spoiled their game. Murray gives me a sorry look. Dylan nods. It feels like being patted on the head by an old relative. The train clangs into the dark of the tunnel. This is the weirdest thing to say, but I actually preferred it when the boys were jerks.

I turn away. I feel a bit sick. I haven't eaten yet today. Couldn't think about breakfast. I take the bottle of Cherry Coke I bought at the newsstand, open it without thinking. Of course it explodes. It's been bumping around in my bag all the way to the station. Sticky brown stuff everywhere. The smell of sugar. The eyes of Ian and his lot are on me again. This would be a perfect excuse for them to pounce. Ian is itching to, I can tell, but he swallows his laugh. *Come on,* I think, *say something, something rude, something horrible, anything.* I shake Coke from my hands, hold the bottle away like a smelly shoe. A puddle has formed on the floor of the car and is traveling toward my feet. I suck drips from the edge of the bottle and take a swig. Warm. Makes your teeth feel furry. I burp. Loudly. Ian looks again. *Say something. Say something.* He wrinkles his nose, pretends he's disgusted. That's rich, coming from him.

I put the cap back on the bottle, put it on the seat next to me. Satisfied.

I have cherry drops in my bag. Nothing goes better with Cherry Coke than cherry drops. Unwrap one, put it in your mouth, crack it with your teeth so the insides come out, then take a mouthful of Cherry Coke. Gorgeous. The shell of the cherry drop fills the gaps in my back teeth like gluey fillings. I click my jaws together, feel the top teeth stick to the bottom.

"Hey."

It's Ian.

"Give us one of those," he goes.

So I do. I lob a cherry drop, hard, all the way along the train car. Ian stands to catch it. It clips him on the forehead.

"Wanker," I mutter as he fumbles to pick it up. Dylan and Murray can't help but crack up.

Ian looks at me, surprised. I'm shocked, shocked that I said that word out loud. So I say it again.

"Wanker," I go. "Can't even catch a fucking sweetie."

Ian moves forward along the aisle, trying to make himself look big. Big, strong Ian. I poke at the cherry film on my teeth with my tongue. He stands there looking at me, wobbling with the train, a skittle that could fall back or stay standing, ready for another strike.

"What did you say?"

Dylan and Murray have stopped laughing. Murray can't get rid of the grin. They've turned in their seats to get a good view, jackets rustling.

"Nothing."

"Didn't sound like nothing."

I look down at the river of Coke parting around my shoe.

Ian raises his voice above the noise of the train. "I said, it didn't sound like nothing."

"I heard you the first time."

I meet Ian's sticky tar eyes. There's something different about them today. Usually they're fiery and wet, full of the joy of being an absolute twat. Now they're unsteady. He knows he should back off, not because he's made my life hell for the last few years, but because of my mum. My dead mum. She's my "get out of jail free" card. I hate that. I hate it because it's a cheat.

We're still staring at each other. *Let me have it*, I'm thinking. *Don't you dare let me off easy.*

"Yeah, well . . ." Ian wobbles, parts his legs to get stable on the train floor. Murray and Dylan are waiting for the final verdict. "Just watch your mouth, yeah?"

I nod at him. "Okay," I say, sarcastic. "I'll watch it."

The lights of Highgate Station appear behind Ian's head.

"Let's get off here, yeah?" The boys pick up their bags, start bundling toward the door, trying to knock each other over. I wonder if they'd planned to get off at Highgate or if Ian is just saving face.

"Mind the gap," I say to the back of their heads.

"Yeah, fuck you, right," Ian shoots back from the platform, giving me the finger.

The doors close and the platform starts moving through the frames of the window like a movie reel getting back to normal speed. The boys are whisked away. The black of the tunnel gulps me down.

They can't bother me now.

Nothing and no one can bother me now.

26 DAYS SINCE

There is a bag for clothes for donation. There is a box for the knickknacks. There's a trash bag. Then, on the bed, there is a pile for Paul to keep. Paul says I can have a pile too. How generous. Whose mum was she after all?

He's also let me choose which bit of Mum's room I want to do. He's all give, give, give. I decide on the chest of drawers. I don't want to watch Paul sorting through Mum's underwear; I'll do it. Though I'm not stupid; I know he's already been through her underwear. If you know what I mean.

Mum's chest of drawers is a Victorian relic like her wardrobe, but they don't match. The chest is a lighter wood and it's a great hulk of a thing compared to the dinky wardrobe that Paul is sorting through. I've chosen the short straw—there's going to be a mountain of junk in this thing. I pull open the top drawer, full to bursting with cheap lace. Nothing really saucy, but still, a drawer filled with sex. I don't want to look. I know Mum did it—she had me, after all—but it makes that thing Mum said about Paul go around in my head. *Black man's cock, black man's cock, black man's cock.*

When I look at Paul, I find it hard to imagine he really has a penis. He's by the wardrobe, folding Mum's clothes like they do in posh clothes shops: laying each top on its front on the bed, crossing the arms behind the back, folding up the bottom hem, then turning the thing over and tidying up the collar. They're only going to Cancer Research. He's such a dullard. So straight. I swear he's made of cardboard.

"How about we put some music on?" he says.

Paul is dead set that this is going to be a joyful experience, excavating Mum's room. A "celebration of her," that's what he called it. Idiot.

"Whatever."

"I know just the thing." The cheerfulness is painful. I know he's going to blub. I'm just waiting to find out which item from Mum's wardrobe tips him over the edge.

Paul goes to the old ghetto blaster CD player by the bed. It's a real antique with a furry coat of dust. I know what album he's going to put on. If we're celebrating Mum, there could be only one choice. It'll be the one with the Brazilian woman who half talks and half sings, a bit like she's bored, or drunk, or both. Mum's favorite.

There's the hiss of the CD spinning into life, and Paul stands over the ghetto blaster, fretting whether he's pressed the right buttons. The man starts dum-dee-dumming, then the slurring woman starts singing her pointless song about the tall, tanned girl who does nothing but walk.

Paul turns to smile at me, does a little shimmy with his hips. I think I might die of embarrassment. I concentrate on stacking thongs and underpants on top of the chest of drawers. A leaning tower of nylon. Mum never went in for fancy coordinating sets. But she liked color. Purples, hot pinks, bright-turquoise blues. Traffic-stopping underwear.

I wonder what color ones she was wearing when it happened. I imagine Paul bringing that underwear and her other clothes home from the hospital in a clear plastic bag. Although I have no clue if that is what actually happens. Do they give you the clothes back when someone dies? Or do they leave them on? Did they cut through her clothes when they tried to save her? Did they just throw the clothes in the trash? When they'd given up on her, did they send her to the morgue naked? I don't know.

People joke about wearing clean underwear just in case you get hit by a car. Not funny. I picture that plastic bag of clothes quite a lot—I can't help it—her things soaked with blood. I imagine it like that see-through sack of guts they give you when you buy a Christmas turkey from the butcher.

Why does everyone who passes the tanned girl in the song say, "*Ahhh?*" Why does she make everyone feel so sad? It makes no sense.

Paul has thankfully stopped shimmying. He's taking more clothes out of the wardrobe, folding them on the bed. Mum and Paul must have done it on this bed. I never heard them. Thank God. But they must have. They could have been as loud as they liked. I always stayed over at Chick's house when Paul spent the night. Or rather Mum only invited him when she knew I wouldn't be here. I never even saw them kiss. I think Mum knew I didn't approve, or maybe she thought I needed protecting from the truth.

Now the tanned girl is ignoring all the people who are

smiling at her. What is the tanned girl's problem, for God's sake?

Mum said in her will that all her stuff was to go to charity — except for anything that Paul or I wanted. Nothing much fits me, not even her shoes, so it's all going into the trash bags. Off to charity. Only the burgundy dress will stay, because it's still in the laundry basket in my room.

It suddenly occurs to me that loads of the clothes in charity stores belong to dead people. Creepy. Those vintagey dresses that Elaine Wilkie and her friends are always wearing, they probably came from some dead granny's wardrobe. That's what the smell of charity stores is — the smell of death. Mum's clothes still have the pinecone stench of mothballs, but maybe they'll start to take on a new smell away from the house.

I've done all the underwear and don't know what to do with them. The bag for charity? I watched a documentary once about how you could donate absolutely anything to charity, even underwear. They send it all to a big central warehouse and find a use for everything. Bras are valuable, apparently. They're expensive to make — all that wire and foam. They send them to Africa and sell them to market traders. The underpants get shredded up and turned into cushion and pillow stuffing. I'm not sure what's worse: wearing someone's secondhand underpants or knowing that you're resting your face on a pillow full of shredded cotton crotches. I shove all of Mum's underpants into the bag for charity. Paul watches me out of the corner of his eye but says nothing.

A saxophone is jazzing over the top of the slurring woman.

Paul's finished with the wardrobe and is going through Mum's jewelry box. Nothing of any value in there. When I was little, I asked to see Yia-Yia's old necklaces and rings from Crete, but Mum said she didn't have anything. I thought this was strange. What did she do with all of Yia-Yia's jewelry after she died? Sell it?

I'll put the bras in the charity bag. Mum would have liked the idea of them going on a long vacation to Africa. She has hundreds of bras—lacy, padded, push-up. I hope African ladies like that sort of thing. Underneath the bras I find a small square yellow photo album with a 1970s print of a flower on the cover. It's big enough to hold a picture per page slipped into plastic sleeves. I've never seen this album before. Mum was never really into taking photos. There is one other photo album in the house. It's on the bookshelf in the living room. The first picture in the book is of my first day at school. Then there are odd pictures of me from each year after that. There are no pictures of me any younger than four. I've never seen a picture of me as a baby. This used to make me think I was adopted, but no one would ever have given a baby to my mum when she was only sixteen years old. Maybe I'm stolen.

I open the photo album from the underwear drawer. I'm expecting Mum to walk in any minute and tell me off for poking around. Although, I actually think Mum would have liked me to have been more of a snooper—you know, steal her earrings, borrow her lipstick, that kind of thing. I did it when I was a little kid. I used to wobble around in her shoes, drown myself in her dresses. But once I was grown up, I was never interested in her stuff.

The first picture in the yellow photo album is of Granbabas. He looks younger than I've ever known him, although his hair is still silver. He's sitting in a wicker chair, smiling. I never saw him that happy in real life. On the next page there is a picture of Mum. I'm sure it's her, although she must be only seven or eight. She looks the same as she did as an adult—same long hair—but her top front teeth are all gappy. She's standing in a dusty yard. She's making a face at the camera. Standing in the background is a serious woman who looks similar to Mum. My *yia-yia*? I don't know. I only have a picture of her in my head based on The Story. The real Yia-Yia doesn't match up with my imaginary photograph. The real one looks harder, more cross.

The next picture jumps in time. Mum looks about fourteen or fifteen in this one. She's in the middle of the shot and has one arm around the shoulder of a skinny boy who looks the same age as her. My heart bobs into my throat. Christos Drakakis?

My dad is Christos Drakakis, and my name is Melon Drakaki—how do you do?

I look into his eyes and try to feel some sort of connection, a piece of thread. Nothing. Mum's other arm is reaching around the shoulder of an older, taller boy. Although it's an awkward position, it also looks like a really comfortable thing for Mum to be doing. Her body is relaxed, slouching toward him, confident. The older boy is sneering with his smile, almost snarling. He is familiar. I am trying to figure out what it is that makes me think that I know him. Then, I realize. He looks like me.

116

The slurring woman is singing a new song now, double-fast, about a girl called Maria whose papa is telling her to go to bed but she goes out hugging and kissing instead.

"What you got there?"

"Nothing." I snap the album shut. I don't want Paul to see it. It has nothing to do with him.

"Photos?"

"Yeah, me and Mum. I'm going to keep this." I hold it hard against my chest.

"Fine, fine, that's fine."

"I wasn't asking permission."

Paul ignores me. He's already cooking up the next thing he wants to say, *umming* and *ahhing* his way into it. He always does that when he has an announcement that he thinks is important. He likes building up his part.

"I'm, errrr . . ." Paul is toying with a small piece of jewelry in his fingers. "I'm going to take this back." He points the thing at me quickly, then pulls it away again, like he didn't really want me to see it. It catches the light, then disappears into his fist. He opens his hand, looks down at the thing, closes his hand, opens it. Pink palms. On the back of his hand, the skin is dark, smooth, airbrushed. He wants me to see what he's holding. He wants me to say something. This feels like a trap.

"What is it?"

"The ring. It was my grandmother's, so I think . . ."

Bingo. He's crying. His mouth stretches into a strange grimace. His shoulders shake.

"Why did Mum have your grandmother's ring?" As soon as the words are out of my mouth, it sounds like the most stupid question in the world. It's the diamond ring Mum is wearing in that laughing photo in the dining room. There would be only one reason for Mum having that ring. Paul looks up at me, his eyes red and wet. He looks as stunned as I am.

"Your mum never said that we were going to . . ."

"No."

"Melon, that's not . . . I'm sure she had a reason for not . . ."

The slurring woman is all out of tune now, demanding we give her a call.

"Who cares," I say. I head for the door. I've had enough. "I don't want to do this anymore."

"Melon."

"What?"

"Ahhhmmm . . ." Paul is brewing up another speech. I don't want to hear it, but he's so upset I feel I have to listen.

"Ummm, do you want to know how it happened?"

"No!" I squeak. I don't want to hear about him taking her on the London Eye or to Primrose Hill or wherever and getting down on one knee. He could have bungee-jumped off the Eiffel Tower with a box of chocolates for all I care.

"I mean, how Maria . . . how your mum died."

Oh.

"I know how she died," I say. "A bus."

"Details, I mean. It's just occurred to me, just now, that no one has been telling you much, the whole story."

"I don't need details."

118

I try to leave again.

"I thought it might help," Paul calls after me. "It might keep you from being so angry."

I spin around in the doorway and glare at him. "Who's angry?"

"You seem very angry, with your mum."

"No."

"She didn't do it on purpose."

"I know that."

"It was an accident. The people who saw it happen said she was looking for something in her bag. Cigarettes probably. Or something. She stepped out and . . ."

"I said I didn't want details."

I reach for the back of my head and remember that the ponytail has gone. Just tight coils of hair. Paul won't shut up.

"She was in a rush, as usual. She was late to meet me and . . . She wasn't paying attention to the road."

"I said I didn't want to know."

"She thought the world of you, Melon."

I spit air. I can't believe that Paul is spouting this rubbish.

"Everything was for you." He's pushing me to say something nice about Mum.

"Nothing was for me," I mutter.

"She wanted to be your best friend."

"I didn't need another best friend."

"What did you need?"

The words come out my mouth without me thinking them first. "A mum."

It takes all I've got not to cry. Not sad tears, angry ones. But I don't want Paul to see even those.

"Yes, a mum." He is nodding, all knowing.

"I said I don't want to do this anymore."

"Okay." Paul places a palm on his forehead. He's run out of speeches. "Is there anything you want to keep?" He gestures around the room.

"No." I tap the yellow album in my hand. "Just this."

The slurring woman is demanding that we call her again, that we trust her.

I go to my room.

6 YEARS BEFORE

I'm nine and a half years old and I'm sitting on a bus.

"Where are we going?" I ask Mum.

There is plenty of room on the bottom deck, but Mum insists we sit upstairs.

"Auntie Eleni's washateria."

"Who's Auntie Eleni?"

"Your auntie. My auntie. You know this."

I do know this. I'm just trying to get Mum to stop being silent.

"What's a washateria?"

"A shop that is full of washing machines."

"Are we going to buy a washing machine?"

"No."

The lady in front turns around to smile at me. Maybe she remembers what it's like to have your mum get snappy with you.

Mum hasn't been herself lately, not since she came back from Crete. She talks about Granbabas all the time, even though it's two months now since he died. She says he had a good life and he's lucky his heart held out this long and it is the fate of everyone in the Fourakis family to die young, so we shouldn't be sad. Still the same stuff over and over.

Mum moans about how English people go on about the weather all the time instead of saying something interesting. She's just as bad.

I still don't know what Mum is really sad about, if it's not Granbabas. I'm pretty sure she's sad about something.

"We are here." Mum elbows me in the ribs. I've wiped a hole in the misted-up window so I can try to figure out where "here" is. Mum presses the buzzer that tells the driver to stop and starts walking while the bus is still moving, which means I have to follow. I bump into people's shoulders and nearly fall down the stairs. Mum doesn't do any bumping; she stays steady, grabbing one pole, then the next, like a monkey swinging through the trees. Mum likes buses. When she's on one, she ignores it, if you know what I mean, pretends it's no bother. I find buses scary. You have to watch what's going on all the time—the other passengers, the traffic outside, getting off at the right stop. I like the Tube best.

When we get onto the sidewalk, the doors shut behind us and the bus does that loud *psss-shuh* noise that always makes me jump even though I know it's coming. The bus chugs away. Mum starts scrabbling around in her bag for a cigarette. She hasn't even turned around to check if I got off okay. I could still be on the bus and halfway to another part of London by now. That's another thing I don't like about buses: you could end up anywhere.

"Where are we, Mum?"

Her hands are really shivery when she lights the cigarette, even though it's not that cold. The sun's out.

"Kentish Town."

"From The Story?"

122

"No. Yes, yes."

She takes my hand and yanks me along. She still hasn't looked to check that I'm there. She could be pulling along a complete stranger and she would have no clue.

Mum is sucking hard on her cigarettes today. Her cheeks go in all the way. Her lips scrunch right up so that they look like Kojak's bum. We walk fast past cafés and charity shops. No one else is rushing like us. We stand out. Twice we almost crash into people standing on the street. We stop outside a big glass window with a door in the middle—a shop full of washing machines. The Papadakis Washateria. From The Story.

Through the window I can see a fat woman folding sheets at the back of the shop. I'm ready to go inside and say hello nicely, like you should when you meet a new person. Mum is standing like a statue. She's staring at the fat woman the same way we stare at the headmaster, Mr. Carling, if he ever comes into our classroom. We're terrified that one of us is in trouble, but we're also secretly hoping for good news.

Mum turns to me and actually looks at me for the first time all day. She takes one big last suck on her cigarette, drops it, and screws it into the ground with her toe. She is wearing proper lady shoes, with heels. She's got on the formal dress she wears when she goes to court with one of the teenagers from her work. Today is Saturday. No work today. No court.

Mum licks her fingers and starts pressing down my hair even though it wasn't wonky in the first place. She really pushes down, trying to straighten the curls. When she's done, she stops to admire her work but looks disappointed. She sighs. She takes a big breath; she turns and opens the door to the washateria.

The inside of the shop smells like a warm blanket. Orange plastic chairs are laid out back-to-back in a row in the middle—like at the start of a game of musical chairs. A man is sitting on one of the chairs, staring at a washing machine as if it's a television. The fat lady at the back of the shop looks up, and when she sees Mum, her face changes. She looked bored to begin with, but now she looks shocked. Then she looks at me and her face changes again. From shocked to all sorry. Then she looks back at Mum and her face goes hard. The whole time Mum and me say nothing. Not even a nice hello, which is rude, really, when you think about it. We just watch Auntie Eleni's face change over and over—*click, click, click.*

Then there is this rumbling sound that isn't the noise coming from a washing machine, and isn't the sound of a bus driving past outside. It's Auntie Eleni. She's sort of chanting, under her breath, "*Óhi, óhi, óhi, óhi.*" It grows and grows like a growl of thunder until she is shouting. "*Óhi, óhi, óhi, óhi, óhi, óhi, ÓHI!*"

"*Thia Eleni,*" goes Mum in her proper Greek voice. She is holding her arms out. Eleni is an angry dog and Mum just wants her to sit.

Auntie Eleni barks something in Greek to Mum and points to the door.

Mum presses down her stretched-out hands, pushing down the bad stuff that's growing tall in the air.

"*Oríste?*" goes Auntie Eleni, still loud, still angry. "*Oríste? Oríste?*"

Is she shouting for Mum to be arrested? The man on the plastic chair turns around for a moment like he might do what Auntie Eleni is asking, then he goes back to watching his washing machine.

Auntie Eleni has her hands on her hips. She is waiting for an answer to the "arrest her" question. Her chest is heaving up and down. This is that moment in a film when the goodie and the baddie finally meet up and you're not sure who is going to pull out their gun first and kill the other person, although all along you know the goodie will win.

I'm not sure who the goodie is in this situation.

Mum mumbles something back to Auntie Eleni and it's obviously the right thing because suddenly Auntie Eleni goes soft, like a balloon losing some of its air.

"Manolis?" asks Auntie Eleni. She looks upset. Manolis was Granbabas's name.

"*Né,*" says Mum, squeaky and quiet.

"*Pós?*"

Mum speaks a little louder now but looks at her feet. Auntie Eleni is still too fierce to hold eyes with. She might bite. Mum carries on explaining. She is probably telling Auntie Eleni that Granbabas had a good life and was lucky his heart held out this long and it is the fate of everyone in the Fourakis family to die young, so we shouldn't be sad. It sounds almost the same in Greek.

Mum finishes her speech and Auntie Eleni nods. Mum nods. I wonder if I should nod too. We all stand still for a while with the washing machines going *whirr-uh, whirr-uh, whirr-uh*. Auntie Eleni looks down at her basket of sheets and then back at us, which even I know means she wants us to go now. Mum stays put. Auntie Eleni starts folding sheets. Mum still stands there. Auntie Eleni picks up the basket of sheets and disappears into the back of the shop. Mum gets the message at last.

"Adío," Mum says all sad and not really loud enough for Auntie Eleni to hear. She takes hold of my hand and pulls me toward the door. Her fingers are icy.

I open the door for Mum and cold air hits us.

"Pos se léne?" Auntie Eleni calls after us. We both turn around. Mum's face looks hopeful.

"Pos se léne?" Auntie Eleni says again. She is saying it to me. Mum digs a knuckle in my shoulder, which means I should speak.

My mouth drops open, but no words come out. I look to Mum for help, but she is just smiling like a big, stupid sunbeam at Auntie Eleni. I feel like I've been asked a question in school when I have no idea what the answer is. Except this is worse, because I don't even know what the question is.

Auntie Eleni rolls her eyes at Mum, as if it's entirely her fault that I don't know what the question is. Auntie Eleni huffs and starts using English.

"What's your name?" Auntie Eleni speaks with less of an accent than Mum, which is a bit of a surprise after hearing her gabbling in Greek.

"Melon," I say. Then I remember the thing about being polite. "Pleased to meet you."

126

"Melon?" says Auntie Eleni. She is using that surprised voice that everyone puts on when they hear my name for the first time. Her eyes flicker up to Mum.

Mum does an apologizing shrug and then smiles. Auntie Eleni is still scowly.

"Yes," I say. "Melon."

"Pleased to meet you too, Melon." I get a smile, but it's quickly snatched away.

Auntie Eleni speaks to Mum in Greek again. Just two words, which sound prickly and painful. She walks away into the back room again. Mum's smile has gone. Bam! Just like that. She looks like she's been punched.

When we get outside, Mum says that we are going to have a coffee in the café opposite the washateria. She makes us sit outside, even though she says English people are ridiculous for sitting outside cafés in the middle of February.

Mum doesn't say anything about what just happened. I want to ask for a translation, but I decide now is the wrong time. Mum is squeezing all the life out of the cigarette in her mouth. Instead, I talk about Chick's ice-skating show, which Mrs. Lacey took me to see during the week. It was *Cinderella*, and Chick played one of the mice. When Chick first told me she was playing a mouse, I said I couldn't remember there being any mice in the Cinderella story, but she said, "Of course there are, silly. There are loads of them. Haven't you ever seen the film?"

I can tell that Mum isn't listening, because she says "yes" and "no" and "really?" in all the wrong places. She smokes lots and stares at Auntie Eleni through the window of the washateria. I think she is hoping that Auntie Eleni will remember something she forgot to say and come across the street to tell us. I get the feeling Mum would really like a hug, but I don't offer her one. I think Mum wants the hug from Auntie Eleni, not me.

Mum makes her coffee last ages. I don't like coffee, so I drink lemonade in a cold can with a straw. This makes me feel really freezing, and my teeth start chattering. Now I know why Mum's hands were shivering earlier on. I want to go home.

Eventually Mum goes, "Come on, we get the bus."

"Can we go back on the Tube?"

"No. Bus. It is better."

We sit on the bottom deck on the way home, which is something Mum never wants to do, but I'm happy to go along with it because it means I won't trip on the stairs. Mum is silent. She stares out of the window in a trance. Usually I have to sit by the window so Mum can make conversation with the grannies and other mums sitting nearby. It feels weird being on the aisle.

I don't understand why we haven't been to see Auntie Eleni before today. After all, she was really nice to Mum when she first got to London and when I was a baby. Maybe Auntie Eleni is annoyed because Mum hasn't stayed in touch.

What was especially strange was the way Auntie Eleni asked me my name. She must know it already. A name like mine isn't hard to remember. Maybe she was just being polite and doing proper introductions. Maybe I should have asked for her name in return.

When the bus gets as far as Archway, I feel like I've left an okay gap and can ask some questions.

"She seemed nice," I go, to start things off. I don't know why I say this because nothing that Auntie Eleni did today was really that nice when you think about it.

"Huh?" goes Mum.

"Auntie Eleni seems nice."

"Oh."

"Will we go and see her again?"

"No," says Mum, and she folds her coat around herself and crosses her arms. It reminds me of Auntie Eleni folding the sheets.

This is the end of the conversation.

35 DAYS SINCE

A few months ago, at my house after school, before the thing with my mum, me and Chick did this friendship quiz. It was in one of her magazines.

FAKE FRIEND OR FRIEND FOREVER?

You had to answer twenty multiple-choice questions and then add up your scores. It wasn't rocket science. If you scored mostly A's, you had a "Friend Forever" and could sit back feeling smug. Mostly C's and you had a "Fake Friend" and the magazine advised you to "dump her." Just like that.

I thought I could just tell Chick that we were "Friends Forever," save us the trouble of having to answer all the questions. But of course, in the real world, no one comes out and says sappy things like that. Also, Chick wouldn't have trusted my word as much as the results of a magazine quiz. So we got out notebooks to write down our scores and worked our way through questions like:

1. YOUR BOYFRIEND DUMPS YOU. WHAT DOES YOUR BEST FRIEND DO?

A. SHE CANCELS ALL HER PLANS SO YOU CAN COME OVER AND CRY. WHAT'S TEN BOXES OF TISSUES BETWEEN FRIENDS?

B. SHE GIVES YOU A PULL-YOURSELF-TOGETHER LECTURE ON THE PHONE. COME ON, THERE ARE PLENTY MORE FROGS TO KISS!

C. SHE ASKS YOUR EX OUT ON A DATE. WHAT'S THE FUSS? HE'S A FREE GUY NOW, ISN'T HE?

You know, real in-depth psychology.

I hardly gave the questions a second look. I wrote down *A, A, A* . . . Chick really took her time, covering her notebook with her arm, as if I was going to copy her or something. That really bugged me, that she took it so seriously. Chick will choose the person she marries because of how well he does in a multiple-choice quiz.

HOT HUSBAND OR HIDEOUS HUSBAND?

Some rubbish like that.

Eventually, Chick went, "Finished!" and turned her notebook over on the carpet so I couldn't see what she'd written. Then she asked, "What was your score for me?"

I thought about saying "all C's" just to annoy her, but I couldn't be bothered.

"All A's," I went. "You are a 'Friend Forever.'"

Chick nodded, smiled, as if she'd known that all along. Spit was shining on her braces. She was waiting for me to ask for my score. I couldn't have cared less.

"Go on, then," I went. "What did I get?"

131

"Ummm." Chick peeled the notebook away from the floor so I still didn't get to see what she'd written. She held it close to her face, counting scores under her breath. Not only had she not given me all A's; it wasn't even clear-cut whether it was mostly A's.

"Mostly B's."

Her head went onto one side, giving me a "sorry" that she didn't really mean. I was to blame. I wasn't a good-enough friend. It wasn't her fault for being harsh.

"Oh, right."

I knew there had to be some C's in there. But I didn't ask her. That was what she wanted.

"Want to watch TV?" I went.

When it was time for Chick to go home, I offered to go upstairs and get her bag from my room. I found her notebook. Just one A. That was for question 8:

IS YOUR BFF ALWAYS GOING OFF AND MAKING NEW FRIENDS?

She'd chosen:

A. NO, SHE'S STUCK TO YOU LIKE GLUE. YOUR FRIENDSHIP IS THE BEST!

So really that answer was about Chick being amazing, not me.

I think of that quiz when I walk through the school gates. My first day back since Mum. Chick is standing by the wall of the sports center all cozy with Lucy Bloss. Lucy is sitting on the wall, so Chick has to look up to her when she talks. Chick is sucking up. She is actually sucking upward.

I'd also given Chick an A for the question about making other friends. How wrong was I? There are plenty of answers to that quiz that I would like to change now. Since Mum died, I look back at the old me and wonder who I was and how I came to think the things I did. That's what you really need to do to find out if you have a "Fake Friend" or a "Friend Forever"—you need to have your mum die.

I wave at Chick. I'm not letting her off easy. Why should I walk past acting as if we don't know each other? Chick watches me come toward her. She's not bouncing from foot to foot like usual. She's rooted to the spot. Guilty. Like a deer in the headlights. She's frozen in the middle of the road and the tires are going to crush her.

Lucy spots me too and stops blabbering drivel down in Chick's general direction. She tries to hold back a smile. Lucy's not really on Chick's side. She's on the side of drama and stirring things up.

"Hey, Chick," I go, all bright and breezy.

Chick nods, half smiles, a quick flash of metal, then she looks down, studies her chipped fingernail polish.

"Hey, Lucy." Normally, I would never, ever, in the real world, ever, say hello to Lucy Bloss.

She doesn't say hello back. She is staring at my head, not at my eyes, higher up than that. She's scrunching up her nose. My hand goes to where she's looking; I can't help it. I stroke the top of my head, expecting to find bird poo there. Nothing.

"What?"

"All your hair's gone." Lucy draws out every word. She's proper gobsmacked.

"I know."

"What happened?"

What does she think happened? Someone burgled us in the night and stole my ponytail? "I got it cut."

"Told you, didn't I?" Chick mutters at Lucy.

"Looks nice, though." Lucy suddenly remembers that my mum is dead and she has to be kind. The thought pops up in her eyes like cherries on a slot machine. She is smiling a big fake caring smile.

I eyeball Chick, waiting for her to say something nice about my hair, even if she doesn't mean it. But no. The line's definitely been drawn. She and Lucy are on one side; I'm on the other. Chick is a "Fake Friend." What now? Dump her?

"Sorry about your mum," goes Lucy, all twangy, not meaning one single word of it.

"S'all right. It's not your fault." I refuse to keep talking up at her, so I talk down at Lucy's shoes instead. They are ankle boots that need a new heel.

"I knooooowww," drawls Lucy, in her big fake caring voice.

I stare at Chick, who couldn't back up any farther against the wall if she tried.

No one says anything. I'm not going to tell Chick she's dumped. I'm going to wait for her to tell me that I'm dumped. I want to see if she's got the guts to do it. I stand there, waiting. I watch Chick silently begging me to take off. Lucy tries to fake-smile me to smithereens. Still no one speaks. We listen to the school yard fill up. Feet on gravel. Snatches of conversations. Talk about TV and who's bitching about who and homework and what's happening where after school tonight. Lucy never stops with the gift-wrapped smile. I smile back. This is a smile-off.

Chick starts to look like she might vomit. She knows she has to say something.

"Mum said you weren't coming back to school."

"Did she?"

"Yeah."

I see Lucy out of the corner of my eye, chewing her lips, eager for things to kick off. For the first time ever, I feel like giving Lucy what she wants.

"Shows what your mum knows, doesn't it?" I say it really friendly, which makes it all the nastier.

Chick meets my gaze. Big eyes. She looks really hurt. She thought she'd come out of this on top, with her shiny new unbereaved friend, and now here she is feeling small. This little deer is going to get squished.

Lucy raises her eyebrows at my last comment. In admiration, probably. It takes one bitch to know another.

"Come back to do my exams, haven't I?"

Chick nods.

"That's sooo brave," goes Lucy, stirring up the pot.

"Nothing to be brave about. I've done loads of studying. When I was staying at Chick's house." I get ready to give the poor, run-over deer a kick in the ribs. "Nothing much else to do when I was staying there."

Lucy pouts away a laugh. Chick looks strangled. She won't retaliate. She has no clue how to—she's never been in an argument in her life. Also, Chick knows that if you're a good girl you can't be nasty to someone whose mum has just died. And Chick is definitely a good little girl. Chop her in half and it's written through her bones.

"You two are the ones who'll have to be brave in the exams," I go on. I'm not being horrible; this is just useful advice. "You two are the ones who aren't that smart."

If you cut Lucy Bloss in half, you wouldn't find the word *good*. She isn't standing for that. She narrows her eyes, turns spiky.

"Is it true you're shacked up with your mum's black boyfriend?" She takes her time with the word "black," really enjoys it, makes it sound sticky and sordid. She never would have said it like that if Dionne Agu—her friend—was here. Suddenly "black" is something that matters. Suddenly it's something dirty. I think about Paul. A nice man in slacks. Lucy makes him sound like a gangster, a Mr. Lover-Lover. The idea is hilarious, but I don't laugh. I glare at Chick, the only one who would know about Paul, the one who has obviously been spreading this story around, letting it grow into something it's not. Chick won't look at me. She fiddles with the hair clip that's doing a hopeless job of keeping her wispy bits back from her face.

Lucy Bloss is all triumphant on her perch. She's not expecting me to answer the question, but I want to.

"Yeah," I say firmly. "Me and Paul. That's right." I will not look weak. I will not crumble.

I have Chick's full attention now. Lucy's face fills with color. She licks her lips at the thrill of hearing what she wants to hear.

136

"Really?" She is unblinking, double-daring me to say it's definitely true. "You're shacked up?" She pops the "p" at the end of her sentence. Grins.

She wants me to backtrack, to scrabble around with words, try to make it sound innocent. Lucy knows that there's nothing going on. She knows I've never even had a boyfriend. She knows I'm the person least likely on the whole earth to start an affair with an older man. She just wants to make me sweat. She wants me to look like a stupid, trembling virgin.

"Yes," I say again, even more confident this time. "Me *and* Paul. That's right."

"Oh. My. God." Lucy's voice is breathy. She leans back away from me, swaps a look with Chick.

She believes me. She really is that stupid. I've got her. I've got them both. Mum's words come into my head and before I can think about what I'm doing, I'm saying them out loud.

"And you know what they say about black men's cocks, don't you?"

Lucy's mouth drops open. Chick, I swear, does a cartoon gulp. I can hardly believe I said it either. No one speaks.

"Well?" I snap, before I lose my nerve. "Do you know what they say, or not?"

"Well . . . um . . . yeah," splutters Lucy.

I eyeball Chick.

"Yeah," she says, a tiny choking rabbity sound.

They both glare at me, startled. I gesture for Lucy to bend down and come closer. She does. I lean in, cutting Chick out of the conversation with my shoulder.

"Well," I whisper to Lucy, "it's all true."

Lucy backs away from me, as if sleaziness is catching. This is more gossip than even Lucy Bloss knows how to handle. Her smile has gone. I still have mine.

I win.

Chick is looking at me like she has no clue who I am. The sounds of the school yard take over again. TV and who's bitching about who, homework, trivial stuff.

"Like your hair, Melon."

Dionne Agu has walked up behind me. She starts eyeing my head as if it's a bizarre art installation. She's arm in arm with Emily Winters.

"It's really short," goes Emily. "Do you like it?"

Their chatter sounds weird after the stuff me and Lucy have been saying to each other.

"Yes," I go before anyone else can answer. "Yeah, I do. Don't you?"

"Yeah, I never said I didn't." It doesn't take much to make Emily huffy.

"What's going on?" asks Dionne. She can sense that something's wrong. Lucy's trap is shut, for starters.

"Ask Lucy," I go. I want her to tell Dionne, see if she bothers mentioning the thing about Paul being black. Lucy drills into me with her eyes. She looks so funny, so desperate, so silly. I start laughing. And that really freaks everyone out—the bereaved girl is laughing!

"You're lying," Lucy goes, cutting me down. She's angry. It's all fallen into place for her now. Three cherries dropping into the slots—*bing, bing, bing.*

"What if I am?"

"Why would you lie about that? You're sick in the head."

"Why? 'Cause he's a black man?"

"I never said . . ." Lucy snatches a look at Dionne. Dionne huddles closer to Emily, looks lost.

"I can't believe you lied about that," Lucy says, attacking again.

"What does it matter to you?"

"You're not even sixteen!"

"So?"

"So that's sick to pretend that you're . . ."

"That I'm what?" This is hilarious. Lucy is fit to explode.

"You could have gotten him arrested."

"Why, because you wouldn't have been able to keep your stupid mouth shut?" I'm laughing again. I'm laughing in Lucy Bloss's ridiculous face. She jumps down from the wall and pushes her nose right up to mine.

"You're fucking mental." She taps the side of her head. "You've fucking lost it, you sick bitch."

I don't want her close to me. Her face powder smells sickly sweet. I put my hands against her breastbone and shove really hard. It feels great to lash out at someone at last. Really great. I wonder why I haven't gone and punched someone before now. I am ready to fight. Lucy skips backward. Dionne pulls Emily out of the way, and Lucy trips on her bag, landing on her backside. Dionne and Emily stifle giggles.

Plenty of faces in the school yard are turned our way now.

"Shut up!" snaps Lucy. "You will fucking pay for that, Melon." My name sounds heavy in her mouth. "You're going to so regret doing that."

She gets up, brushes down her skirt. I want her to try to hit me, but Lucy Bloss isn't going to fight. She won't get dirty.

"I never believed it for a second." Lucy's face looks hot, sweaty, close to tears. "As if anyone would want have sex with you, you fat bitch."

We all let that insult land.

Dionne, Emily, and Chick stare at me, waiting to see what I will do. But Lucy has finished with me now. She's picking up her bag. And she knows that I am done with her too. She has spoken the final truth of it all. I am a fat bitch who no one would have sex with. Where do we go from there?

Lucy looks to the others. "Come on."

They fall in behind her like soldiers. Chick too. Loser.

"Let's go," hisses Lucy. They walk off. Lucy is smoothing down her long, blond hair. "And your hair looks like shit!" she yells back over her shoulder.

The others are nervous about laughing at me, the girl whose mum is dead, but they do it anyway.

I watch them head off toward the science lab. Chick doesn't look back. Not even once.

3 DAYS SINCE

Ian and the others get off at Highgate Station. I stay on until Tottenham Court Road, change to the Central Line, and then get off at Oxford Circus. I was worried I wouldn't remember where to find the place, but here I am. Not far from Regent Street. I feel sick—still. The Cherry Coke and cherry drops were a bad substitute for breakfast. I stand outside for a while, willing the sick feeling away. I stare through the glass doors at the marble floors inside. I imagine a massive puddle of pink puke in the middle of the shop, spreading across the shiny floor. Gross.

This is definitely the place. All the perfect staff in their perfect black outfits. Me and Chick had walked right up to the doors with Mrs. Lacey that day. She had told us we could go off and do whatever we wanted while she was in there, but we must meet her in the café at the end of the street in exactly two hours. No excuses, thank you very much. She'd checked Chick's digital watch to make sure it said the same time as hers. She'd actually made Chick take it off so she could fiddle with the buttons and change the time by two minutes.

"There," she'd gone when she plonked it back in Chick's hands. "Now there's absolutely no reason for you to be late."

Before Mrs. Lacey went inside, Chick had asked if she could spend some extra money on her credit card as a special treat.

"No."

"But Dad said you—"

"I said no."

Chick's parents are loaded, but they're pretty stingy with Chick. You'd expect Chick's allowance to be huge, but it's not. It's bigger than mine ever was, of course. Chick's credit card has her name on it, but it's not really hers; it's just an extra card on her mum's account. Mrs. Lacey pays the bill. Chick knows she can't spend any more than her allowance.

Once Chick's mum had gone inside, Chick said she'd share her credit card money with me all the same. I was really embarrassed by that. What was I, some sort of charity case? I just mumbled a thank-you and hoped it wouldn't get mentioned again.

We had stood outside the doors for a while deciding where to go, Chick sticking her nose in her *A to Z* guidebook. Inside, a man was kissing Mrs. Lacey on both cheeks and helping her out of her coat. It had a fake-fur collar. Cruella De Vil. Mrs. Lacey told us we weren't to go anywhere on the Tube; we had to stay close. She said, "The London Underground is a dangerous place—unless I'm with you." Being with Mrs. Lacey made us bombproof.

"She never said we couldn't get on a bus," I'd whispered, leaning in over Chick's *A to Z*.

"Better not," said Chick.

Mum wouldn't have cared less if I'd tubed it from High Barnet to Morden on my own ten times over. She wanted

142

me to feel free. She wanted me to be the proper Londoner she never really was. Not with that Greek voice of hers. Mrs. Lacey is like a normal parent: she wants to keep Chick locked up and protected. Chick might be a nervy tourist in her own city, but at least she knows someone is keeping her safe.

We'd walked to Carnaby Street that day and tried on shoes. We'd each bought a little pot of lip balm that cost too much money. I'd made sure I paid for mine. When we got back to the coffee shop (ten minutes early, just to be sure), we'd tested out each other's flavors. Chick had bought mint; I'd bought cherry (of course). Mrs. Lacey was late.

If Chick isn't allowed to go into central London on her own until she's sixteen, I guess I fall under those rules, now that I live with the Laceys. I am officially breaking the Lacey law.

I put my hand in my jeans pocket and rub my finger over the rounded corners of Chick's credit card. Money burning a hole in my pocket. I want to get inside. The sick feeling isn't going to shift, no matter how much fresh air I puff in and out, though I'm pretty sure I'm not going to actually be sick. That's what it feels like when you're pregnant, Mum said. Constant nausea.

I shove one of the glass doors. It's stiff and doesn't budge. I have another go, really barge at it this time, and I'm in. The air is blow-dryer hot and clanging with music and chatter. I'm in one of those dreams where I'm walking around school wearing nothing but shoes, but no one has noticed yet.

The woman at the reception desk has hair that looks like it's been ironed flat, then sealed in plastic. She gives me a massive smile.

"Hi! You okay this morning?"

I wasn't expecting nice. I was expecting suspicious.

"Hi, um, I don't have an appointment but I wondered if . . ."

The woman eyes my hair quickly and nods. She buries her concentration in her computer screen.

"Hmm, I can maybe . . . fit . . . you . . ." She's clicking and scrolling like this is the most important request she's ever had.

"Scott!" Suddenly she's turning and yelling above the music, some chill-out album being played really loud. "You okay for a cut after this?" She flicks back to me. Her hair doesn't move like normal hair. "It is just a cut, isn't it?"

I nod.

"Just a cut!"

Scott is wearing skinny gray jeans and a tight black V-neck. His hair is styled so it looks like he is standing sideways in a wind tunnel. He is doing a blow-dry on a woman, yanking her neck each time he stretches out her hair with a big, round brush. Scott steps back from the woman to give a thumbs-up, then goes back to inflicting his torture, bobbing along with the music as he does.

The plastic-hair girl throws me another massive grin.

"Take a seat. Scott will be over in a minute."

It's that easy. I was expecting a lecture on how expensive it is here. I was expecting the third degree on how I was thinking of paying. I'm disappointed that I haven't had to put up a fight. I sit down in the waiting area. Really I wanted them to say, "No, go away," so I wouldn't have to go through with it.

The middle-aged woman sitting next to me on the leather bench smells luxurious and has skin that's stretched too tight across her face. She's reading one of the magazines that have been put inside leather folders and stacked up on the glass table. On the page that the woman is reading, there are bits of other people's snipped hair in the crease of the spine.

Also on the table in front of me is a menu of prices in a plastic stand. I pick it up and scan down for the cost of a haircut. It's more than Chick's monthly credit card allowance. On the back of the hair menu there is a list of coffees and sandwiches, all at silly prices. I think about what I will order to make the sick feeling go away.

"All right. I'm Daniel. D'ya wanna come with me?"

A boy in a black T-shirt and black cardigan, all covered up with a black apron, is hovering over me. He looks my age. He has acne on his neck.

"No," I tell him. "I'm with Scott."

"Nah, nah." He's grinning like this is hilarious. "I'm just gonna wash your hair for Scott, ain't I."

"Oh, right."

"Gis ya jacket." I wonder if he's putting on the East End accent just to be cool.

We walk over to the coatroom and I realize I'm still holding the plastic menu.

"Want me to take that, yeah?" He smirks at me again and puts the menu back on the table. I don't know what he thinks is so funny. He's as out of place in here as I am.

"Stick your arm in there." Daniel holds out a floaty gray smock. I turn my back as if I'm putting on a coat. "Nah, nah, this way. Forward. It does up at the back, dunnit. That's got ya. Sorted. Follow me."

We walk through the middle of the salon, watched on both sides by the faces of customers reflected back by the mirrors. We go down some stairs to a low-lit area filled with armchairs and sinks. "Womb-like"—that's what they would call it on one of those snobby decorating programs. A bit dark is what they really mean.

Daniel points to one of the chairs and I sit down. He hands me a TV remote control on the end of a spiral cable. There are no TVs. I'm confused.

"For the chair, innit." Daniel snatches back the control and presses a button. A footrest takes me by surprise and starts to lift up my legs. Daniel skips to one side to avoid getting kicked.

"Wey-hey. There you go. This one does the headrest, dunnit. Lean back. Get comfy." He hands me back the control. I pull the ponytail band out of my hair and have a last feel of the curls. Past my shoulder blades. A couple of years and it would be long enough to sit on. But what's the point of that now? I drop my head into the neck rest of the sink behind me. I wonder whether I'm supposed to keep my eyes open during the whole thing or keep them shut. I once overheard Lucy Bloss telling Emily Winters that you should close your eyes when you're having sex;

otherwise, you look like a prostitute. Daniel turns on the water. It makes me jump.

"Wey-hey, steady there. Too cold for ya?"

"No, it's fine."

"How old are you, then? You don't look very old to me."

"Fifteen."

"Yeah, yeah, thought so."

"I can pay, though."

"Yeah, yeah, course you can. Never said you couldn't, did I. Shouldn't you be at school?"

"Study leave."

"Right, yeah. Exams. Nightmare. Just done mine. You want a head massage?"

Do I want a head massage? What is the right answer? If I say no, will I sound frigid? If I say yes, will I sound like a prostitute? "Yes. Please."

"No worries. I can do that for ya."

I like the feeling of someone else washing my hair. Mum used to do it when I was little in the bath, scrubbing her fingers against my scalp. "No nits for you! *Agapoula mou!*" She used to cut it too. I've never been to a hairdresser before. She said it's easy when it's curly because you don't have to worry about straight lines. That's how come she could cut her own hair as well.

Daniel is lifting and then dropping my wet, heavy hair in the sink, getting rid of the soap.

"Gotta lotta hair, intcha."

"Yes."

"S'nice."

"Thanks."

We would cut our hair in the kitchen, me and Mum, because you needed to be able to sweep up every curl afterward. The hair trimmings would then get wrapped in newspaper so they couldn't escape when the trash was thrown out. If a bird took some of your hair, even a strand, and made a nest with it, you would lose your mind, Mum said.

Daniel has turned off the spray head. For a minute I think he's finished, but then I hear him pumping one of those big bottles on the counter behind the sink. There's the squelch of something being rubbed between his hands, and then he's touching my hair again. It's different now, though. He's not being rough and scrubby like before. He's stroking my hair gently like it's a cat. Then suddenly he drives his fingers, hard, forward through my hair toward my forehead. He reaches my temples and presses a little, then drags his fingers back again, slowly. When he reaches the back of my head, he pulls my hair, just enough to feel good, not painful. Then he's pushing forward again, hard, pulling back, slowly. Again and again. I close my eyes and see the ghosts of the ceiling spotlights on the back of my eyelids.

"That pressure all right for ya?"

"Yeah, it's . . . Yeah."

He keeps massaging. Forward, hard, backward, soft, a strong pull. Forward, hard, backward, soft, a strong pull. Then he stops, his hands resting at the edge of my face. He leans forward and speaks quietly.

"Need a cold rinse?"

My eyes ping open. I am officially a prostitute.

148

"It's good for your follicles."

"What is?"

"A cold rinse."

"Oh."

He blasts me with icy water and I want to squeal.

Daniel ties my hair up in a towel and walks me back through the salon and over to a chair. He introduces me to Scott, who shakes my hand, which is the weirdest thing. I see my washed-out face looking back from the mirror, the turban of towel piled on top. I look like an utter dickhead. A sickly, pale dickhead.

"Get you anyfink to drink?" Daniel asks me. He's faffing around, tidying up Scott's hair dryer and brush from the last customer.

"Yeah, a Coke please."

"Okay, gotcha."

"And a smoked salmon bagel." I'm trying to remember what else was on the list. "And a hot chocolate."

"Hungry now, yeah? Coming up."

Daniel disappears and Scott beams at me in the mirror. He pulls away the towel and starts combing my wet hair.

"And what are we having done today?"

"Cut it all off."

Scott asked me three times if I was sure. He tried to talk me into a shoulder-length bob, but I said, "No, short." When Daniel came back with my sandwich and drinks, he looked shocked at the huge strands all around me on the floor. There was enough there to make a whole nest. A huge, insane palace for the London pigeons.

Scott chewed gum and danced around to the music while he snipped. At one point he said to me, "Got any plans for the weekend?" and I just stared at him like a loony for the longest time before I could get myself together to answer. Mum used to say that in a silly voice when she was cutting my hair in the kitchen. Her pretend English voice. I never really got the joke. "Doing anything nice this weekend?" she'd go. "Going anywhere nice for vacation? Nice weather we're having, isn't it?" *Ha-ha, snip, snip.*

"Well?" asked Scott.

"No plans," I'd told him.

"You want to speak to Daniel about that, then," he'd said, and winked at me in the mirror.

I was a bit upset when it was all finished—about my hair being short, I mean. I tried not to look Daniel in the eye as he hovered around, taking off my smock, brushing hair off my neck. I didn't want him to see me looking like I might cry.

"Looks nice," he'd gone. "Proper edgy."

I couldn't speak. I knew Mrs. Lacey would keel over when she saw me.

At the counter, the plastic-haired woman told me how much I owed. I repeated it back to her, the figure sticking in my throat. My hand went into my jeans pocket and I pulled out Chick's credit card. When the woman went to take it off me, I held on to the card just a little longer than I should have. She gave me a look. I loosened my grip. She put the card in the machine and then turned the keypad to face me. My stomach lurched. A PIN? I hadn't even thought about needing a PIN. I tried Chick's birthday. It

150

didn't work. I gave my birthday a go. I don't know why — it was just something to try. Then I did *1,2,3,4.*

PIN REJECTED.

"Have you got any other way of paying?" went the plastic-haired woman, still friendly but a bit firm. I stood there, feeling wobbly, my hand on the back of my neck, holding onto the spiky hair that was there in place of my ponytail. I shook my head.

"Can you ring my mum for me?" I asked her, sounding snively.

This haircut was going to make even more of an impact than I'd first thought.

The plastic-haired woman's smile was fading.

"Her name's Rowena Lacey," I told her.

And I'd given the woman the number.

THE STORY

4

This is the recipe.

Take five pounds of hulled whole wheat. Hold it in your arms. Feel that it weighs nothing compared to the load that lies heavy on your heart. Wash the wheat; let your tears join in. Strike a match, strike up faith, light the gas. Watch the wheat bubble and boil. See steam rising like hope. Take the pot from the heat and pour the wheat through a sieve. Lay the grain on a sheet overnight to dry. Rest your head on your own sheets. Dream of a flower dying, shedding its seeds, allowing another flower to grow.

In the morning, on the day of remembrance, put the wheat in a bowl with walnuts, almonds, and parsley. Add a message of devotion, a wish for the future, your gratitude to God. Sprinkle in cinnamon, not guilt. Throw in sesame seeds; throw away your fear. Turn out your mixture and create a mound—a monument to love. Brown some flour and sift. Add a layer of sugar. Press flat. Finally, crush the skin of a pomegranate with the remains of your fury, and spread the seeds with love, in the shape of a cross.

Maria did not dream of a flower dying. The night before her mother's funeral, she did not sleep at all. She pressed one of Mama's cardigans close to her face, letting it transport her back to a farm where cistus shrubs turn the air bittersweet. She listened to Melon's snuffling breaths, envying the way her daughter remained untouched by grief. She thought of the day ahead, the day she would return her mother to the earth. She was not ready to let her go.

Auntie Eleni had outlined the ceremony and recommended a plot. She had also pressed into Maria's hands the pamphlet containing the recipe for the traditional *kollyva*—the boiled wheat.

"But I can't cook," said Maria, scanning the recipe. "I can't do it."

"You will find it within yourself," Eleni insisted.

And so she had.

Letters and phone calls to the farm received no response. With his silence, Babas made it clear that he would not be journeying to England to bury his wife. Maria and Eleni would go to the funeral alone. Melon stayed with a considerate neighbor, playing with a collection of toys on their hearth rug, unaware of the furious rainstorm outside.

Maria couldn't help but find the downpour fitting. She wanted to feel the rain on her skin, have it cleanse her of her grief. She imagined the ancient river Lardanos, the river of holy water, evaporating into the air in Crete and falling on London's streets. With her hair soaked through, Maria walked behind Mama's coffin, and she listened to them read the psalm:

For I acknowledge my transgressions, and my sin is ever before me.

Maria placed the resurrection icon in Mama's hands, and on her forehead they placed a wreath.

Behold, I was shapen in iniquity; and in sin did my mother conceive me.

Maria and Eleni took up candles, received light from the priest, and watched the fire burn.

Purge me with hyssop, and I shall be clean.

They gave their kisses to Mama and they told her good-bye.

Wash me, and I shall be whiter than snow.

At the wake, Maria took a spoon to break through the crucifix of pomegranate seeds. She passed among the small gathering, scooping boiled wheat into their cups, but soon found she could not hold herself up. Maria fell to her knees cradling the bowl and began crying with such a force she feared she would never stop.

Indeed, the crying continued for weeks. A vast flood swamped Maria, pulling her beneath the surface of life. When the tears eventually dried, they were replaced by the soft, suffocating fog of depression. She was numb. Maria looked back on her days of rage and sorrow with a twisted sense of fondness. At least then she had felt something.

"You need time to recover," Auntie Eleni decreed. "We will find someone to care for Melon."

"No," said Maria, the first word she had said with any real passion since the depression had taken hold. "A child needs its mother."

And slowly Maria returned, piece by piece. The green hue to her olive skin began to fade, she put food in her belly, her shoulders uncoiled, the pupils of her eyes reconnected with life. The brick lodged within Maria's ribs began to crack, and though the splinters still caused jerks of pain, Maria found a new feeling growing inside—the fire of ambition. Here was rebirth—a flower dying, shedding its seeds, allowing another flower to grow. Her mother's death had not been for nothing. Maria went back to school.

It is a joyous moment when a life finds a target and a purpose, when a person realizes what makes them special. It is like a stylus falling into place on a record. Music begins to play.

The sign on the double doors of the office read, "Congratulations to Maria Fouraki, who will be joining the Adolescent Resource Team as a trainee social worker." Maria pushed through those doors, found her new desk, and on it placed the framed picture of her daughter on her first day at school.

Melon had found her English voice, and every day Maria marveled at the clean-edged words that spilled from her mouth. She would be the Londoner Maria could never truly be.

And they would go on to buy their own home in the city, not far from Kentish Town.

And soon Maria would earn enough to afford the regular airfare to visit Crete.

"I have this piece of thread," Maria explained to little Melon. "The piece of thread that connects my heart to yours. This thread, it also binds my heart to home and to Babas. When something is tugging at Babas's heart, I know, because I feel it too."

Maria understood that the past could not be forgotten and that history could not be altered, but the truth could be viewed from a new angle, an angle that pleased everyone.

Forget what you know, what you feel about everything that has happened.

This is how Maria would explain.

Come and see things in a new way, she would say. *Purge me with hyssop, and I shall be clean. Wash me, and I shall be whiter than snow. The view from up here, it is rosy. The future from here, it looks good.*

36 DAYS SINCE

"You can take your jacket off, you know."

"I'm not staying." I fold my arms across my chest.

"You're not staying?"

"No."

"Oh." Amanda looks disappointed. These last few weeks she's convinced herself we're getting somewhere. If she was one of those detectives on TV and I was the villain, she'd be talking about "breakthroughs" and about how she'd "worn me down," stuff like that.

"No, I'm not staying. Sorry." I'm such a pain.

"But you came."

"Only to tell you I'm not coming anymore."

"You felt you owed me that."

"Yes."

She smiles. I am dumping her and she's smiling.

"So, why have you decided not to come anymore? What feelings have led you to that decision?"

"I don't want to do that."

"What?"

"The feelings stuff."

"Right."

The schoolkids are playing field hockey on the grass outside the window today. There's something really satisfying about hitting a really hard ball with a big wooden stick. Amanda follows my gaze out of the window.

"Do you think that you're all better now, Melon? All fixed?"

"No, I think . . ." I've fallen for it again. I am talking. "I think I'm better off broken."

Amanda is looking even less dumped. She's not listening to what I'm really saying.

"Or maybe what I mean is . . ." How does she do this, get me saying things that I don't want to say? "What I mean is, I've written it all down, all the stuff about my mum, like you told me to, and I don't feel any better."

"Maybe that suggests you haven't written it all down yet."

"Maybe."

"Maybe there's more to say."

"Maybe."

I can see Amanda has photocopied some handouts. She's fiddling with the corners of the stack on her lap. Amanda likes handouts. They're good for papering over the damage.

"I've photocopied this for you."

She hands me the top sheet. She has a copy for herself too. The title reads, WHAT IS ACCEPTANCE? There is a cartoon girl next to the title. She is looking up wonderingly but confusedly at a rainbow.

"What do we mean by acceptance?" asks Amanda. She has switched into teacher mode. I like her better when she's off script. I stare at the confused cartoon girl. Isn't acceptance just a matter of saying "yes"?

"I found some photos," I tell her. Who else can I tell?

"Photos of what?"

"Mum."

"Where were these photos taken?"

"In Crete, when she was little."

"How did it make you feel finding those?"

I refuse to answer that. Amanda doesn't know how to talk about anything without bringing feelings into it.

At our second session, I talked about the frumpy social worker they've assigned to me. She's named Susan. Poppy isn't allowed to do my visits anymore because she knows me too well. They think it's better that a complete stranger invades my house—a complete stranger who wears navy pantsuits that have gone pilly on the thighs where her legs rub together. Anyway, I was telling Amanda about how funny I think it is that Paul, who is a social worker, is being checked up on by another social worker. He's getting a taste of his own annoying medicine. Amanda goes to me, "Does that feel like a victory for you, that Paul is feeling uncomfortable?" as if I'm the bad person in all of this. It was only meant to be a joke.

"What's this acceptance sheet, then?" I go.

"You don't want to talk about the photos of your mum?"

"No."

Amanda looks down at her own copy of the handout,

reading it for a moment as if it's the first time she's seen it. She must have hassled tons of teenagers with this thing before.

"Okay, so, what do we mean by acceptance?" Amanda fixes me with an eager look.

"Well, it says here . . ."

"No, what does the word mean to you, Melon, in relation to your mum?"

I start reading from the first bullet point on the sheet. "Acceptance does not mean you feel happy and contented about what has happened. Acceptance is . . ."

"Melon, don't just read the sheet. What do you think?"

"Why did you give me the sheet, then, if I'm not supposed to read it?"

"Well, hand it back and we'll talk first."

I thrust the sheet back at her with a huff. Amanda straightens out its creases and puts it facedown on the pile on her lap. She looks at me, that hopeful face again, waiting for me to talk about acceptance. She'll have to wait until dinosaurs walk the earth again.

At our third session, last week, Amanda tried to talk me into joining some of the group activities at the counseling center. If I wanted to, Amanda said, I could share my feelings with other teenagers who have lost someone. My feelings—everything is always about feelings! I said no. Who wants to sit around with a bunch of sad kids (both meanings of the word *sad*) and have some kind of sob-off? We'd all be competing to see who has had it worst. I'm not interested.

"I found pictures of my dad too," I go.

"What, with the pictures of your mum?"

"Yeah, they knew each other as kids, except . . ."

"Except?"

There is a poster on the wall behind Amanda, a kind of flow diagram of what grief feels like. There are angry arrows of "guilt" and "fear."

"His name is Christos Drakakis. My dad is Christos Drakakis." *And my name is Melon Drakaki*, I want to say. *How do you do?*

"You don't know him, do you, Melon? You haven't met him. But have you seen photographs of him before?"

"No."

"Gosh. Were you pleased to find these pictures?"

"I look nothing like him."

"No?"

"No."

I have studied the photo album more closely since I found it in Mum's underwear drawer. When I can't sleep, I take it out from under my mattress and flick through the pictures. I stare at Christos Drakakis's face and try to feel like he really is my dad. I will and wish for that, but it never feels true. I'm just looking at a picture of a boy who is younger than me. The older boy in the picture, the one with the sneery smile, his hard face drills into mine. He laughs when I do this willing and wishing, trying to make Christos fit the jigsaw puzzle in my head. The older boy is Yiannis, I have decided. He must be. He is the boy who had sex behind the goat sheds.

"Would you like it if you and your dad looked more alike?"

161

"I don't want to look like a boy."

"No, but do you wish there was a family resemblance?"

"Not bothered, really."

The field-hockey girls are in a huddle in the center of the field now, their heads down. They could be having a jolly strategy talk or be getting a telling-off—you can't tell from up here. There could be someone in the middle of that huddle being quietly kicked to pieces.

"Do you still want to know what I think about acceptance?" I ask Amanda.

"I'd like to know what you think about the photos. Are you pleased that you found them?"

"I don't know."

On the flowchart poster on the wall behind Amanda there are also angry arrows of "denial" and "confusion."

Paul wants me to go to Crete with him. He wants us to scatter Mum's ashes on the melon farm like she requested in her will. Paul asked if Auntie Aphrodite might be happy to let us stay with her. I told him she wouldn't even let me and Mum stay, so she's hardly likely to give her spare bedroom to Mum's black boyfriend. I said it to him exactly like that—I said "black." It's the first time I've brought it up. Paul looked a little shocked.

"It doesn't bother me that you're black," I added, just to be clear that I wasn't the one being a racist. "I'm just saying Auntie Aphrodite wouldn't like it."

He nodded at me. No smile.

Since then, Paul's been bringing home travel brochures. Piles of the things. Pages and pages of bright-white apartments with bright-blue pools next to bright-green spiky trees. He wants me to join in and help pick out a place to stay. He wants us to have a cracking adventure. A celebration of Mum. There's nothing to choose between these brochure apartments; they all look the same.

"Where did you and your mum used to stay?" Paul asked me.

"Can't remember the name of it," I told him. I don't want to go back to the same place with him.

Without her.

I told Paul I might look for my dad if we go to Crete. I didn't really mean it. What would I do if I found him? He's obviously not interested in me. I just said it to wind Paul up, to make him think he wasn't doing a good enough job of playing dad himself. But it didn't ruffle him up like I'd expected. Paul just went quiet. He looked at me like I was a little deranged, as if he was scared of me. Then he gave me another one of his nods.

"I would like you to throw away the idea of acceptance," says Amanda.

"Acceptance of what?"

"The idea that you should accept what's happened."

"I should fight it? The fact that she's dead? That doesn't make much sense."

"No, what I mean is, no one expects you to suddenly feel happy again."

"Well, good."

"Acceptance just means acknowledging that the person has really gone."

163

"So I shouldn't fight it? Make your mind up."

Amanda sighs and wipes a hand down over her forehead and eyes.

She goes quiet for a moment.

When she looks at me again, she has transformed. This is a new Amanda. "What is it that you think you're fighting, Melon?" This is tough Amanda. "Why are you fighting against everything?"

"I'm not fighting anyone."

I sit next to Justine Burrell at school now. Chick sits next to Lucy. Justine Burrell is clever and intelligent and a high achiever, which means she has no friends. Obviously. I actually quite like her. I see how it must be for her now, being on the outside looking in. Not that I was ever really an insider. But I definitely wasn't a proper outcast until now.

Whatever we have in common, we're not really friends, Justine and me. It's my fault. I don't say much in class. My mind wanders. I try to listen to all the exam recap stuff we're doing, but before I know it, I'm off thinking about The Story. I play around with it in my head, deciding how I should write the next part in my book. I think of new words, prettier ones, better sentences, because English was never Mum's strong point. I struggle to remember how Mum told The Story. I can't bring her voice back anymore. My memory of her hasn't gone mute, exactly. I can still hear the chip-chop way she used to speak—it's just there are no real words coming out of her mouth. Maybe this chattering sound will be the next thing to go. Then the image I have of her will lose all its facial features. She'll become just an outline. Then—pop!—she'll disappear.

"So you say you've finished writing everything down?"

"Yes."

"Can I ask you what kind of thing you've been writing?"

"The Story."

"The Story?"

Amanda thought I was working on some weepy essay about how sad I am.

"The Story that Mum told me," I explain.

Amanda looks confused. "A bedtime story? A fairy tale?"

"No." A fairy tale? Who does Amanda think I am? A baby? "No, it's not a fucking fairy tale."

"Okay, I'm sorry, Melon. I'm really sorry if what I just said upset you."

"It's not a fucking fairy tale!"

"No, no, I understand that now. But will you tell me what it is? Please."

"No, fuck off. I don't want to talk about it now."

I get up. My face is prickling. I feel a real fury burning in my belly. It's come out of nowhere, this red-hot rage. I'm not even sure why I'm so offended. All I can think is, how dare she say that? How dare she call my book a fairy tale?

"Melon, sit down. This story is obviously really important to you and I would really like to hear about it."

"It's not important to you. It has nothing to do with you. You know nothing about it."

There is a *thwack* and a cheer from the field outside.

"Where are you going, Melon?"

I head for the door.

"Home."

"Tell me about The Story."

"It's just a fucking story, that's all, okay?" I am outside of my body looking down at myself. It's like watching some other girl going crazy.

"No, it's more than that, isn't it, Melon?"

I'm possessed. I'm doubled over, screaming at Amanda. "It's just a fucking story! All right! It's just a fucking fairy tale!"

I stop and feel the silence putting its hand over my mouth.

There is nothing left inside of me.

I walk out of the room and slam the door.

5 MONTHS BEFORE

"Hurry up! I need to pee."

Mum shut herself in the bathroom over an hour ago.

"What is problem? I am not locking door. Come in."

"I don't want an audience."

"Oh, for goodness' sake, Melon. Is only me. If you just need to pee . . . You need a poo?"

"No! God! You're so . . ."

I push my way into the bathroom and stomp past Mum, who is lying in the bath, all boobs and bubbles. Her face is smeared in green gloop. I pull down my sweatpants and underwear, make a porcelain crash as I sit. I stare straight ahead while I pee. Mum wants to make eye contact, but she's not getting it. I wipe, stand, pull up my clothes, flush.

"Wash your hands!" The face mask is setting, and Mum can't move her mouth properly. The words come out all rigid. *Wah yer hans.*

"I was going to anyway."

"Tan coo," she goes.

"I'm turning the music down," I tell her on the way out. "It's scaring Kojak."

Mum has had the same song on repeat for an hour, blasting out from the CD player in her bedroom, loud enough to fill the bathroom with music. She was dancing around her bedroom to it earlier, weaving her feet around, clicking her fingers, flapping her elbows like a chicken, flirting with her reflection in the mirror.

"It's like the sad fuckers' salsa club in this house." I dry my hands.

"Meyo, du nu si dis eff wud," Mum grunts over the music.

"So-rree," I say. I leave.

In Mum's room, there is a burgundy dress on the bed. She has laid it out with tights poking out the bottom, shoes at the end of the tights, a bra and underwear on top, and a necklace, bracelet, and earrings all in the right place. It looks like someone has stretched out on her bed and then evaporated, leaving their stuff behind. There are still tags on the dress. It's new. I finger the fabric. I've never seen this dress before. I walk around the bed to her CD player and turn down the volume so it's just a mumble.

In the hallway I give Kojak a rub behind the ears. He's sitting outside Mum's room with his ears pinned back, squinting. He is standing his ground—making a protest against crap Latin music. He hasn't figured out that he can just leave. How lucky is Kojak? He can just pop out the cat flap and escape. I have been told I must stay here and not go to Chick's house because I am getting my first proper introduction to Paul when he comes to pick up Mum. Cannot wait.

People go on dates all the time, every single day of the week, but Mum is acting like Paul and her are Adam and Eve. This isn't even a first date. She's been knocking around with Paul for weeks. Tonight is far from monumental. It is the Social Services Christmas Ball. Calling it a "ball" makes it sound like some glamorous thing in a castle in Vienna, but really it will be a crappy buffet in a municipal hall in Barnet. Mum has built it up to be the red-carpet event of the year. I'm not allowed to spoil the illusion.

"You are spoilsport," Mum yells from the bathroom, now that the music's gone. She must have cracked her face mask because she sounds normal again. As normal as Mum ever sounds.

Mum suggested we have a "pampering afternoon" to get ready for tonight. It's what they tell you to do in sappy magazines. I wonder if anyone in real life actually has "pampering afternoons." I bet the women who write those articles have chipped nails and stubbly legs like the rest of civilization. I told Mum I didn't want to do it.

"I'm not going out, am I?" I said.

"So? You join in with me. Just for fun. Help your skin."

She'd licked her thumb and rubbed at the concealer on the zit on my chin. I yanked my face away, told her to get off. I try really hard at feeling good about myself, and she has the power to take it away with one wipe of her thumb.

"You are looking much better without this stuff on your face. Makes it worse. All cakey. You prettier underneath."

Mum knows nothing. You have to keep covering up. You have to keep battling. The last thing you must do is admit defeat. An ugly disease gets hold of you at about thirteen years old and turns you zitty and lumpy and greasy, and if you don't fight it you'll never come out the other end. You have to keep concealing and hiding and disguising and hoping for something a tiny step nearer to perfection. You have to tell yourself that it's a good thing that you have curvy thighs and not bamboo canes for legs, like Chick. And you have to tell yourself that your frizzy hair is interesting, while Lucy Bloss's perfect, perfect hair is just fake. And you have to tell yourself that you are lucky to have only a few zits and not a big, mad rash of acne, like Georgina Holcroft, who has it across her cheeks and—even grosser—her shoulders. At least no one stares at your gross back when you're getting undressed for PE, trying to work out where the zits start and where they end. It's cruel to think of your classmates like that, but you have to focus on their weaknesses to survive. You have to make their problems and insecurities seem worse than your own, otherwise how can you live with yourself?

Especially when you have a mum like mine.

Mum walks out of the bathroom wrapped in a towel, trailing the smell of her bath bubbles. She's done that thing with her hair where she twists it around and around on top of her head and it just stays there in a bun by itself. All so easy. I think about the jokey stuff Mum says about Auntie Aphrodite. *Flowers they are growing wherever she is walking; birds they are flocking wherever she is flying!* Those words are about Mum, really. Mum is the elfin fairy queen and I am her lumping great monster offspring. How did this happen? Was she cursed, or am I? Either way, I never inherited her cheekbones. I got dark hairy arms as extra punishment.

No.

She is the one who's the embarrassment. This is how I have to think about it, or else I will die of self-hatred. Mum is the one who dresses like a scruffy student. She is the one who collects cheap jewelry like a thieving magpie. She is the one who accidentally on purpose forgets to put on makeup and comb her hair because she thinks she's all floaty and poetic. She is the one who insists on speaking like she just came over on the last plane from Greece even though she can write English perfectly, better than me. She is the one who laughs that little bit too loudly in public and makes everyone stare and stare. She is the one with the problem.

"Come, help me choose what I am wearing," Mum goes, dripping water along the hallway. Kojak feels crowded out and hightails it down the stairs. I get up from where I've been crouching next to him. I throw a look into Mum's bedroom.

"Looks like you've already decided."

"Is not final." She's lying. That dress is like nothing else she owns. That dress is especially for tonight.

"S'okay, I'm going to write my Christmas cards."

"Oh." She looks disappointed. "Okay, then."

I head back down the hall to my room and close the door.

Writing Christmas cards is a political business. It's best to write too many and include the people you don't really like. This is insurance. If someone gives you a card and you don't give them one straight back, it's awkward. You just stand there not knowing what to say, your mouth opening and shutting—goldfish lips. If you have the backup card ready and written, you're safe. In the same way, you must never give a card to someone unless you are absolutely sure they are going to give you one back. Otherwise, you'll be on the receiving end of the goldfish lips. Total shame.

I start by writing a list. Lists make you feel better. It seems like you're doing something productive when really all you're doing is making a list. They work with everything, not just Christmas cards.

I AM BETTER THAN MUM BECAUSE I . . .

- SPEAK PROPERLY
- DON'T DRESS LIKE A GYPSY
- DON'T TELL STORIES ABOUT MYSELF ALL THE TIME
- ACT MY AGE

This makes me feel better for all of a nanosecond. Then I feel like a bitch for actually writing it down. I am a bad person and therefore not as good as Mum after all. Mum wins.

On my Christmas card list, I put:

CHICK

ELAINE WILKIE

GEORGINA HOLCROFT

CARA MORAN

FREYA NIGHTINGALE

LOUISE SHINE (JEWISH, BUT STILL SENDS CARDS. WEIRD)

POOJA VARMA

SHAKIRA ANWAR

KAYLEIGH BARNES (INSURANCE)

EMILY WINTERS (INSURANCE)

DIONNE AGU (INSURANCE)

LUCY BLOSS (ONLY FOR AN EXTREME EMERGENCY)

I put no boys on the list. Boys don't send you anything—
unless they're your boyfriend.

I take the pack of cards out of my schoolbag. They have
a picture of a snow-covered house on them. The house is
perfect—door in the middle, four symmetrical windows,
a garden fence. Other people have houses like this. Other
people also have perfect, symmetrical lives. I turn the pack
over. It says there are only ten cards inside. Two people have
to go from my list. Who won't bother to send me a card?
Lucy and Kayleigh are the obvious ones to ditch. They could
come over all "season of goodwill," but it's unlikely. I'd
be less surprised if a new baby Jesus turned up in East
Finchley.

I've bought a silver ink pen for the writing. I saw a really
lovely one in a shop that wrote in shimmery red, but I
couldn't use that for my cards, even if I was writing one
to Lucy Bloss. I don't hate her enough to want her dead.
I give the silver pen a shake, listen to the ink mixer inside
rattling up and down. I take off the cap and give it a quick
sniff. Kayleigh Barnes says you can get really high with one
of these things if you put your mind to it. Can kill you
too, though, make your heart stop.

DEAR CHICK,

I write,

MERRY CHRISTMAS. HAVE AN AMAZING NEW YEAR.
LOVE, MEL XXX

Next year will be amazing, because our exams will be done and finished. I lick the envelope, seal it up, write "Chick" in curly letters on the front. I'm just about to start writing Elaine's card when Mum cranks the music back up, earsplittingly loud. I am being attacked by salsa. I put down the silver pen and go out into the hall.

"Turn. The. Music. Down," I yell over the plinking and plonking of a deafening piano.

The music dips. Mum wobbles out of her room in high heels. She's finished getting dressed. She is a different person. Neat. Chic. The burgundy dress clings to her. It says, *Look, here are my boobs and here is my bum.* The dress has raised seams running up the side of Mum's thighs, crisscrossing over her belly and under her chest. It looks expensive. I should have checked the price tag when I was in her room. Her hair looks different too. It's scraped back and twisted tight at the back of her head. It's tidy for the first time in history. Her makeup is heavy, immaculate, smoky. Perfect. Mum has been promoted. She's no longer the elfin fairy queen; she's a goddess. I want to tell her how nice she looks, but I feel too winded to talk. This is my mum—a woman who has sex. I hate her. I hate her.

She watches me looking her up and down, then breaks into a cackle.

"What's so funny?" I go. The laugh makes me feel small, left out. I don't get the joke.

She's holding her belly, putting her hand up to her mouth.

"What's so funny?" I try to find some laughter in me too, but there isn't any.

"You." She can't catch her breath because she's laughing.

"What?" I look down at my baggy T-shirt and my sweatpants. The same old me. Nothing new, nothing funny.

"We the wrong way around," she splutters. "Should be me telling you 'shush.'" She lets the cackle take over, crosses her legs like she's going to wet herself. She comes up for air and speaks again. "And this"—she sweeps a hand up and down herself—"this should be you."

Now, that really cracks her up. Doubles her over. I watch her laugh. The hand covering her mouth again. I look down and notice the tomato-sauce stain on my T-shirt. I look back at Mum, gift-wrapped in burgundy Lycra.

It should be me.

I try to picture myself going on a date. I have to borrow a corny scene from an American movie. A boy with perfect teeth and slicked-down hair arrives at our house with a corsage for me to wear on my arm. Mum has on one of those prim fitted dresses with a sticky-out skirt and a dainty apron tied on top. Her hair is in big curls around her face. Mum makes sure that my date measures up by asking what his parents do for a living. *What car does your father drive?* she inquires.

Mum is still giggling.

This is never going to happen to me. I will never meet anyone. I will never leave home. I'll be stuck here, watching Mum go on date after date, listening to music getting louder and louder. I will get grumpier and more and more bitter as the days go by. I have fallen under an ancient curse. I am doomed to grow old too quickly, while Mum will miraculously grow younger. I will sit back and watch while she lives my life instead of me.

"I'm going to watch TV," I say. I go downstairs and leave her giggling on the landing.

Mum comes into the living room while I'm flicking through the channels. She's pulled herself together. She wants to be "serious Mum" now.

"I wish you could come too," she says. The TV light flickers against her face in the dark of the room. "Is so exciting," she says.

I give her a quick, pitying look.

"You're acting like you're fourteen years old or something!" I try to make this playful and teasing but my heart isn't in it.

A rich girl on TV is arriving at her own birthday party in a horse-drawn carriage.

"I quite like the chance to be fourteen again, actually," Mum says. She is grinning in a meaningful way. I know where this is going. I burrow my body into the corner of the sofa.

The rich girl's friends are whooping and cheering as she steps out of the carriage.

"When I was fourteen . . ." Mum goes, "I was . . ."

I stop listening. I tune Mum out and concentrate on the birthday girl on TV. I know how it goes. This is The Story. When Mum was fourteen, she was young and innocent and everything was perfect down on Tersanas Beach. Then she got knocked up with me, and Babas said "pah" instead of good-bye, and the final slivers of her childhood slipped away.

The rich girl is air-kissing friend after friend, acting like she is better than all of them.

"The rent did not pay itself . . ." Mum is still going. She's on to the London phase of The Story. When will she stop? Her arms are gesturing wildly. She loves every word of her story, all the misery.

Shut up, shut up, shut up, I go, inside my head. *Shut up, shut up, shut up.* I give her a quick smile to show that I am satisfied, that I've heard all I need to, that she can be quiet now.

The girl on TV is twirling in the center of the dance floor. Everyone is watching as she throws her hands in the air and gyrates her skinny hips.

"When I hear Greek words spoken on the top deck . . ." Mum says with a sigh. "Above the fast talk of those English teenagers . . ." On and on she goes, poor little Maria who had no friends so had to find them on the buses.

Then the polite lid that has been on top of all my feelings flies off.

"Oh, God!" I growl. "You should have just had a fucking abortion if it was so much trouble."

I clamp my mouth shut as soon as I've spoken.

Mum stops talking.

I have never answered her back like that before in my life.

I can't look at her.

On TV, the air-kissing goes on and on.

"What did you say?" Mum heard me the first time. She is daring me to say it out loud again.

"I said"—I try to make it sound like a fair and reasonable comment this time around but it's no good; I am angry. I look her in the eye—"had you never heard of abortion?"

All the life drains out of Mum's face. The girl on TV is squealing about how "awesome" everything is. Mum's mouth opens and closes, opens and closes, but nothing comes out. She is doing the Christmas card goldfish face.

"Don't do this tonight, Melon," Mum goes, eventually finding something to say. She is wobbling her words. "I feel . . ."

"Oh, grow up!" I snap. I just want to explode. The last thing on earth I want to hear is how she feels. *What about me?* I want to yell at her. *What about me?* But I manage to stop myself. I bundle up the anger, push it down, replace the lid.

I curl myself tighter into the corner of the sofa. The rich girl on TV is disappointed because some boy she's invited to the party hasn't shown up.

The doorbell rings. Mum doesn't move. I can see her out of the corner of my eye. A drip of mascara is rolling down one of her cheeks.

"Aren't you going to get that?" I say, gentle now. I just want her to leave. I can't bear her standing there, silently punishing me for the things I just said. I cannot win. When I keep quiet, it hurts inside, and when I say something, I hurt her.

I aim the remote at the TV and flip through the channels, working my way through the music videos. Mum leaves the room.

I hear the front door open, hushed voices in the hallway. I'm waiting for Paul to be dragged into the living room for his embarrassing introduction.

I hear the front door close. All quiet. They've gone.

52 DAYS SINCE

I'm sitting on the sofa with Susan, the social worker. She's at one end; I'm at the other. I don't want to get too close. I stink. I haven't showered for eight days.

Susan is sipping the tea that Paul made before he left the house. He hasn't given her a mug; he's given her a cup and saucer. I didn't even know Mum had cups and saucers. Every day I discover another thing I didn't know about Mum.

I'm not sure what Paul is trying to prove to Susan by using a proper teacup. Is it a well-known Social Services fact that men who abuse children never serve tea in nice cups? Paul hates being checked up on by Susan. I think it's made him take a long, hard look at himself. Now he knows how it feels when he goes around to strangers' houses, breathing down their necks, trying to get their kids put into foster care for no reason whatsoever.

Susan puts her teacup on the saucer with a clink. A horrible noise. It makes me squirm. So polite. She picks up a chocolate-chip cookie and takes a bite. (We always have cookies in the house now that Susan comes around.) I watch her jaw work, listen to her chomp. How can she still have an appetite when all she hears are stories like mine, or worse? Maybe if you hear terrible things all day long, it just starts to sound like a whole bunch of nothing. Maybe the chocolate-chip cookies cancel out the horror.

"Is there anything else I can do? Anything else I can get for you?" That's what Paul had said before he'd eventually left the house. He'd buzzed around Susan like a gnat. Susan made it clear when she first started doing her visits that Paul needs to make himself scarce so I can speak my mind with no eavesdropping. Yet he always comes home early from work on the days when I have an appointment, just so he can open the door to Susan, then disappear. He has this need to show his face, prove he's not neglecting me. Sometimes when Susan is here, Paul goes outside with a cup of coffee and dithers around our little square of yard with some clippers and a trowel, pretending he knows what he's doing. Today he's popped to his mum's place in Southgate. He was clutching one of my mum's sturdy canvas supermarket bags to his chest as he left. He'll come home carrying one of Irene's rocket-hot casseroles in that—guaranteed. He will try to make me eat. I haven't eaten for three days.

I have been thinking about the last day she was alive.

I start the argument in my head before I get home. On the way back from school, I'm firing myself up. I have Ian Grainger's words in my head. I see his face, pouting, waggling his tongue, mouthing my name. I haven't been able to think about anything else all day. Inside I'm fizzing.

"We were just, like, you know, yelling out names of food and stuff. Bananas! Cake! Mickey D's!"

Idiot.

"Why do ya think everyone's always talking aboutcha, Melon?"

Because they are. Because everyone is always laughing at my stupid, stupid name.

I want to go straight home after my last class — that's how ready I am to fight it out with Mum — but I have to stay for basketball practice. I hate basketball. I'm no good at it. I spend most of our games on the bench. Then when I do go on, I get the crap positions where you can't score. Melissa Dobbs and Dionne Agu get to be guard and point guard every match. They get all the glory.

In the game at the end of practice, Nina Greco shoulder-barges me so hard that I skid across the ground on my knees. I'm left picking bits of gravel out of bloody flesh. Nina Greco is such a great fat heifer. I would have told her so, but why get mouthy with Nina Greco? I need to save it all up for Mum.

Susan is still chomping, dropping bits of cookie onto her lap. We both watch the crumbs fall. Susan catches me looking and smiles. She flicks at her pilly trousers with the back of her hand.

I want to take one of those fuzz-away machines to Susan's thighs. Or, better still, buy her some new trousers. I want her to appear on one of those makeover TV programs and see her life transformed via the miracle of a new haircut. But then, who am I to give advice on haircuts? Chopping off your hair makes no difference in the world at all.

"And how do you feel about this trip to Crete with Paul?"

Susan's voice is gluey with chocolate chips. There are crumbs on her lipstick lips.

"Fine."

"There is no element of the trip that worries you at all?" Susan pops the last bit of the cookie into her mouth.

"No, it's fine."

"Where will you be staying?" she asks with her mouth full. "With family?"

"No, Paul's found a villa."

"And that's okay, is it?" She slurps her tea, clinks her saucer again.

I cross my arms tighter across my chest. "It's fine."

"Are you happy with where you'll be sleeping?"

"It's . . ."

"Fine?" Susan finishes my sentence with me, and smiles.

I look across at her from under eyelids that feel like slabs of concrete.

"It's okay to tell me what you really think, you know," she goes.

I clasp my hands together and push them down between my thighs. I'm cold. "I've got a separate bedroom in the villa to myself, if that's what you're getting at," I go.

"Well, no, not exactly. I just . . . I just want to make sure you're absolutely comfortable. This is a very big undertaking, traveling all that way, with Paul."

"Not all black men are trying to have sex with teenage white girls, you know."

"I'm not saying they are, Melon."

"No?" I lift an eyebrow, an eyebrow that weighs a ton.

"No."

"Because that would be racist," I slur back at her.

"Yes, Melon, it would."

I can't stop myself. Everyone who tries to help me, I attack them.

I take the side gate when I get home, go in the back door. It's unlocked. Mum's already home. It must have been one of her court days, and she's come home without checking back in at the office. Lazybones. I slam the back door hard to let her know I'm there. I get a muffled "hello" from upstairs. There's the smell of cooking. A frozen meal is doing a twirl in the microwave. Just one frozen meal. I'm obviously going to be eating on my own, unless I go over to Chick's house and time it just right so that I get asked to stay for dinner.

I chuck my bag onto the kitchen table, hard. It slides right across and falls off the other side. Kojak, who was asleep on one of the kitchen chairs, squawks and jumps down as the bag hits the floor. Drama queen. It was nowhere near him. I work my way along the breakfast bar, prodding at a loaf of bread, a bag of doughnuts. Kojak starts winding his body around my legs. I nudge him aside. I'm not in the mood to be nice.

I hear Mum hightailing it down the stairs, and I strike a pose, ready for combat—arms folded, chin down, square to the door. She comes skipping into the kitchen wearing her fancy court suit with the blouse untucked. She doesn't pay me any attention at all.

"Bloody meal. Cook, will you, yes?" She goes over to

184

the microwave and puts her hands on her hips, as if
glaring at the countdown will make it go quicker. Kojak
rubs his face against Mum's legs to see if he can get any
love from her instead. There's a run all the way down
the back of her right calf. I drop my fighting stance, walk
over to the kitchen table, and pick my bag up off the
floor. I do everything with a huff so Mum knows she's
in trouble.

Me and Susan have only been talking for a few minutes and already I'm exhausted. I screw my palms into my eyes.

"You okay, Melon?"

"I'm . . ." I was going to say "fine" again, but I stop myself. "I'm tired."

"I hear you haven't been to school for the last ten days."

Paul is such a bigmouth. Just as I was beginning to wean myself off social workers. Just as I was beginning to convince them that I don't need checking up on anymore. Just as I was about to be left alone. Now they are all on red alert again.

I can't face school. I can't face getting up and getting out of bed. I can't face putting on a uniform. The walk to school is only ten minutes, yet it makes me ache to my bones. I walked to the corner shop on Monday, only because I had to, and that nearly killed me.

I got my period at last. They disappeared when Mum went. Something good to come of it all, I suppose. But when they started again and I went to the medicine cabinet in the bathroom, there was nothing there. Obviously. Paul would never think to buy stuff like that. And nor did I.

Mum always did it. I walked to the corner shop with toilet paper stuffed in my underwear.

The idea of the school yard fills me with dread. No one daring to catch my eye, no one knowing what to say — their silence hangs around my shoulders like a cloak made of lead. Ian and his lot still ignore me, despite our argument on the Tube. What I wouldn't give for him to pick on me now. I deserve it.

Only Justine Burrell has the guts to talk. Constant chit-chat, kind words, all the right things. She's so understanding, it kills me. I didn't even get any joy from watching Chick fall from grace. She's not allowed to sit next to Lucy Bloss anymore; she has to sit with Emily Winters. Chick's time as top dog was short-lived. I feel nothing for her. Not sorry. Not pleased. Nothing.

"Do you want me to speak to the school about putting off your exams for a year?" Susan is speaking ever so gently. She is coaxing a kitten down from a tree.

"No."

"Or at least speak to the exam boards, let them take your circumstances into account."

"No."

I don't want any more fuss. I want everyone to leave me alone. All these people sticking their nose in and trying to help has just made things worse.

"I go out tonight. For dinner." Mum gets a fork out of the drawer and waves it at the microwave. "This is just a snack. So I not get hungry." The microwave pings. She opens the door and takes out a full-size lasagne.

I pull back a chair with a long, teeth-grinding scrape. I sit down at the table and yank books out of my bag, slamming them down hard on the table.

"You'll be okay? There is lasagne for you in the fridge." Mum flips her plastic tray of food upside down onto a plate, scrapes the rest out with the fork. She uses her finger to wipe up the last of the sauce. "Ow, is bloody hot."

I sigh loudly, start flipping the pages of my French textbook so roughly I almost rip them. Finally Mum notices me, my anger, and turns to look. She blows on a huge forkful of lasagne. A dollop of meat falls, and Kojak pounces to lick it up off the floor.

Mum's forehead has creased into a "w." "What is matter with you?"

I'm so wound up I can't speak. I wrench open my French exercise book and try to concentrate on what I'm supposed to be writing.

MA MÈRE EST UNE *ANNOYING COW.*

"Melon, you go deaf? What is wrong?"
"Nothing."
"Oh, okay. You just be rude for no reason."

MA MÈRE EST UNE <u>GRANDE</u> ANNOYING COW.

She shovels in more steaming lasagne. "You just be in this bad temper for fun of it."

"You!" I slam down my pen. "You! That's what's wrong with me."

187

Mum cocks her head to one side and smiles, finding
it all so funny. She shrugs. "What I do?"
"You have made my life HELL!"

I have been spending a lot of time in my bedroom the last few days. I know it really well now, in detail. The way the lining paper under the paint on the walls is starting to peel, just to the side of my chest of drawers. The way the cream carpet gets darker around the edges of the room. The way the swirls in the plaster on the ceiling have pictures hidden in them—goats jumping fences, miserly old men with huge noses, boats bobbing beneath clouds, dinosaur birds with terrifying beaks. There is a dent in the bottom panel on the back of my door. There is a stain on the carpet, like an island, in the doorway.

I have taken the posters down off my walls because the faces were annoying me—all those smiles and moody pouts. There are oily splodges where the tack used to be. Those splodges also started to annoy me, so I got a marker and joined up the dots. My wall is filled with crazy scribbles, boxes joined to boxes—a mad family tree with no names. I tried sniffing the marker, desperate for a high, but it just made me feel sick.

"When was the last time you changed your clothes, Melon?" Susan is eyeing my sweatpants and baggy sweater.

"Last Thursday."

Susan smiles and winces all at once.

The sweatpants have gone loose from being worn so much. The knees stick out when I stand up straight. The fleece of the sweater feels thinner and floppier every day.

I go to bed in these clothes and lie awake sweating under my duvet. Then I sit around the house in them all day feeling cold. It makes no sense; these clothes are too warm and not warm enough all at the same time. But still, I don't want to take them off. They've started to take on this thick, sweet smell that I'm getting attached to. I find it comforting. The smell is mine. It proves I still exist, that I haven't been completely swallowed up by what has happened. That I haven't been chipped away to nothing by all these people poking and prodding me, telling me how to think and feel. I'm still me. I hope the smell is getting up Susan's nose. It must be repulsive.

I cannot concentrate on my French homework. I just want to kill someone. I shut my books, start stuffing them back into my bag.

"How I do that?" She doesn't stop shoveling. Her chin is greasy. "How I make your life hell?"

"You gave me a stupid, STUPID name."

She nods, all smug. Such a know-it-all. "They tease you at school again, yes?"

I sling my bag over my back, give her my best drop-dead look, and make for the fridge.

"They make fun of your tits?" Mum spears her fork through the air and points at my chest.

It takes everything I've got not to grab her by the throat.

"No! For God's sake! They were not making fun of my TITS!"

I yank open the fridge door, stand in the light, looking

at half-empty shelves. There's nothing I want. I'm breathing so hard, I feel like I might explode.

"So what they say?"

"I don't want to repeat it," I hiss. I smash the fridge door shut.

"Is just words."

"Why?" I turn and spit the word at her. "Why did you have to give me such a stupid name? Why?" I will not cry. I will stay angry, not melt into a sobbing heap.

Mum takes a big breath, smiles. Here she goes. "On an island far, far from here, where . . ."

"Don't you dare talk to me about that stupid fucking FARM."

"Melon, do not say this f-word."

"What? 'Farm'?" I laugh, a nasty sound. I back away from her. "I'll say what I fucking like!"

"You want to know why, so I tell you why." She shrugs again, shovels more lasagne into her mouth.

"Change the record!" I jut my chin at her, stick two fingers down my throat, pretend to puke. That's what I think of her story.

She's leaning back against the counter. So relaxed. Couldn't care less.

"Maria is boring name. Everyone in Crete called Maria. You yell 'Maria' in the street, every girl turn around. You don't want that."

"I want to be normal. I want you to be NORMAL!"

I turn my back on her and stomp out of the kitchen. My fat braid whips around and strikes me on the

cheek. It stings so badly that I can't hold back the tears.
I run up the stairs, punishing each step with a stomp. .
I go to my room. I slam the door.

"Are you still seeing your bereavement counselor?" Susan puts her elbows on her knees, bends over her lap, rests her chin on her hands. She's making herself small. Unthreatening. She's trying to get inside. She's not coming in.

"No."

"Why have you stopped going?"

"Wasn't helping."

"Were you finding it difficult?"

"That's not what I just said, is it? I said it wasn't helping."

Susan sits back again, looks at me for a long time. Sighs. I can feel her disappointment. I am not what they want me to be. They try and try to mold me, but I never measure up. I'm ashamed that I'm such a failure.

"Things have become a lot worse for you, haven't they, Melon?"

Susan pats me on the head with her words.

I drop my chin to my chest, close my eyes, and take a deep breath. I inhale the thick, sweet smell coming off my sweater.

"Do you think maybe you should go see your doctor, have a chat about how you're feeling?"

Another person to prod and poke at me, to assess me and find me coming up short.

"A doctor may have some other ideas on how to get you through this difficult time."

They want to drug me now.

"What do you think about that, Melon? Do you think that's a good idea?"

I tip my head back and try to find pictures in the swirls of the living-room ceiling. "Fine," I say. The word means nothing anymore. "Fine."

"What I think a doctor might be able to do is . . ."

I stop listening. I can still hear Susan's voice, but the words lose their shape. It's like unfocusing your eyes when you read a book. Who cares what's being said.

I throw my bag at the dressing table. Bottles of hair spray and deodorant fall like bowling pins. I take a teddy bear from my bed and launch it at the back of my bedroom door; next I send a toy rabbit, then Arthur the lion. Thud, thud, thud. My hands are aching to tear something apart. I scream at the ceiling, clench my fists, collapse onto my bed.

Why does nothing I ever say have any effect on her? She is untouchable. Why can't she just say sorry and admit she was wrong? Just once. She can sympathize with drug dealers and child prostitutes and gang members and trainee burglars, but she can't find a scrap of sympathy for me. I should mastermind an armed robbery just so she will give me the time of day.

Mum's footsteps come up the stairs. She treads slowly along the landing. She is outside the door. For a long time she doesn't speak.

"Melon," she goes eventually. "I come in?"

I flop onto my back on the bed and bawl at the ceiling,
"No!"

"Okay."

She's still there, standing by the door.

"I get ready and go out now," she says.

"Fine." I still don't hear her feet on the landing. She's
not shifting.

"Melon?" Her voice goes quieter.

"What?" I yell back.

"Was very . . ." Her voice is still small, sucking me
in. I just want to shout her down, and she makes me
listen. I hate her.

"Was very . . . difficult for me . . . I was . . ."

I move onto the edge of the bed. She sounds like a
different person, talking like this. Humble for once. In a
moment she will say sorry. She will say sorry and I will
have won.

"I choose name when . . ." She stops for the longest
time. She's dropped her script, The Story. I get a prickle
up my spine. Anticipation. I am going to hear her say
something that means something.

What? I want to yell back. What? You chose my
name when what? But I keep quiet. I stay cool. I hear
her sniff, sniff again, blow her nose.

Then when her voice comes back, it is bright and
chirpy again—she has changed her mind. She isn't
going to say it after all—that something that means
something.

"I went against my mother to call you 'Melon.'" She is

working her way back to the script. "She want traditional name; she don't want reminding of home. She homesick."

"Yeah, yeah," I shout back. "When a sense of longing goes unanswered, an illness takes over. *Now that's my fault, is it? Yia-Yia's cancer, just because I had the wrong name.*"

Quiet.

"I no say that, Melon."

"That's what it sounds like."

"No, that not what I say. It just very hard for me . . ."

It's always about her. Everything is always about her.

I scream at the closed door: "Your mother's dead now! So what? Get over it! I'm the one still alive! I'm the one suffering!"

I grab the nearest thing: a souvenir snow globe of Crete. A ridiculous thing—a reminder of a place that means nothing to me, a place where it hardly ever snows. I hurl it at the door. It strikes the wood with a satisfying crack. It leaves a huge dent. I hear Mum walk away.

I hear Paul's keys in the front door and I leap off the sofa. I have never felt so pleased to have him come home. Jumping off that sofa is the most sprightly movement I've made in days.

"Paul's here," I trill at Susan. I pull my sweater down over my bum and head for the living-room door.

She watches me go, confused by my burst of enthusiasm.

"Have you told me all you wanted to say?" Susan calls after me, speaking to my back.

"Yes," I say. "I have, thanks."

Paul arrives in the living-room doorway.

"Hi, Paul," I go. Too enthusiastic. He looks just as confused as Susan.

"Have you two finished? Because I can . . ." Paul points behind him, searching his mind for a pressing task he can go perform. "I can go and . . ."

"No, we've finished," I say.

"Right," goes Susan, trying not to sound irritated. She gathers together her bag and paperwork.

Paul walks through the living room to the dining room and places Mum's canvas shopping bag on the table. He could have taken it straight through to the kitchen, but that would have meant missing out on a chance to eavesdrop.

"So, would you like me to make this appointment with your doctor, or shall I leave you to do that?" Susan goes, fastening the catches on her briefcase.

Paul looks over his shoulder, worried.

"You do it," I say as breezily as possible, trying to waft the conversation away.

"What's this?" presses Paul. As if he would let a comment like that just drop.

"We decided it might be a good idea for Melon to talk to a doctor about how she's feeling, didn't we?" Susan stands, holding her briefcase in front of her pilly thighs.

"It's Susan's idea," I mutter. "There's no 'we' about it."

Music is coming from behind Mum's bedroom door. I move quietly across the landing, avoiding the loose floorboard that runs down the middle. I can hear Mum singing, all out of tune. I can hear her squirting body

195

spray. I've changed into my denim skirt and cleaned up the snow globe. When it hit the door, the plastic cracked and a pool of glittery water leaked onto the carpet.

I go down the stairs and into the kitchen. I grab the pad of notepaper on the table. It has the windows and balconies of city skyline printed down its sides. I tear off the top sheet, which reads milk, lightbulbs, lasagne *in Mum's scrawl. I scan the room for a pen and see one sticking out of the fruit bowl on the sideboard. I grab it, scribble on the blank sheet on top of the block to get the ink flowing. Red ink. Kojak, who had been asleep on one of the kitchen chairs, jumps onto the table and forces his head against the back of my hand. I take a minute to give him a rub under the chin, then I write.*

MUM. GONE TO CHICK'S.

I can hear Mum's superstitious voice in my head. I look at my message. Think about crumpling it up and rewriting it in blue. No. I can't be bothered. I push the notepad into the middle of the table, roll my eyes at Kojak. This'll give me and Mum another reason to have an argument tomorrow. Guaranteed.

"What you thinking?!" she'll squawk at me. "Writing in the red ink!"

"What's your problem?" I'll shoot back. "You're still alive, aren't you?"

I go over to the dining-room table, to where Paul has placed Mum's canvas shopping bag.

"So, what's Irene cooked for us tonight?" I ask.

Paul steps toward the table—a blocking move.

"Just leave it, okay?" I mutter at him.

I'll go see the doctor if that's what they want; anything for a quiet life. I don't want a heart-to-heart with Paul about it.

Paul starts yabbering. "No, Melon, that's not . . ."

I maneuver around him. "What's she cooked? Not Jamaican rundown again?" I pull at the side of Mum's shopping bag.

"Melon, leave that for a minute." Paul reaches out to grab the bag, but I slide it away from his grasp.

"No offense," I go, "but I can't stand that mackerel thing she makes."

I look in the bag. I shut up. Paul shuts up. There's no casserole bowl, no dish with a tinfoil lid. There's a wooden box. On the top of the box there is a picture of a dove cut out in a paler wood.

"What's in the box?" I go.

Paul is looking at his shoes and covering his eyes with a hand. Susan is craning her neck on the other side of the room, trying to see.

"What's in the box?" I go again. My voice has gone reedy, high-pitched.

Paul takes a businesslike breath, puts on a businesslike face. "I think you can go now, thank you, Susan." His smile is strained.

"Right. Well, I'll see you next week, Melon," goes Susan.

"Okay," I go. My voice is shaking, and my hands are joining in. I have no idea why.

197

"I'll let myself out," she says, crabbing sideways out of the room.

"Yes, yes, thank you." Paul does not go with her to the front door. How can this bag be more important than impressing the social worker?

We hear the front door open, then close. I still have a hand on the bag. We both stand there, not moving at all. The house is so quiet. Just the rumble of cars and trucks passing on the main road.

"What's in the box?" I ask again. I feel water dripping down off my chin, and it takes me a few seconds to realize that it is tears. Tears are streaming down my face.

Paul looks at me, his face in pain. I look back hopefully, willing him to say something, anything other than the answer I know he's going to give me.

"Your mother, Melon," he says blankly, calmly, not letting himself cry. "Your mother's ashes."

My chest heaves. This awful sound chugs out of my throat.

"I'd been keeping the box at my mum's place until I felt you were ready to have it here, but . . ." He stops. He can't talk.

My chest heaves again, as if my body is trying to get rid of something, to bring something up. I look at the box, the carving of the dove. *Agapoula mou, peristeraki mou. My little love, my little dove.*

"Oh, God," I wail.

A strange, dark monster breaks free of its cage in my ribs and comes hurtling out of my throat. I roar. I cry as if I will never stop.

Part Two

133 DAYS SINCE

The sky is an unreal blue. Murky. Inky. It clashes with the fat orange vapor trails from the aeroplanes — jagged lines disappearing downward behind the curve of the earth. The aeroplanes themselves are insect-small and motionless. They're just hanging there, ready to be squashed between giant fingers.

"You scared of flying?" Paul doesn't take his eyes off the road when he talks. He drives slowly, carefully, like a nice middle-aged lady.

"No. I like it. It's fun. You?"

"Doesn't bother me," he goes.

A car slices in front of us, too close, and disappears down the road. Paul doesn't swear or shout like Mum would have done. He slows down as if he's been given a warning. I eye the speedometer. Fifty-five mph. You can go seventy mph, faster if there are no police around — even I know that and I don't drive.

"Actually, I am scared of flying," Paul says. His hands are clutching the top of the steering wheel too tight. His arm muscles are tensing with the strain of it. "I'm scared, but in a healthy way." He pauses to check over his shoulder.

Are we going to dare to break out into the middle lane?

"When I get on a plane, I'm thinking, 'Oh, well, we might crash, that's that.' I just accept it."

No. We stay dribbling down the slow lane.

"That way, when we land and I'm still alive, it's a bonus. It's an especially good feeling." Paul is smiling. "I embrace death!" he goes with a big flourish. He takes one hand off the wheel and waves it around, quickly clamping it back in position when a truck zooms past, gusting us toward the shoulder.

We both laugh. Not real laughing, just the nervous kind. It's still not okay to laugh properly.

Embrace death.

I haven't embraced death. These last few months, it's been embracing me. It's had its arms tightly around my throat. It pulled me down, under the surface. It could have won, it could have drowned me, but something made me swim upward for a gasp of air. Maybe it was the promise of this trip. But since when did I ever look forward to going to Crete?

Paul peels his eyes away from the road to look at the dashboard clock. "Shall we stop for a breather?"

"Aren't we nearly there, though?"

"Ah, yes. But we've got some time to kill."

He's right. We left stupid-early. Everything has been planned to the minute, and then an hour or so has been added on in case of a traffic jam, or a flash flood, or the outbreak of the next plague.

"You never know what it's going to be like at the airport," he goes, all serious. "Might be lines around the block, and then we'd wish we'd stopped for a pee."

"Okay," I go. "Fine. Whatever you think."

He starts slowing down and puts on the blinker, even though there's still a mile to go. We trundle along, ticking and flashing. Finally we pull into the rest stop.

"What shall we do with Mum?" I ask.

He doesn't answer. He is concentrating on trying to find a parking space.

"We can't leave her in the car, can we?" I go on. "Someone might steal her."

"No."

Paul is reversing slowly, very slowly, into a parking space.

"So?" I push.

"How close am I to the car next to you?"

"You're fine."

"You can get out okay? You can open your door?"

"Yes!"

"We'll put her under the seat."

"No," I go. "That's not right."

I get out of the car and pull the lever that tips my seat forward, so I can reach Mum. She's in the wooden dove box, strapped in with a seat belt, so she doesn't fall and spill into the footwells. I sling my backpack over my shoulder, lift up Mum, and hold her close to my chest.

"Let's go."

I slam the car door. Paul locks up.

Amanda said seeing Mum's box of ashes for the first time was a "catalyst." I looked it up in the dictionary.

CATALYST: A SUBSTANCE THAT PRECIPITATES OR SPEEDS UP A CHEMICAL REACTION WITHOUT BEING PERMANENTLY CHANGED IN THE PROCESS.

I see what she means. Mum is still ash, like she always has been since the funeral, but now I am different.

A catalyst.

It makes me think of that chemistry experiment where you mix baking soda and vinegar and it makes the beaker bubble over. When I first saw the dove box, everything inside me came fizzing out. Amanda seemed pleased about this, which meant I was really angry with her for a while. I was still furious with her for being rude about The Story. There was a time when I thought I would never forgive her. But now I can see that all the crying and shouting was a good thing. At least it was honest.

Inside the rest stop everything is bright and plastic and colorful. The few people ambling around are tired and spongy and gray. You'd think that rest stops would be happy places. Everyone there is off on a journey—the promise of something new. But they're not happy places. They're shiny on the surface, miserable underneath.

Me and Paul go our separate ways for the bathroom.

"Meet you in the coffee shop," goes Paul. He nods over to a counter where a tall, skinny boy in an apron is yawning his face off.

"Okay."

"Whoever gets back first gets the coffee." He grins over his shoulder. A challenge. Paul has been paying me an allowance out of the money that Mum left, so I have the cash to buy coffee if I have to. I'm bound to take longer, though. I'll make sure I do. The drinks are on Paul.

He disappears into the mens'. I follow the sign for the ladies'.

Paul is really looking forward to this trip to Crete—he's about-to-burst, can't-think-about-anything-else excited. He's made an itinerary of all the things we must achieve while we're there. Just reading the list is exhausting. Every day in the run-up to us leaving, he's been calling someone to sort out something. I came home one day last month and he was on the phone to the airline, talking about taking Mum through airport security.

"It's not a box of drugs, or explosives. I don't want you thinking that . . ."

He got it sorted out, but I told him it's not customs he needs to be stressing about. If we're going to scatter Mum's ashes on the melon farm like she asked, he should be worried about getting past Auntie Aphrodite. Paul can't get ahold of Auntie Aphrodite. She hasn't answered his letters.

When I get into the toilet stall, I'm not sure what to do with Mum. It seems wrong to put her on the floor, so I put her under one arm while I pull down my jeans and underwear with the other hand. Then I sit with her on my lap while I pee. Mum wouldn't have minded; she was never cringey about bodily functions.

When I wash my hands, there's room to put her box down by the tap. The mirrors over the sinks make me look even more tired than I am. They pick out every vein and blotch. My skin looks yellowy green; my hair looks lank. I pull my curls back with a band that I have around my

205

wrist. The hair reaches into a tiny ponytail now—just. I'm pleased that it's growing back fast. It's something familiar and reassuring from "before." Chick is still off the radar. I have a ponytail but no best friend. No, that's not true. I have Justine Burrell. We got through exams together.

I study my face now that my hair isn't messing up the edges. I am different, more grown-up, more steely, as if my bones are made of stronger stuff. Is this what happens when you become an adult? Have the final slivers of my childhood slipped away?

Back outside, Paul has already sat down with the drinks. He has bought me a cup of coffee. I never used to like coffee. Paul started making it for me when I was really depressed because he didn't know what to say and he seemed to need to do something. I drank it to make him feel like he was being useful, then I got a taste for it.

I sit down and Paul pushes a steaming mug toward me. I put Mum on the table. He stares at the box for a moment, then smiles, all affectionate.

"I've stopped counting the days, you know." He sips his coffee and gets a milky top lip. I point at my own mouth and nod in his direction.

"What? Oh." He wipes his face with the back of his hand. "Thanks."

I sip my coffee. I have it black and strong, which Paul says makes me hard as nails.

"Counting what days?" I go.

"Since."

We both watch an old man in a blue jacket scrape back

a chair at the next table and sit down. He moves gradually, in stages, like he's in pain.

"Me too," I say. "I've stopped counting."

"I used to be able to tell you to the day, to the hour, how long it was since it happened. But now . . ." Paul is smiling, nodding, pleased with this revelation about himself.

"It doesn't matter anymore." I nod too.

"No, it's not that exactly. It still matters. It's just that I've been thinking forward now. I've been counting down the days till we get on that plane."

"Yeah?"

Paul's excitement makes me anxious. I want the trip to live up to his expectations, I do, but every time I've been to Crete, it's just been awkward and painful. I want him to understand this, but I can't find the words to explain.

"We'll finally be able to put her to rest, like she wanted," Paul says.

"I suppose."

A middle-aged woman comes away from the coffee counter and puts down two mugs on the table in front of the blue-jacketed man.

"There you go, Dad," she says.

She opens up the small handbag that she has strapped across her body and pulls out a packet of chocolate-chip cookies—cheap supermarket ones brought from home. She catches us watching. Paul raises a hand in a half wave, smiles to show that we don't think bad of her for not buying the coffee shop's expensive biscotti. The woman looks at Paul, then at me, then back at Paul. Then she shoots me this look of concern. A sort of silent, *Are you okay?* I smile back, confused. Paul repeats his nod and wave, more reassuring this time, and the woman sits down opposite her dad.

Paul turns back to me, shaking his head a little. He rolls his eyes. I stare at him, thinking for a minute that he knew the woman. Then I see what that woman sees: a tired-looking teenage white girl and a thirty-something black man sitting alone together in a rest stop at five a.m. I go where her mind goes. And then I think, *Oh, God, if we're getting looks like that here in London, what will it be like in Crete, in the villages, where they've never even seen a black man?* I look down into my coffee.

I should say something, warn Paul what it's like on the island with the family — the way they used to treat me and Mum, the way they'll treat him — but it's hard to tell him things like that. He has this image of how it's going to be, and I feel bad for spoiling it. In a way, Paul is quite delicate. He doesn't understand that it will seem weird to the family that we're scattering ashes. To them, Mum doesn't belong in Crete. To them, she shouldn't have been cremated in the first place. It's against their religion. Or maybe they would have approved — burn the witch.

I want to tell Paul that I feel weird about scattering Mum's ashes too. There's a part of me that doesn't want to do it. I think of Mum as more real now, more real than when she was alive, and I'm not sure I'm ready to let that go. I say things to the ashes that I could never have said to her when she was actually here, living and breathing. I tell her that I'm sorry for the red ink, for hating her, for not listening to The Story. I tell her I'm sorry for not being at home when the police came to tell me she was dead.

Mum used to say that people's spirits carry on doing things after their body has gone. She would have gone home after the accident to tell me what had happened and I wasn't there. I have a lot to make up for.

Paul is toying with a packet of sugar, spinning it around on the table.

"It's 133 days," I go.

"What is?" asks Paul, not looking at me.

"Since Mum died."

"Yeah, I know," he says quietly.

He swigs his coffee again, but this time I don't tell him about the milk mustache.

133 DAYS SINCE

We're at the villa and I'm starving, so I eat the Coco Pops. Paul has brought a variety pack with him in his suitcase. He thinks we've come to a third-world country where they've never heard of a cornflake.

When Nikos, the villa owner, showed us around, he pointed out a welcome basket of food on the kitchen table.

"To say, 'Hello to Crete,' and to get you starting."

I gave Paul a look to say, *See? They eat food here too.*

Then Nikos explained that there was a supermarket just down the hill in the village, where you can buy Marmite and PG Tips.

"All these important things," he went, with a big-eyebrowed smile. Then he laughed, loud, while Paul looked at his feet. Ha-ha.

Nikos also told us not to put anything down the toilet and to move the toilet-paper roll when you take a shower because Greeks don't believe in shower curtains and you'll only get your toilet paper wet. So basically he filled us in on all the important things—eating and shitting.

Nikos's son lugged our suitcases from the rental car into the villa. Haris, his name is. Well, that was how Nikos introduced him. When Nikos was ordering him around, he called him "Haralambos." Hilarious. Haris is about the same age as me, with shiny, tanned skin and gelled spiky hair that you're just dying to reach over and squash. Once he'd fetched our suitcases, Haris stood in our doorway gawking at me while his dad ran through the local tourist attractions. I tried staring Haris down, but that just made him smirk. I don't know why he was acting so pleased with himself. He was wearing the tackiest T-shirt I've ever seen. It had this ridiculous English slogan:

ITS THE NEW THING!

LIFE THE DREAM, USA

At one point when his dad was speaking, Haris piped up with, "The pool, it is very deep at one end."

"Yes," went Nikos. "Is very deep. More than two meters. You share with other guests. You be very careful."

Haris grinned at this, like the pool being deep had some kind of double meaning.

In the welcome pack of food, there is a bottle of olive oil, a jar of olives, a bottle of wine, and some rock-hard bread, so in a way I'm thankful that Paul has been an idiot and brought half of the Tesco grocery store with him. I know he has tea bags and marmalade in that suitcase of his. He was even talking about bringing bacon.

Paul is standing on the small terrace that leads off from the kitchen/living room to look out across the swimming pool, hands resting on the back of his head. His hair has been clipped really short for the trip. His silhouette against the bright-blue sky is all head and ears. He does a dramatic oh-it's-all-so-beautiful sigh. "Let's get in that pool before it gets dark," he goes.

It's five in the afternoon but the sun is still hot enough to strike you dead.

"Wanna eat these first," I go, dribbling chocolate milk down my chin.

"I'm going to find my swimming shorts." Paul bustles back through the living area, off to his suitcase in one of the bedrooms. He's called dibs on the double room. I'm stuck with the twin.

The Coco Pops are hitting the spot. Mum always used to buy variety packs.

"This way," she used to say, "you are not getting bored every morning."

Paul obviously shares this philosophy.

I stayed overnight at Chick's once and mentioned to Mrs. Lacey at breakfast that we have variety packs at home, and Mrs. Lacey said they were a really bad thing. I thought she was going to say because of the sugar or the lack of fiber, but no. She said, "Variety packs don't teach a child that you have to make choices in life and commit to things." When she said "a child," she meant me.

Next breakfast with Mum, I parroted back what Mrs. Lacey had said, and Mum cackled to herself for about five minutes straight.

I'm shoveling down the Coco Pops double-quick, silently thanking Nikos for leaving us a "Hello to Crete" half liter of milk in the fridge too. I'm so hungry. The last thing I

212

ate was in a coffee shop at Gatwick at seven thirty this morning. Paul dragged us up there, away from all the good places on the ground floor, and told me to get a sandwich, as there wouldn't be any food on the plane.

"Yeah, there is," I told him. "There's a hot meal."

"Only if you order it," he went. "I decided against paying for it. They always taste awful."

I couldn't believe it. The best thing about the flight is the food. Everyone knows that.

"Have a sandwich," he goes, "because they'll only have chips on the plane."

I scanned the glowing fridges. "But I don't want to eat a chicken-and-avocado sandwich at seven in the morning."

"Have a croissant, then."

So I had a croissant and I ate it under protest, while Paul scarfed down a crayfish-and-arugula sandwich like it was the middle of the day or something.

We didn't speak. How could he cancel the in-flight meal? I couldn't look at him. I pretended to be interested in the posters advertising how fresh everything was, and the dead-eyed staff who looked the total opposite of fresh. I wondered if they kept them in the dark, in locked cages in the basement of Gatwick Airport, only letting them out to brew up cappuccinos.

"Ta da!" goes Paul. He slides on bare feet across the tiles of the living area. He's put on bright-blue Bermuda shorts, a Hawaiian shirt, his shades, and a floppy hat. I'm supposed to laugh, but I can't find the energy. The whole journey has left me feeling sad, washed out.

213

"Ready to swim!" he announces, clicking his heels and saluting. I still can't find a laugh.

Flying just wasn't the same without Mum. With her it was all about the anticipation. Not about coming to Crete, but about each moment on the journey itself—the takeoff, the meal, the Toblerone from the cart. There was something really thrilling about knowing what to expect. Mum would always get nervous, struggle with her seat belt, and then try to have a smoke in the bathroom. Looking back, I see now that she wasn't actually scared of flying; she was scared of the family at the other end. But now I am scared of flying.

On the plane with Paul, I was terrified. Without Mum there to be the scaredy-cat, I had to take on the role. As we walked down the boarding tunnel, all I could think about was how people who've had near-death experiences say they go down a tunnel. Flying is exactly like dying—you end up in a different place. I hyperventilated; I nearly fainted. Although maybe it wasn't a fear of flying exactly. Maybe it was *my* fear of what's at the other end. In Crete. And at the other end of life too.

Paul drops the clown act and sits opposite me at the kitchen table. He watches me slurp the dregs of the milk.

"They good, were they?"

"Mmm." I nod.

"Excellent."

"Did you know breakfast cereals really do actually have iron in them?" I say this to avoid the heart-to-heart conversation that I can see hurtling my way. "You know, like actual iron filings, not just injected vitamins."

"Yeah?" goes Paul.

"I saw this thing on TV where a scientist rubbed a magnet over a clear plastic bag of crushed cornflakes, and all these bits of gray came to the surface."

"Wow, that's good knowledge, Melon."

Patronizing words. He's softening me up.

"You'd never have known it was there, would you?" I go, running out of things to say.

"What do you want to do this trip?" Paul asks.

This is it—the serious talk.

"Nothing much. Get her ashes scattered. Get a tan."

"We'll go out for some shopping and lunch on Friday, for your birthday, of course."

"Thanks," I say.

"Sixteen!" He does jazz hands when he says this.

"Yes." I smile. Just a day and a bit left of being a child. Just a sliver.

"And I have a list of archaeological sites that are supposed to be fantastic," Paul goes, "and then there's the cathedral and the museums in Chania. So much for us to do." He says Hania all wrong, with a hard "ch" at the front.

"Yeah?" I push the bowl away. "Great."

"But what do you want to do while you're here? We're here for the ashes, yes, but it's about you too." Paul has flicked on his "social worker" switch. "It's about tying up any loose ends you might have; it's about building some bridges."

"What, with Aphrodite, you mean?"

"If that's what you want."

"You must be having a laugh."

215

Paul gets up and takes my empty bowl to the sink. There is no dishwasher. Nightmare.

"There is one thing I'd like to do." It's easier to say these things without Paul sitting right in front of me.

"What's that?" Paul turns, nodding hard, an eager beaver.

"I know I've said this before, probably just to annoy you, but the more I think about it, maybe I should do it, just to see, just to kind of know . . ." I feel silly saying it out loud.

"What?"

"I thought I might try to find my dad." There. "No offense."

"No offense taken. You mean, find out about his childhood here."

"No, actually find my living, breathing dad."

Paul makes that worried face, just like the last time I mentioned Christos.

"Your father isn't here, Melon," he says firmly. "You won't find him in Crete."

It's strange the way he says this, so definite.

"Oh, yeah?" I say. "Well, where is he, then?" I smirk. Paul may be an expert on crumbling monuments, but he's no expert on this piece of history.

"Ahhhmmm . . ."

That voice. Like he's preparing a difficult speech.

"He . . . He came over to England with your mum, and then . . ." He puts his hand up to his forehead and pinches a section of skin. "Your mother really never told you anything about this?"

"Yeah, I know plenty, thank you very much."

216

My turn to speak. My turn to show off my knowledge.

"His name is Christos Drakakis and he was the neighbor's son and he liked to draw and he was skinny and he never left Crete *actually* and . . ." I'm running out of facts. "And I have a picture of him."

Paul looks at me, broken. "Your mother told me a different story."

"I bet she did. To keep you smitten."

"She . . . No . . ." He closes his eyes, massages his forehead with his thumb now—hard. "She told me a . . . worse story."

"Worse?" I snort. "How could that story get any more bloody tragic?"

Paul puffs himself up with air, rests his chin on his chest, then lets it out. . . . "Your father is dead, Melon, I'm afraid. I really think I should be honest with you about this and . . ."

The floor disappears from under my seat. Suddenly nothing in the room, in the world, is in the right place. How can Paul know this?

He can't. That's how. He just can't.

"He died when you were a baby," Paul goes on, looking me in the eye. He seems utterly convinced. "You wouldn't have known about it at the time. It was . . ."

"No."

"Yes, Melon."

"That's bullshit."

"No." He flattens down the air with his hands. "It's not. Don't you think we would have tried to contact him after . . . after your mum . . . if we knew that he was alive?"

Poppy asked me for Auntie Aphrodite's number when she visited. She never asked about my dad.

"Okay, then," I go. "How? How did he die?"

He studies me for a few seconds before saying, "A drug overdose."

"What, he killed himself? With painkillers or something?"

"No, he didn't do it on purpose. It was . . ."

"No," I say. Enough. I scrape back the chair to put a stop to all this stupid talk.

"Let me finish, Melon."

"No." I keep calm. "Because you have got this all wrong. This is not how The Story goes. I should know. I've heard it enough times. It's even written down." I stride off toward my bedroom. "And I have pictures," I call back at him again, in case he didn't hear it the first time.

In my room, I pop open the catches of my suitcase and pull the black bikini from the zipped compartment inside. My book with The Story is in there too. I flip it open. The photo of Mum with Christos and Yiannis is inside the cover. I examine Christos's lopsided smile. He's not dead. I can feel it. I undress and put on my bikini.

Mum's dove box is propped up against the pillow on one of the beds, watching me. I glare at it. *So speak, will you? Settle this for good.* It keeps its trap shut.

I walk back out into the living area with a towel wrapped around me.

"Are you coming for a swim, then, or what?" It is my turn to be the cheerful, determined one.

218

Paul is sitting at the kitchen table, sulking.

"I'm going to skip it, actually, Melon. You go ahead. Watch out for the deep end."

"Suit yourself."

I should stay and talk to him, tell him how things really were, but I'm not in the mood. Mum lied to him, but he'll get over it. After all, it's just a story.

134 DAYS SINCE

When I wake up and wander into the living area, Paul isn't there. We didn't mention my dad over dinner last night. We went down the hill to the village and ate at a taverna with a blue-painted terrace and dusty metal chairs. The waiter spoke perfect English, but Paul insisted on getting out his phrase book and practicing his hopeless Greek. He was *parakaló*-ing and *efharistó*-ing all over the place. He was still thinking about the conversation about my dad, though. I could tell.

There is a pot of coffee brewing in the kitchen, so I pour a cup and move out of the dark cool of the villa into the blaze of sun on the terrace. The sound of cicadas seesaws in the air. Paul is in the pool, doing laps. Up and down, swift and expert. Paul is a new person like this, with the water washing away his goofiness.

A cat jumps over the wall as I watch, and starts slaloming around my ankles. Its white limbs are bone and fur; its face is pinched and meatless. It makes Kojak seem like a monster by comparison. I go inside and pour a saucer of milk and head for the terrace, have second thoughts, go back and tip Special K into the milk for extra calories. It feels mean giving diet cereal to a skinny cat, but it's my least favorite of the variety pack. And anyway, when I put it down on the terrace, the cat chomps it down as if it's prime steak.

Paul is out of the water now, dripping up the path to our terrace.

"You're up," he calls, cheery.

"Yeah, just going to get my bikini on."

"Oh." He stops at the terrace edge, brow furrowed. My plan to sunbathe obviously doesn't fit in with his timetable for the day.

"What?"

"I was just going to tell you to throw on some shorts and come with me. I'm going up the road to see this late Minoan tomb. Nikos has just been telling me all about it." Paul thumbs in the direction of the pool. Nikos is spraying a hose at the base of a tree that looks like a giant pineapple. There is no sign of Haris.

"This tomb is relatively intact, apparently," Paul goes on. "And it's not in my guidebook. Quite a find."

"A tomb. Nice." That's what this trip needs. More death.

"Then we should maybe try to find the farm tomorrow?" Paul adds, tagging it on like I won't notice.

"At the end of the trip, maybe," I fire back. "Save the worst till last."

"Whatever you think." Paul has gone back to tiptoeing on eggshells around me, just like when he first moved in. We've slipped back to that.

"It's just that meeting the family isn't going to be fun, you know that."

"Your mother did tell me."

221

"Yeah"—I tilt my head to one side, give him a grin—"but are you sure she told you the whole truth?"

Paul ignores this, dries the last of the swimming pool water from his body. He has small coils of black hair on his chest. I have the urge to touch them—not like that, not pervy or anything—I just want to know if they feel as wiry as they look. Paul starts folding his towel.

"Your mother told me all about the family," he says.

He lines up each edge of the towel carefully, exactly.

"About how they punished her, about how angry they were about everything that she did. But she also told me that she understood their anger and wanted to put the work in to earn their forgiveness. I know they will be frosty, Melon, but I also think that Maria's death will have changed them. Like it has me. Like it has you."

The towel is a neat square now. He holds it close to his chest.

"Mum did nothing wrong," I say, then I walk back into the kitchen to fill up my coffee. "Getting pregnant is hardly a crime," I mutter as I go.

Paul follows me. "I wasn't talking about getting pregnant."

"What, then?"

Paul opens his mouth, then closes it. He has tumbled through a hole in his story.

"I don't know," he offers, in the end.

"I'll get my bikini, then." I take my coffee to my bedroom. "Enjoy your tomb," I tell him.

*   *   *

222

There is no one else by the pool. The other guests must be on a mission to see every dug-up scrap of Greek history, just like Paul.

I sit on the edge and drop my legs into the water. The cold slices though my calves. I pull off my T-shirt, let the sun get a look at my shoulders. Me and Chick always used to see who could get the best tan while we were away. We never mentioned that it was a competition, but we both knew it was. I always won because Chick was so pale to start with. I don't think Justine Burrell is into pointless tanning competitions. Better things to be worrying about.

I have my book with The Story on my lap. I have also brought one of those pens with the sliders—one button for each of the four colored inks. I might add some drawings in red ink. This might sound like a terrible thing to do, but I see it as a way to destroy the superstition, release me and Mum from its grip.

I told Amanda about the note—in the end. That was hard to confess. I thought she would be angry, that she'd see how I had caused Mum's death and then wouldn't want to help me anymore.

But she just sat there blinking for a minute, and then she went, "You don't actually believe that, do you?"

Amanda did some research. She discovered that in Greek tradition, red is actually a symbol of love; it's in Korea that they see writing in red ink as a bad omen.

"There you go," I'd said. "That proves there's some truth to it."

"But you're not Korean, are you?"

"I'm not Greek either."

"You're more Greek than you are Korean," she'd said.

I couldn't argue with that.

I've also decided that The Story, as I've written it down in my book, isn't good enough. I need to rewrite it, do it justice, make it more special. I have the voice of Mrs. Castleman, my English teacher, in my head, telling me to set the scene, to work harder on my descriptions. I scan the gardens around me for inspiration. Large red flowers shout out from the beds in between trailing pink vines. There are these orange fans that look like birds' heads on the end of huge stalks. I'm trying to remember if there are palm trees like these ones near Tersanas Beach. Is "palm tree" even the right name? Don't you have to go to the Caribbean to see real palm trees? I don't know.

Ripples break across the flat surface of the water. The blue mosaic underneath jiggles out of focus. Haris is at the other end of the terrace, dragging a long pole with a net across the tiles on the bottom of the pool. I start writing, try to look busy.

"What you write?" Haris calls across, squinting into the sun.

"Nothing."

I wish I'd kept my T-shirt on now. I tug at the black Lycra of my bikini, make sure it's covering my boobs as much as possible.

"Is for school?" he asks.

"No, I've left school."

"No!"

"Yeah, I'm sixteen."

"You're not sixteen!"

"Well, tomorrow I will be, actually."

Haris pulls the net out of the water and flips it inside out, dropping leaves onto a soggy pile on the poolside. He slides the pole back into the water.

"Is too noisy for you?"

I don't know what he means. The only sound is the sparrows squabbling, the odd sheep bleat. I try to hear what he hears.

"You mean the cicadas?" They are grinding and squealing at full volume, but I find every time we come to the island, after a day or so, you train yourself to block out the noise.

"*Tzitzikas!*" Haris announces. "Is not legs rubbing together; is muscles going in and out. Only men do it, only men *tzitzikas*. The women, they keep quiet." He mimes zipping his lips and then laughs.

I'm not sure whether to smile. I can feel the sun crisping my shoulders already. I put my head down and go back to writing. Haris doesn't take the hint.

"Is your boyfriend?"

"Who?"

"The man. The black man."

"No! He's my . . ." I can't think how to put it. "He's my stepdad."

"Your mother, she not here?"

"She's dead."

Haris stops, lets the submerged end of the pole sink

to the bottom. He leans on the raised end. He drags a hand through his hair.

"But you are young. Just fourteen, no?"

"I told you, I'm sixteen, actually. Tomorrow, I'm sixteen."

"Your birthday?" He puts too many *s*'s in it, makes it "births-days."

"Yes."

"I bring you a present."

"No, it's okay."

"No, I bring it."

He pivots the pole against the edge of the pool and pulls the net back up through the water. It's hard work; his brown arms go tense.

I glide my feet forward and backward through the water, make my own ripples.

"You on vacations?"

"No."

"Why you here, then?"

"My family is from here. My mum comes from near Tersanas."

"Your mother very beautiful like you?"

I roll my eyes. Look down. "Prettier," I mumble. "I'm the freak."

"What you say?"

"My mother was much prettier than me," I say, loud and clear. "I am the freak."

"What is 'freak'?"

I shrug it away. Haris stares into the distance as if he is still trying to find the Greek translation for what I've said.

I'm bracing myself for the next question, but when I look back at Haris, all his attention is on something he's found at the bottom of the pool.

"*Ela*," he says. "Look."

Haris wrenches the pole up through the water, his brown arms stiffening again. He pads around the edge of the pool toward me. His bare feet make sweaty prints on the tiles. He feeds the pole through his hands so the net is close to him, then he holds it out for me to inspect.

"Look."

He stands close—close enough for me to see how the sun has turned the hair blond on the lower half of his legs, close enough for me to smell his boy smell, a whiff of cigarettes.

I lower my head over the net, then pull back. It is a frog.

"Dead," Haris announces.

It is on its back, its pathetic front legs folded over its white bloated chest, clutching its now-still heart.

"Last week I catch scorpion," he tells me. "But it alive."

I shield my eyes from the sun to look up at him. He's beaming. Am I supposed to be impressed?

"No, you didn't," I say.

"Is true. You find one in your bedroom, you scream, I come rescue you."

I snort, look away, down at the white page of my book. Haris flips the frog into the flower bed behind me.

"Let cat eat it," he says.

I want to get up and go, but I don't know how to do

that without Haris getting a full-length view of me in my bikini, the sweaty creases across my belly. Haris scuffs back around to the other side of the swimming pool. He skims the water again.

"If black man not your father, where your father?" he asks.

I open my mouth, close it.

"He not here?" Haris goes.

Then I say, "He's dead."

I don't think this before I say it. The words just fall out of my mouth. I look down at the water, watch the sunlight jag across the surface. I imagine my words sinking through the blue beneath my feet. *He's dead. He's dead.* I want Haris to fish my words out of the pool so I can put them back in my mouth, unsay them, make them not true.

Haris nods for a while. Then he goes, "You are 'orphan.'" He doesn't say this gently at all. He's just pleased with himself for knowing the right word in English.

"I suppose so," I say.

Haris pulls the pole out of the water, shakes the last of the insects and leaves into his pile, then scoops it all up with one hand.

"Okay, 'freak,'" he says, loud and perky. "Friday I am bringing you present."

Then he wanders away from the pool terrace, dragging his net behind him.

Just before sunset, Paul drives us to a sandy-colored building set in the olive groves not far from the airport, not far from

Auntie Aphrodite, not far from the farm. We climb the front stairs to a stone archway, stop to watch the sun shrink to a spark and drop behind the mountains, and then we continue into the courtyard. The bells in the tower are ringing, harsh and pushy, a sound that doesn't quite mask a squawking sound, a meowing. I follow the cries, while Paul takes photographs of the front of the chapel. I find the stray cat that is making the noise. Its fur is as honey colored as the buildings that surround us. A scrawny tomcat with long matted hair is on the female cat's back. His teeth are sunk into the fur at her neck. The tomcat notices me, fixes me with one eye, but continues to thrust with its hindquarters. I wonder if the female cat is squawking in pleasure or pain. After a moment, I feel weird watching and I walk away.

Paul is staring up at a tree, his guidebook hanging from the tips of his fingers.

"Melon, come here," he says, looking up into lime-colored leaves. "See? This is several trees all growing together."

There are oranges on the wide green branches. I scan right and see that there are lemons growing there too.

Paul glances down at his guidebook. "There is one 'rootstock,' which is one tree, then there is an orange tree and a lemon tree grafted onto it."

I can feel him watching me, making sure I understand.

"It's kind of like a limb transplant, I suppose," Paul goes on, enjoying playing the schoolteacher. "This way the tree is stronger, it has healthy roots, and it avoids disease."

"Wow," I say, just to humor him.

"So you see," goes Paul, "things can grow happily alongside one another."

I nod.

"That's a lemon tree," Paul goes on, pointing to the fruit, "and that's an orange tree. They are different, but they are the same thing."

I watch the leaves ruffle in the dying light.

"You're not talking about trees, are you?" I say.

"Yes, I am," he says, not looking me in the eye. "What did you think I was talking about?"

Fallen fruit is going moldy at the base of the tree, and I wonder why the monks who live here don't collect them up and use them, why they leave them to rot. I turn to Paul.

"But you still need a solid root for it to work," I say. A statement, not a question.

Paul nods. The air is getting cool fast, now that the sun has left us.

"You mean you need the truth?" he asks, turning to face me.

"I thought we were talking about trees," I say.

On the way out of the courtyard, I read a framed sign on the wall by the archway entrance:

MONASTERY AGIA TRIADA (HOLY TRINITY) OF
JAGAROLOU HAS BEEN FOLLOWING A COURSE, WHICH HAS
BEEN WRITTEN DOWN IN HISTORY WITH GOLD LETTERS
SINCE 1632.

This sign has got it right. History is so big, so heavy, that it needs that capital letter. But also this sign is wrong. Because no one cares what is written down. Writing something down, in gold letters or red ink or whatever—it makes no difference to anyone.

135 DAYS SINCE

I am officially sixteen. I can do what I want.

I let Paul talk me into doing some sightseeing before lunch.

This is all stalling, I understand this. We are squeezing things in and spreading out time, making the inevitable seem further away. As soon as we sit down for my birthday lunch we must finally acknowledge that I am grown up. Paul will find it impossible to back off. If he doesn't have someone or something to fret about, he's not happy.

I put on the burgundy dress. I packed it especially for today. The sleeves are long and I will cook in this weather, but it's the only thing I could possibly wear. I will be fine. Pregnant women on the island wander around in the heat of the day bundled up in thick jogging suits and they don't even crack a sweat. It's the cool Greek blood. I have that blood too.

As we leave the villa, we find a small, lidded cardboard box on the doorstep outside. Written on the top in felt-tip pen, it says:

HAPI BIRTHSDAYS

HARIS X

Paul looks confused. I haven't mentioned to him that I have spoken to Haris. Paul, on the other hand, has recounted in detail every single conversation he has had with Nikos.

"How does he know it's your birthday?" Paul asks.

I shrug, pick up the box. I'm nervous about opening it. Will I find a dead frog, or worse, a scorpion? Will I scream and have Haris come rescue me?

I lift the lid. Paul peers over my shoulder.

Inside is a small bronze figure of a man with horns and an animal's face.

"The Minotaur," goes Paul. "Half man, half bull."

"I do know." I roll my eyes. "I have been to Crete, like, a million times."

I turn it over in my hands. It's weighty and warm.

Paul locks up the villa. "Odd gift, though."

To me it makes perfect sense. King Minos of Crete refused to sacrifice the white bull in Poseidon's honor, so Poseidon made Minos's wife, Pasiphae, fall in love with a bull. She gave birth to a monster—the Minotaur—who was locked away in a labyrinth on the island. Haris did understand what I was saying by the pool yesterday after all. Me and the Minotaur: we are both freaks.

We drive into Hania along the coast road, past small villages and resorts. We pass car rental offices and restaurants called Zorba, balconies strung up with lines of drying laundry, and houses with steel supports worming their way out of the concrete like stray pubic hairs.

"It'll be nice when it's finished," Paul says.

233

"When what's finished?"

"Crete."

Paul drives even slower than he does at home. A car sits with its nose on our bumper through the curves and passes us as soon as we hit the straight road again. The driver takes his hands off the wheel and throws them toward the sky.

"What was his problem?" says Paul. He laughs nervously.

There are no road markings, no rules. Everyone drives where they like, on the shoulder, the middle of the road, in the shade. Paul can't cope with the anarchy.

We drive on, past peeling billboards for Winston cigarettes, past *kafeneon* terraces lined with frowning gray men. This is my culture, but it feels as foreign to me as it must to Paul. Then the sea starts to creep into view around the corner. A stone jetty with a doll's-house chapel stretches out into the water. The road is now lined with car showrooms filled with shiny new models that look out of place alongside the old bangers on the street. Are they just there as a reminder of what a real car should look like?

In Hania, we start our tourist marathon at the cathedral—a huge bright-white stone building that is surprisingly tiny inside. The ceiling strains under the weight of too many chandeliers, and above the altar is a painting of a giant Jesus, crossing his fingers and hoping for the best. Hoping that all he said turned out to be true.

We leave and Paul steers us into a courtyard and up some stone steps to a folklore museum. The shoebox-small rooms are filled with embroidery, photos from the olden days, and frozen-faced dummies in traditional dress. Paul lingers longer than he needs to over the reconstruction of a traditional Cretan nuptial bed. I know that he is thinking about Mum. He casts his eyes down, holds his breath, frowns.

Back out in the courtyard, Paul spies a Catholic church.

"Wow, look how different this looks from the Orthodox places of worship." He is poring over his guidebook for some facts about this new find. To humor him, I agree to go inside. Jesus is crossing his fingers here too, a model of him at the altar this time, not a painting. I light a thin orange candle for Mum. Water surrounds the gold tray of sand and candles. I suppose you wouldn't want to start a fire with all this hope and emotion.

"Can we go shopping now?" I ask.

No. Paul wants to take a trip in a glass-bottomed boat. Mum would have been appalled to see us behaving like such tourists. We sit up on deck with a bunch of sunburned English families, some chattering Germans, and a loud American group. We wait to leave, swaying and rocking, feeling queasy. That's when I notice the boat's name— *Aphrodite*.

In the middle of the trip, we moor up by an island where a tiny shrine stands over a small smattering of beach. A beautiful white bird rainbows through the air and lands on the sand.

My little love, my little dove.

"I think it's a heron," Paul says, all excited.

"Nah, seagull," says one of the Americans, butting in.

We speed back to Hania, kicking up a great whale tail of white water.

When at last we get to browse in the shops, Paul buys me my birthday present—a silver string bracelet with a small evil eye. Mum used to wear a leather strap with an evil eye to ward off bad spirits. I don't know where this bracelet is now. I hope she has it with her, wherever she is.

Then we walk around the harbor, past a stall selling pottery plaques that clank on their display in the sea breeze, past the restaurants, each with their own "sidewalk bully"—a waiter who can lure in tourists in any language. Paul chooses a taverna overlooking the old mosque because it is quieter and we'll get better service. And because their sidewalk bully is particularly pushy. This isn't how Mum would choose a restaurant. *Neoplouti*, she'd have called this place. *New rich*. Mum would find the busiest café, somewhere full of locals. And certainly not a restaurant on the harbor. They're for the gullible. When she was in Crete, Mum suddenly became Greek again. Until she found someone who would listen to her show off about her amazing life in *Lonthino*.

I am sweating in the burgundy dress. I take a seat in the shade. Greek music *chink-chink-chinks, strum-strum-strums, plink-plink-plinks*.

Paul orders two glasses of champagne and I am stunned. Goody-Two-Shoes social worker Paul is buying me alcohol. He must have sunstroke.

"One glass." Paul waggles a finger near my face. "I know you'll go and do this anyway. Might as well do it responsibly with me."

I nod, trying to keep a serious face.

"Did you know that people believe there is still a palace to find underneath Chania?" says Paul, his nose back in his guidebook. "It's buried over there, they think." He waves in the general direction of the mosque's concrete dome. "They found Roman mosaics under the cathedral square, near the market, so they're pretty sure there's something near. They've also found Linear A and Linear B scripts together here. Two ways of writing. Further proof."

"Did you see they've got a Starbucks now too?" I say.

The wind ruffles the stand of napkins on our table, and the salt pot tips over.

"Quick," I say, "throw some over your shoulder."

"Which shoulder?"

"Left," I tell him, repeating what Mum used to say to me. "Spite the devil." We both pinch up some grains and throw.

The waiter brings over our champagne and takes our order. Pizza for me and something meaty and Greek for Paul. He knocks the rim of his glass against mine.

"Cheers."

"Cheers," I say.

"To being sixteen!"

"To being an adult."

Paul laughs at this. "Well . . ."

He's in denial.

We watch the restaurant's sidewalk bully ask a passing couple, in English, where they're from. Denmark. The bully pauses, rifling through his brain for some Danish words, but he's too late—they get away.

"So, what are you going to do now that you're sixteen?"

I feel like a child being asked what I want to be when I grow up. A ballerina? A princess? A mummy?

"Dunno, do my A-levels."

"Then what?" Paul is a fan of life plans.

"I don't know."

We watch the glass-bottomed boat called *Aphrodite* trundle out of the harbor again.

"What are *you* going to do now?" I ask.

"What do you mean?"

"Well, you were going to marry Mum, weren't you?"

This is the first time we've talked about this.

Paul nods. "Yes, I was."

He takes a gulp of champagne, stares at the harbor lighthouse.

"How come you and Mum were engaged? I mean, you'd only been going out for, like, a few months."

"A year."

A whole year? I scan back through my mind, trying to figure out how this is possible. I gulp some champagne too. It tastes yeasty, like lemonade gone wrong.

"Still," I go, "a year. That's quick."

"Sometimes you just know when someone is the right person."

For some weird reason, Ian Grainger comes into my head. Idiot.

"What if the other person doesn't know?" I go.

"Know what?"

"That they're the right person for you."

"I don't think I follow you, Melon. If you know, they know."

"So if the other person doesn't feel the same, then it's not meant to be?"

"You can't make someone love you." Paul gives a defiant shake of his head.

"No?"

"No, that I'm sure of."

Two dark-haired kids in baggy clothes come wide-eyed to our table, offering their palms. "Very poor," the eldest one goes. "Please you be kind."

The entrance bully dives over and shoos them away as if they were nothing but pigeons.

The Greek music *zing-zing-zings* and *ding-a-ling-lings*, getting faster and faster.

Back at the villa, we sit drinking coffee on the terrace, watching the sunset. It is a relief. I've felt too hot in the burgundy dress. It is soggy under my armpits. I'm ready for the cool of the evening.

"Has it been a good birthday?" Paul asks as the dark starts to come.

"Yes," I say.

It has.

"You missed your mum?"

"Yeah, a bit."

If I am honest, not really. How can I miss her? She is here. She is everywhere on this island, just like she is in every room back home.

"Yeah, I missed her too," Paul says, nodding. The scrawny white cat is balancing along the low wall of our terrace. It stops next to Paul, and he rubs it behind the ears.

But the other reason I didn't miss Mum was because of how Paul organized the day, structured it, made it reassuring. If we'd spent this day with Mum, it would have been unpredictable, chaotic, a little scary.

"Is there anything else you wanted to do for your birthday?"

"Yes."

And I think I say this because of the champagne and because of the glass of *tsikoudia* that Paul let me drink when we got back to the villa. And I say it because I am a grown-up now and I should be able to handle it. I say it because I am feeling brave, feeling ready.

I say, "I would like you to tell me your version of The Story."

Paul studies me for a moment. I don't need to say anything more. He knows which story I mean. He's been bursting to give me the truth. His truth. And that is all it is, I tell myself, to make it easier to bear. It will be just one version of the truth.

"Okay," he says.

And he starts talking, gently at first, watching me to see how each word lands. This is his story, the one Mum gave to him. And it is exactly like mine but everything has been moved around. It is one of those puzzles where you slide squares within a square to build up a picture. Only this picture, this story, is clearer. There is a "rootstock"—the truth—and then there is my story, a foreign branch grafted to the stalk, winding its way around the trunk, making you believe that the tree is full of fruit. But really the fruit doesn't belong.

240

I concentrate on the stars, clear and defined in the sky. I can hear Mum's chip-chop voice in my head telling me The Story, but as Paul goes on, there are no real words coming out of the mouth of my mother. She goes mute. The image I have of her starts to lose all of its facial features. She becomes just an outline; she withers to dust.

Pop—she disappears.

I get out of my chair and run.

I run from the truth.

ANOTHER STORY

On an island far, far from here, where the sea frames the coastline like a barbed-wire fence and where the sunshine throbs like a time bomb, there once was a farm. At first glance it was like any other piece of land on the Akrotiri Peninsula, but here was where fifteen-year-old Maria Fouraki fell in love for the very first time.

Maria's *babas* worked hard on his relationship with his daughter, his only child—a precious gift.

"Just a week is all it takes," Babas explained as he sowed that season's melon crop. *"Agapoula mou,"* he called Maria, *"peristeraki mou." My little love, my little dove.* "Just a week and the growing will begin."

"I know!" Maria bit back, rolling her brown eyes. "Only the strongest seed will survive. So what!"

Then she jumped across the line in the earth that divided Babas's land from the Drakakis farm next door, calling after herself, "Who cares about darkling beetles and melon aphids and yellow-striped armyworms? Certainly not me!"

And Babas watched her go, his forehead a pinched "w" of concern.

* * *

Maria was off to meet Christos, the small and wiry youngest Drakakis boy, even though an ever-widening gully was forming between them. Maria had told Christos of her dream to one day run away and become an artist, but he had disappointed her, saying he just wanted to stay in Crete and take over his father's farm. Maria looked on as the chickens ignored Christos's timid commands, and she found herself drawn to Christos's older, sturdier brother. Her only thought: *How will I love anything more than I love Yiannis Drakakis?*

Maria and Yiannis became inseparable. On Tersanas Beach, secluded in the mouth of a cove, they would stand nose to nose, barefoot in the sand, a pill dissolving beneath each of their tongues. At the farm, late at night, Yiannis would lead Maria behind the goat sheds, where she would arch her back and lift her face to the moonlight.

Christos spied on the pair and asked what they had been doing to produce such peculiar sounds.

"It's called making beautiful music," Maria told Christos, and she and Yiannis walked away, their heads falling backward with laughter.

This was when Babas and Maria's arguments became as omnipresent as the sea breeze from Kalathás Bay, as dependable as the melon harvest, as sure as a girl grows taller with every passing summer.

"I keep my borders free of weeds, do I not?" Babas would bellow.

"Yes," Maria would answer.

"I would not let my land grow wild?"

"No," Maria would mutter.

243

"And so it is with my child as it is with my land," Babas roared. "Drakakis will keep his pestilent, druggy son away from my baby daughter."

But Babas did not realize that while he concentrated his fury on his daughter's relationship with the oldest Drakakis boy, he'd neglected to notice housekeeping money and jewelry disappearing.

Maria and Yiannis snuck away from the Akrotiri peninsula in the enveloping dark, with a small suitcase of stolen goods and a big dream that London would be more understanding of their love.

Before she left, Maria took one final look at her sleeping parents.

"Pah!" she said, instead of good-bye.

In the morning, Maria's mama, always in the background, stepped forward and became the industrious one. She established which aeroplane Maria had boarded, and she made her way to London too, even though Babas refused to take any part in the search. When your little girl, your melon prized above all others turns into a thief, it changes everything. Forever.

In the early morning, London's streets look like the aftermath of a disaster. Stop for a moment in one of the city's filthy alleys and you will hear the murmurs of last night's sorrows, last year's sorrows, the sorrows of centuries ago. But London is not a place for looking backward. It moves relentlessly forward. In this ruthless city, Maria and Yiannis made their new home.

They began with a tiny flat above the Taj Mahal Tandoori

House, where the stench from the trash below infiltrated the windows and where the arms of the sofa bed were chewed through by mice.

The rent did not pay itself, so Maria sold Mama's jewelry and tried to get a job at the Mount Olympus Restaurant across the street. But the owner didn't believe Maria's story that she was old enough to earn a wage. So they relied on cash from Yiannis's ironing work, sourced from a contact from the island, a front for making deliveries of a less innocent kind. And the pair would have survived on this income alone had they not been tempted to use more of Yiannis's stock than he was able to sell. They lost their flat and were forced into a filthy squat.

Maria missed home. She wrote letters describing her anxiety as they had boarded the aeroplane, the strange, cold air when they landed. She told Mama and Babas of their achievements — *Yiannis, the thriving businessman!*

And she tried to explain.

At first she could not find the words, but driven by the desperate feelings that possessed her at night, the sentences came. *You are two bricks, side by side, strong, building the walls of our family. I want to come back to you. I need you. I love you. Your devoted Maria.*

Babas never replied. Babas's interfering sister Aphrodite did. *You should have thought of all this*, read Aphrodite's scribble, *before you brought shame upon your family.*

And so Yiannis put an arm around Maria's shoulder and told her, "I have found an answer to all our sorrows."

And Maria stopped, and Maria listened.

This is the recipe.

Take a knife edge of powder. Feel that it weighs nothing

compared to the load that lies heavy on your heart. Drop it into a torn-off Coke can. Add cold water; let your tears join in. Throw in lemon juice; throw away your fear. Strike up a cigarette lighter; watch the powder boil. See steam rising like your hopes of relief.

With the remains of your fury, rip the soft fibers from a cigarette butt. Add a message of devotion, a dismissal of your future, your ingratitude to God. Take a needle and draw your mixture through the filter. Tap twice for air, once more for luck. Clench your fist in anger, release. Pierce the skin, see blood rise, let your head drop onto dirty sheets.

Let the final slivers of your childhood slip away. Know that nothing that has happened before this day has really meant anything. Or rather, everything that has happened before this day has only been leading up to this. Feel a man push himself between your legs, thrusting hard. Say a familiar name, although you can't be sure it belongs to him. Imagine you are in a farmyard, lifting your face to the moonlight. Dream of a flower dying and a weed growing in its place. In the morning — on the day of remembrance — regret what you have done, but do it again and again and again. Become addicted.

Germination took on a whole new meaning for sixteen-year-old Maria. While the others around her shrank, their cold bones pushing through skin, she rested her hands on a taut, expanding belly, feeling the warmth within, encouraging her baby to go away. She wandered the tablecloth of concrete that spread out around her new home, wondering how this strong seed had survived.

And that was when she was found — by Auntie Eleni, who

had left Crete ten years before and, with her husband, Vassilis, now owned the Laundromat on Kentish Town Road.

"You're coming with me."

Maria took hold of Eleni's hand, which was surprisingly soft considering she spent all her time dealing with the dampness of other people's laundry.

"She came looking for you, your mama," Eleni explained, leading Maria toward the station. "But she found a lump in her breast. She went home. She died."

Maria could not hold herself up. She fell to her knees, cradling her heavy belly, and began crying with such a force she feared she would never stop.

"You musn't be sad," Eleni told her. "She knew this when she married your father and took his name—all the Fourakis family dies young."

Eleni extended a warm welcome in her small house near the train station.

"I can't believe you found me," Maria mumbled through mouthfuls of sausage and stewed cabbage.

"I have this piece of thread," Eleni explained. "The piece of thread that connects my heart to yours. When something is tugging at your heart, I know, because I feel it too. The thread, it also binds your heart to Babas, to Mama. You must go home."

"I can't," said Maria, putting down her spoon.

"You will find it within yourself."

And Eleni pressed into Maria's hand a pamphlet of soothing words—the recipe for the traditional *kollyva*—and sent Maria to bed with one of Mama's cardigans, left behind when she had returned to the island.

Maria did not sleep at all. She jerked and sweated, her skin crawling, itching, anticipating a dose of something that she could not get. She pressed Mama's cardigan close to her face, wishing for it to transport her back to a farm where cistus shrubs turn the air bittersweet. She envied her unborn baby untouched by grief and desire. She thought of the trip ahead of her, the day she would return to face Babas. She thought of her love for Yiannis, the bliss that could be found at the end of a needle. She was not ready to let that go.

Before she left, taking with her Eleni's jewelry and the earnings from the Laundromat, Maria took one final look at her sleeping aunt and uncle.

"Sorry," she whispered, instead of good-bye.

The night brought with it a furious storm that Maria couldn't help but find fitting. She wanted to feel the rain on her skin, have it cleanse her of her sin. She imagined the ancient river Lardanos, the river of holy water, evaporating into the air in Crete and falling on London's streets. With her hair soaked through, Maria walked back to the squat and told Yiannis they needed a new place to hide.

And before long, in the fluorescent light of an operating room, hair glued to the pallor of her hollowed-out cheeks, Maria had her baby girl cut from inside her. Maria examined the creased and swollen features of the new person squirming in her arms, someone she never expected to see alive, and then she lied to the woman from Social Services about the warm welcome she would find at her auntie Eleni's home in Kentish Town. She took the baby back to another grubby squat, back to Yiannis. She got high.

And despite her state of intoxication, she remembered the hospital's instructions to register the baby's birth.

"What shall we call her?" Maria asked Yiannis, as the registrar sat poised with her fingers over the keyboard. "Something English? Something from home?"

"Onomase to 'karpouzi' tote!" slurred Yiannis. "Call it 'Watermelon,' then."

"Yeah," said Maria, collapsing into laughter, as the baby screamed its objections, "our daughter will be called 'Melon.'"

And that was how Melon got her name.

But this was momentary joy. Maria could no longer stand the life that London offered her—the bawdy banter of car horns, the tinny bass lines of other people's music, the way her baby stopped breathing a few days after she took her home, the way the hospital explained she had been born an addict and had almost died of withdrawal. The way Maria winced when she told the nurses the baby's ridiculous name. The way the woman from Social Services said she was very sorry but the baby belonged to them now. The way Maria returned to the squat to find Yiannis lying on the floor. The way Yiannis's empty eyes were staring at the wall. The way vomit was bleeding around his stone-heavy head. The way Maria called for an ambulance and then ran away to save herself.

Here it was, her first lesson in how to love and lose.

A vast flood of grief swamped Maria, pulling her beneath the surface of life. The tears dried and were replaced by the soft, suffocating fog of depression. Maria looked back on her days of rage and sorrow with a twisted sense of fondness. At least then she had felt something.

She rode red double-decker buses all day, paying no attention to numbers or destinations—she just wanted to be lost among the Gothic buildings with their sooty faces. And then one day she heard Greek words being spoken above the fast talk of the English teenagers. This was Anastasios "Tassos" Georgakis from Agios Nikolaos in Crete, a lean older gentleman with slender wrists and inviting eyes. Tassos had come to the U.K. as a theology student many years ago and had found his calling in London helping addicts like Maria. He said his work consisted solely of helping people find a target and a purpose, their "something special," but Maria suspected there was more to it than that.

She went with him to the Saint Elias Center, where she was given a single room, which contained no decoration except for a crucifix hung above the bed. The door was kept locked between visits from Tassos and the others who came reciting their words of redemption.

For I acknowledge my transgressions, and my sin is ever before me.

Tassos placed a resurrection icon by Maria's bed, and Maria clawed the walls, her forehead beaded with sweat.

Behold, I was shapen in iniquity; and in sin did my mother conceive me.

Tassos lit a candle for Maria and fitfully she watched the fire burn.

Purge me with hyssop, and I shall be clean.

Maria offered up kisses to her old life and told it good-bye.

Wash me, and I shall be whiter than snow.

Slowly Maria returned, piece by piece. The green hue to her olive skin began to fade; the pupils of her eyes reconnected with life. The brick lodged within her ribs began to crack, and though the splinters still caused jerks of pain, she found a new feeling growing inside — the fire of ambition. Here was a flower dying, shedding its seeds, allowing another flower to grow. Tassos offered Maria work at the Saint Elias Center, but though the word of God had brought her back, it had never truly entered her soul.

"No," said Maria, the first thing she had said with any real passion since she had arrived in England. "I can't. My child needs her mother."

At first she visited Melon at her foster home, watching her play with a collection of toys on the hearth rug. Melon was growing strong and broad, a sign of Babas's Fourakis blood staking its claim perhaps, as Maria could not be sure the genes of Yiannis Drakakis had played any part in the child before her. Melon was attending playgroups, places where she was learning accentless English. *My daughter,* thought Maria proudly, *will talk like the teenagers on the top decks of buses.*

Gradually a timetable was agreed upon for Melon to return to her mother.

"But in the meantime," said the woman from Social Services, "what about you?"

And Maria went back to school.

It is a joyous moment when a life finds a target and a purpose, when a person realizes what makes them special. It is like a stylus falling into place on a record. Music begins to play.

The sign on the double doors of the office read, "Congratulations to Maria Fouraki, who will be joining the Adolescent

Resource Team as a trainee social worker." Maria pushed through those doors, found her new desk, and on it placed the framed picture of her daughter on her first day at school.

Maria's vocation was Mama's love reborn, Yiannis's lost future reclaimed, Tassos's nurture repaid. Maria would help others as she had been helped. She would go on to buy Melon her own home in the city, not far from Kentish Town, so one day Maria could forge a reconciliation with Eleni. And soon Maria would earn enough to afford the airfare to visit Crete so she could apologize to Babas and introduce him to his granddaughter.

"I have this piece of thread," Maria explained to little Melon. "The piece of thread that connects my heart to yours. This thread, it also binds my heart to Babas. . . ."

Maria understood that the past could not be forgotten and that history could not be altered, but the truth could be viewed from a new angle.

Forget what you know, what you feel about everything that has happened. This is how Maria would explain. *Purge me with hyssop, and I shall be clean. Wash me, and I shall be whiter than snow. The view from up here, it is rosy. The future from here, it looks good.*

135 DAYS SINCE

I run.

Down the gravel track toward the village.

My hands on my ears to begin with. Then I pump my arms, feel them scuff the dry wall, the prickly shrubs.

The night is black. Paul chases me. He bellows my name. Then I hear him yelp in pain. He wasn't wearing shoes when we were out on the terrace.

I turn the corner, shy away from the lights and music of the taverna, keep my face in the shadows. I am a freak, a Minotaur, born as a punishment for doing wrong. A car growls past and I run faster now, away from the village, toward the sea, tears stinging my sunburned cheeks. I hear my own breath. I hear Paul calling my name, his voice getting smaller.

"Melon! Melon!"

I reach the main road. The dark looming mass of the sea is in front of me.

On an island far, far from here, where the sea is woven from strings of sapphire blue . . .

No. All lies.

I am the daughter of a liar. The daughter of a junkie. I am nothing but a joke.

I run, on past the junction. Dust covers my sandaled feet, turning them to stone. The insect buzz of a motorbike sends me onto the curb, backs me up against a tree. The burgundy dress snags on the bark, and I lose my footing. I fall, yell out, then clamp a hand to my mouth. I don't want anyone to hear me, to see me. But the motorbike has stopped. It is turning around. It pulls up close and I draw back from its thundering motor.

It is Haris. And he looks at me like he knows.

Did everyone know? Everyone except me?

I take his hand. I have no choice. It is just like he said it would be—I will scream and he will come rescue me. We stare at each other for a moment, until I feel too ashamed and have to look away. I wipe tears and snot from my face. He pulls me toward the bike.

"You want come with me?"

What else do I have? Nothing. Nothing.

Nothing that has happened before this day has really meant anything.

I get on the bike behind Haris.

Or rather, everything that has happened before this day has only been leading up to this.

I am no one. No past. No truth. Now is all there is.

I grip Haris's slim, hard waist, smell the leather of his jacket, the faint edge of cigarettes. The bike belches forward and my heart jams in my throat. I hold on tight, as if my survival depends on the warmth coming from his body. We take off down the coast road, the air cold against my bare shins. Inside my stomach there's a somersaulting beast. Trapped. We are going too fast and I am going to die.

All the Fourakis family dies young.

"Where are we going?" I shout, but my words are stolen by the squeal of the bike. We lean sharp into a curve, and I see the roadside fall away, see the car wrecks at the bottom on the scrubby rocks: a warning of what happens if you go too crazy. Then we are upright again, high above the harbor, where the lights from the ships make the waves look like oil. We speed, too fast, too fast, until the road becomes built-up again and we have to slow down. But still we dash past blank-eyed shops and banks, dry cleaners and hardware stores. Cars line the streets and I tighten my thighs, scared that my knee will hit a side mirror. Then there are no cars anymore. The storefronts lose their dowdiness. They grow shiny. Local faces are replaced by pink peeling cheeks. Haris slows down again, the engine *phut-phut-phut*-ing. He navigates tight corner after tight corner. Tourists scatter like birds from a gun.

We are at the old harbor. I can see the restaurant where I ate with Paul just hours ago. But that was the old me, not the real me. Not the me who knows the truth. Haris plows forward, as if he's going to drive us straight into the inky waters, end it all.

All the Fourakis family dies young.

But he turns, swift, and we bounce across stones instead, the fairy illuminations of the harbor lighthouse behind us. We zip past fish restaurants that smell seaweed strong. Are we supposed to drive so close to the restaurant tables? Haris doesn't care. I don't care either. After all, what do right and wrong mean anymore?

We swing around a corner, our shoulders dipping low to the road, past a playground with its swings sitting empty, past a fresh stretch of seafront cafés. Busy. Infested. Locals, not tourists. We stick close to the seawall, people skipping out of our path like they knew we were coming all along. The water below us is shallow with fish. They group; they swirl.

This is our destination — a bar with a terrace of stretched cream canopies. Clustered underneath are low white sofas, sophisticated, upscale, with kids my age lounging across them. Are they holding the places until the adults show up? Haris lurches into high speed to make an impressive arrival. Faces swarm, sipping on straws. The music throb-throb-throbs. My heart joins in. I wasn't expecting an audience for my tear-swollen face.

"Get off the bike." Haris is enjoying the attention. I'm scared to let go.

You will find it within yourself.

The concrete sways beneath my feet after the thrill of the ride. I pull down my hem. A girl with dark eyeliner looks me up and down, gives me a gravelly *"yassou."* Haris is still straddling the bike, gabbing to a boy in a red padded vest. He is smoothing the heel of his hand along the edge of his gelled hair. Everyone is in sneakers and sweaters, and I am too dressed up in the burgundy dress. I am an effigy of my unreliable mother.

"Give me your coat, Haris. I'm cold," I lie, shouting it again a little louder to compete with the *dumf, dumf, dumf* of the music. "Your coat. I'm cold."

He climbs off the bike, props the kickstand, hands me his leather jacket.

The boy in the red vest says, *"Anglidha?"*

She English?

And Haris nods. *"Né."*

Another boy, in a checked shirt, pushes through the crowd to give Haris a high-five. The girl with the dark eyeliner smiles at me, half friendly, half sorry. I shouldn't be here. But where should I be? Nowhere. I belong nowhere.

I let Haris sling his arm across my shoulders and move us over to a rectangle of sofas where a boy with a shaved head is flicking a cigarette lighter on and off in time to the dance track. A girl with a matted beehive watches us sit, popping gum against her cherry lips. I am special because I'm with Haris. I see that now. Is this the only way I'll find my "something special," via the glow of someone else?

The boy in the checked shirt hands me a tall glass of

dark liquid. It looks like Coke, but when I drink, the taste is stinging, as if I'm downing nail polish remover. I cough, splutter, and the girl with the beehive laughs.

I lean close to Haris's ear. "You get served?"

"Served?"

"They give you alcohol here?"

"Yes, why not they give me alcohol?"

"The police . . ."

"Police suck," he says, and I watch him tip back his head, screw up his eyes, take a long draw on his cigarette.

How will I love anything more than I love . . . ?

Then I watch him yabber, quick and confident, holding the attention of the table. I can barely hear over the *bam, bam, bam* of the bass line, and even if I could, I wouldn't understand. Are they talking about me? I swig more of the drink and wonder what Paul is doing. Calling the police? A car swings past and I turn away. The guy and girl next to me start kissing, their faces suctioned together. I nod my head along to the music. I keep drinking. This is the only way I can join in. And when I empty my glass, the boy in the checked shirt hands me another full one.

"English," he says. "You like drink. Too much you like drink."

"I'm Greek," I shoot back.

But then I think, *Am I? Am I?*

I drink, faster, faster.

I watch the girl with the dark eyeliner tell off the boy

she's with. In any language, you know when you're in trouble. She counts off the things he's done wrong on her fingers.

Ena—one—you did this.

Dio—two—you do that.

And *tria*—three—I will never ever forgive you.

"We go."

Haris has hold of my hand and is pulling me away from the sofas, away from the soothing pulse of the music, toward the bike. When he lets go to swing himself into his seat, the seashore spins. I concentrate hard, really hard, on hitching up my dress and climbing onto the bike without falling over. I take hold of Haris's waist, rest my face on his T-shirted back.

"I want to go home," I think I say.

"I take you somewhere very pretty," says Haris, and he strikes the pedal. The bike comes to life. Vibrations roar up between my legs.

We are flying past the bay again, with the sheer drop and the car wrecks and the sea and the ships and the lights, and then, and then . . .

I fall asleep. I must have. There is this gap. We are speeding fast through the night, speeding fast toward death, and then I fall asleep.

I wake as we bump along a dirt track, still close to the coast. We are traveling across grass. Light from the bike's headlight bounces off shrubs and piles of rocks. Then I see it—the fortress at the edge of the cliff. Haris kills the engine. We coast as if we're trying to catch the deserted building unaware. When he turns off the bike's lights, my eyes take an age to adjust to the starlight.

"*Ela*. Come on."

We go the rest of the way on foot, weaving through the rocks. Haris pulls me tight. It must be late. No, it must be early. I want to go home, but I have no clue where that is, so I might as well be here. The fortress looks like something out of the Wild West, a movie set with its insides shot out. Haris walks us around the back wall. Bam—there is this amazing view.

Somewhere pretty. Somewhere really pretty.

The future from here, it looks good.

The moonlight hits the sea. The military base below sulks on the coastline, winking its lights. It is stunning. Insects chirp in the undergrowth. The waves sigh and shush.

"Yes," I say. "Really pretty."

But Haris is not looking at the sea anymore. I can feel it. His breath is near my ear, getting heavy, slowing down. This is when I'm supposed to kiss him, but I've never . . . I don't know how you . . . What do you . . . ?

"Here." Haris puts a small bottle in my hand and I swig from it, feel the blast of it in my throat. I could breathe fire. I could . . . I could . . .

Haris puts a hand to my chin and pulls my face away from the view. I have no choice. He puts his mouth over mine. No. I choose this. My groin aches; my stomach pulls toward him. Haris is breathing fire too. His tongue is hot and tastes of ash. He winds it around my mouth. He clamps his hand over my backside and pushes my hips into his. I tense as his fingers squeeze into my flesh. I hear Lucy Bloss telling me that I am a fat bitch who no one would have sex with. But, oh, God, this is it, I'm about to. And I don't know what to do. I don't . . .

You will find it within yourself.

I feel like I am going to explode. What do I do with all this fire?

Haris pulls away, and for a moment I think that he has noticed his mistake in choosing me, the freak, the fat bitch, but he just says, "More," and puts the bottle to my lips. I gulp some down. He does the same. He is in a hurry now. He needs to get somewhere fast.

"This way." He grabs my hand and pulls me through one of the doorways of the fortress. Its roof is open to the stars. The gravel inside is spiked through with grass.

"This way." We head toward a stone stairway. He knows where he's going. He's taken girls here before. *Who cares?* I think. *Who cares?*

Here it was, her first lesson in how to love and lose.

The stairs take us to a stone platform with battlements, to a better view of the sea, but we're not here for that. Haris edges me back against the stone wall, fixes his mouth over mine, grabs at my chest.

"No!" I react lightning fast, pull away his hand.

"Is okay," he murmurs, and starts groping again. And I let him. I let him run his hand up the inside of my thigh, push up my dress. He clamps his hand over my underpants, and I jump like I've been given an electric shock.

Throw away your fear.

I tell myself to relax. And he sees my body release. He works his hand inside my underwear. And I listen to a breathy moan—a sound that is coming from my own mouth.

"Happy birthsdays." Haris sighs.

And I let him push me down onto the floor, ignore the stones digging hard into my back, the smell of cigarette butts. I hear the click of his belt buckle, hear the crinkle of a condom wrapper, feel his hand fumbling between us. He pulls hard at my underwear, and I feel cold air between my legs. I am wet and I'm worried that this is not how I am supposed to be.

Forget what you know, what you feel . . .

"You okay?" Haris asks, and I can feel him against my leg, hard—the hot, smooth skin.

"Yes," I say, but I'm ready for pain. This is what Lucy Bloss says—it hurts, you bleed, and you should close your eyes.

I keep my eyes wide open, just to spite her, look into

Haris's black pupils that have swelled, large and round, making him look possessed.

He pushes my thighs apart. My legs are shaking, and I can't do anything to stop them.

"Relax," he says, and oh, my God, oh, my God . . .

It's called making beautiful music.

A bird cries in the undergrowth and it's a weird sound, like a cork being pulled from a bottle.

It hurts. God, it hurts. Why does everything have to hurt so much? It takes all my self-control not to push him off. But I do not move. I listen to Haris make low, horrible sounds, like he is being tortured, as if he doesn't want to be doing what he's doing. I suck in my breath, concentrate on the stars.

Dream of a flower dying, shedding its seeds, allowing another flower to grow.

Haris pushes, pushes, pushes and kneads at my chest. The sharp pain inside of me turns into an aching roughness. I feel I should do something with my hands, but what? I don't know. I wrap my arms around the back of his head, feel the spikes of short, sweaty hair. This is the right thing. He pushes his face closer to my ear. My cheek is sore from the brush of his stubble. His belt buckle *clank, clank, clanks* against the stone floor. The skin at the base of my back has been grazed. It's burning. Haris's breath gets tighter, raspier.

Something inside my belly wants to break free. I want to climb up a mountain and jump off the other side.

"Né, né," Haris groans in my ear, and it's all so scary, I just want to laugh. I shut my eyes and see that picture from biology class—my pelvis cut in half and Haris inside. This is ridiculous and impossible and terrifying and oh, God, oh, God, oh, God.

She would arch her back and lift her face to the moonlight.

I lift my hips off the floor to ease the pain and suddenly Haris's body shudders, violent, as if he's having a heart attack. He goes rigid, pushing a strangled sound through his nose. I freeze. Haris opens his mouth, roars, like a dog does when you step on its tail.

Is this right? Did I do something wrong? Is this it?

And my sin is ever before me.

Haris collapses, silent, a dead weight. I am still thinking about biology class.

He comes back to life, rolls off me, fumbles for a cigarette.

"Thanks," I say, which sounds so stupid, too formal and polite. And I start crying because this is all too much, too much, and I want to go home, but I don't know where that is.

"You cry because this is first time," Haris says.

And now I am so embarrassed that he could tell that I was a virgin that I cry even harder. I curl up into a ball, holding my aching belly. I can feel grit on my cheek.

Let the final slivers of your childhood slip away.

"Is okay," Haris says. "You get used to it."
And then he wraps his arms around me, covering my dirty face with kisses.

136 DAYS SINCE

Morning.

Haris drops me near the taverna, away from the villa. I spring away from him just as he tries to kiss me. I can't do it. I feel sick and I doubt Haris's cigarette breath will taste very good in the morning.

So this is a hangover. The somersaulting beast has left my stomach and invaded my brain. I wave and walk away, and Haris looks disappointed, maybe because I have taken over his job of being the heartbreaker.

I walk up the hill, feeling the bruising ache between my legs. I go through the gates to the villa, down the path lined with shrubs, toward our terrace. Someone is in the pool doing lazy laps. There is the gentle *slip-slop* of water. The sky is the bluest blue, and the birds are perky, shrill — taunting my throbbing head. Someone has engineered this morning to be too wonderful, too perfect, so that last night feels like the strangest dream.

I want to go inside and sink my face into a cool white pillow. We slept on the dusty stone floor of the fortress last night, curled into each other, spoons, sharing Haris's jacket as a cover. When I woke up, I could see that we'd been lying on a bed of cigarette butts and food wrappers and other people's used condoms. I want to shower myself clean.

But I'll have to get past Paul first.

The white cat is on our terrace wall. It yowls at me, but I'm feeling too jangled to spend time rubbing its ears. The patio doors are open, but I can't make out any shapes in the shade of indoors. I take a big breath, step inside.

He is sitting on the sofa in yesterday's clothes. His nice white shirt with the blue flowers, the khaki shorts. Crumpled now. He has his head in his hands, but his neck wrenches up when he hears me come in. I stand there, waiting for him to start crying, lecturing. He takes in the sight of me. He takes in a great big breath of me.

"Oh, Melon, thank God, thank God." His head sinks back into his hands. His body relaxes, collapses. "Thank God, thank God," he mutters.

He looks odd, exhausted, as if he's run a marathon and has got no blood or muscle left for anything else.

I want to go through to the bathroom, strip off, but I stay put. If I move, I will trip some sensor that will set Paul off. Already a small earthquake is starting—his hands are shaking as they clasp his head. He lifts his face, his eyes fierce. I look away.

He can tell.

I must look different. I must look more ripe, like a piece of peeled fruit. I mustn't shift. If I do, he'll definitely be able to tell, just from the way I move.

"Where have you been?" he asks, low and serious.

"I ran away."

"Where?" There isn't any niceness in his voice. The ground beneath us is about to crack.

"Away."

"Away where?" His voice is quivering, rising.

"Just away."

"Where, Melon?" he roars at me. He gets to his feet, fingers clawing the air for something. I flinch as he grabs *The Rough Guide to Crete* from the coffee table and hurls it into the kitchen. The metal fruit bowl goes flying. Oranges bounce across the tiles. The mouth of the bowl spins and spins against the floor, a howling clatter that goes on and on.

I shrink into my shoulders. I have never seen Paul get angry.

"Where? For fuck's sake, Melon, where have you been?"

I've never heard Paul swear.

"Look at you. Look at the state of you."

There are gray smears of dust on the burgundy dress. My feet are filthy. My face feels sticky, oily. I put my hand up to feel the tangled mat of my hair and see that there is a bloody scratch up my right arm. Now that I've noticed it, I start to feel the sting of it too.

"Look at the state of you!" Paul yells again.

He launches himself toward me and I think he might grab my throat, but he stops, strides away toward the kitchen. He kicks the upturned fruit bowl. It clangs against the kitchen cupboards. He turns, paces toward the front door, huffing, panting. He swivels again, pushes his crushed white shirt up his arms, plants his hands on his hips. He keeps his back to me. His shoulders go up and down with the weight of his breath.

268

"I'm going to ask you again," he says, quiet now, a lawyer summing up, "and you're going to give me an answer."

He turns to stare me down.

"Where have you been?" He bites the whole of his bottom lip, keeping back his fury.

I open my mouth to speak, but what can I say?

"Where?" He jabs at me.

"I don't . . ."

"Where?!"

"The sea," I say.

Paul's eyes drill into me. I need to say more.

"I saw the sea and then . . ."

"And then what?"

"I saw the sea and"—I start to tell a story—"and I know this will sound weird and everything, but it felt like the sea was talking to me, in a way. And I was sort of talking back."

I am my mum's daughter. I can do it. I can tell a good story.

"And it said, 'You want to come with me?' So I went. I went down onto the beach and the sand felt warm and it felt good to just sink into it all and lose myself, kind of. If you know what I mean."

The earthquake inside Paul fades to tremors.

"And it's not like I really understood what the sea was saying, not words or anything, but I understood, I guess. Then I watched the lights of the ships and the harbor, and they were really pretty. Really beautiful."

I am my mother.

"And then I must have fallen asleep. I just curled up where I was and I cried and I fell asleep."

That's how you do it. That's how you tell a story. Truth and lies, truth and lies.

Paul nods. Calmer now.

"I called the police," he says. "I need to tell them you're . . . okay." His voice breaks at the end of the sentence. There is this choking sound. He looks away.

Then it comes—the sobbing. Paul is shaking again, this time with tears. He staggers to one of the armchairs. His head falls back into his hands. I still haven't moved. I am stuck to the floor.

"I thought . . . I thought you were . . ." he manages. His back heaves with the sobs. His voice is all mangled. "You could have been . . ."

"Dead?" I offer.

Paul chugs out more tears.

"Sorry," I say.

"No, *I'm* sorry . . . I'm . . . Anything could have . . . Oh, no, I can't . . ." He can hardly breathe from his crying. "I thought . . . I thought that . . ."

I want to run away again. I have seen Paul cry before, but not like this, not anything like this. This is awful. The earthquake has turned in on itself.

"It just brought it all back . . . You disappearing and . . . I shouldn't have . . . I shouldn't have told you all that and . . . I'm supposed to be looking after you and . . . Oh, I can't . . . I just can't . . ." He gets pulled down under the sobs for a moment, then surfaces again. "It just brought it all back . . . Losing Maria . . . Losing your mother." He gasps and splutters. Snot and tears stream down his face, into his hands.

270

Me and my mother, we are the same person. We do the same things to people.

"I'm sorry," I say again. I just want him to be okay.

"No, *I'm* sorry." Paul sniffs, snorts. He lifts his face to the ceiling, gasps for air.

"S'okay," I say.

His chest hiccups. He starts to recover his speech. "No, it was too much, too much to tell you, all that, just like that."

I shake my head. I look down at my fingers—there is a half-moon of dirt under each of my nails. "I knew it all anyway," I say. "I knew my story wasn't true."

This surprises him. I can tell.

"Well, no, I didn't know," I say. "But, yes. I can see now that I knew it wasn't true. All along I knew. It's just . . ."

Paul nods.

"I just thought," I go on, "that people who were in denial knew they were in denial. So I couldn't have been in denial, could I? But I was."

Paul smiles. "No, people don't know they're in denial. That's the whole point."

We both fall quiet at that. There is just the sound of Paul's hiccupy breath.

Then he says, "So, are you going to rewrite your book?"

"What book?" I follow his gaze to the kitchen table.

And there it is. My book. The Story. The one I left in a drawer in my room. He's read my version of The Story.

I gasp. "That was none of your business."

I dart for the table, pull the book to my chest. The picture of Mum and Christos and Yiannis slips to the floor.

The three of them look up at me. I bend down to pick it up and feel the graze on my back drag against the fabric of the dress. I can't believe he has read it. My story. The fairy tale.

Just a fucking fairy tale.

"I didn't know where you were, Melon," Paul says, offering me his palms. "I thought there might be something in there that might help me find you."

"No, you didn't," I spit back. "You're just fucking nosy. You've been dying to know what I've been writing. Couldn't just let me have my privacy. It's none of your fucking business. You're always interfering."

I am stuck to the floor again, a furious mass, my arms clenched around the book. I want to run, but where can I go? Where? And I am so sick of running.

We fall silent. Paul nods. He is not going to fight back.

"I liked it," he says eventually.

"What?"

"Your story."

"Yeah, but it's not true, is it," I mutter.

"Some of it is."

I close my eyes.

"The sea is blue."

I shake my head.

"The island is magical," he goes on. "The farm, the melons—she loved them. She did."

"She hated all that. . . ."

"When she was a teenager, maybe. She loved it as a kid, as an adult. She wanted it back. People change."

And yes, this is it. This is what I don't understand. How

272

a person can change, even when they're dead. My mother is a chameleon, a magician's rabbit. Now you see her, now you don't.

I have no energy left to be angry with Paul.

"Why did she lie to me?" I say.

"Because she loved you."

I frown at that. How can lies be love?

"And if you say something enough times, it becomes true." Paul makes a steeple of his fingers, examines his fingertips. "Your story is beautiful. The rest of us didn't get anything as lovely."

"You got the truth. You all knew. Poppy, the kids at Mum's work, everyone."

"Take what you've been given as a gift," Paul goes on. "She did it because she wanted you to love her."

"I did love her," I say.

"And now? Now that you know the truth?"

"Yeah, still." I sound unsure. I know I do. "I don't know. I do, of course, but . . . it's . . ."

"Complicated."

"Yes."

He smiles. I try to smile back but a wave of something horrendous—a feeling of terror—takes over my body.

"Oh, G-g-od," I stammer, and I run from the room. I dash for the bathroom, skidding to my knees by the toilet. I puke so violently, I feel as though I will turn inside out.

Paul calls after me, so I get up and shut the bathroom door. I'm in a cold sweat, but I feel better. I flush the puke away. Then I think—blood, I'm ready to look for the blood. I pull down my underwear and there it is. Not a lot, just

273

smears of pink. My thighs ache. I sit down. I pee. I take off the underwear and bunch it into a ball in my hand. Then I think about how Paul will be waiting outside when I open the door. I don't look forward to trying to get past him with underwear in my hand. I put them back on.

When I open the door, Paul is leaning against the wall.

"You okay?"

"I'm fine."

"So you had quite a bit to drink on the beach last night, then?"

"No." I try to laugh him away, but Paul's not having that.

"So where were you last night? Really."

"The beach."

"The real story, please, Melon."

He smiles a gentle smile.

I give in. I take a breath. I tell him another story. No lies this time. I tell him about the motorbike ride and the kids at the bar and the drinking and us sleeping at the fortress. Paul's been told stories worse than mine; he can handle it. I just leave out one little thing, of course, because I know I would die if he gave me a lecture about all of that.

Paul can do what I've got to do now.

He can fill in the gaps.

137 DAYS SINCE

"This is it," I say, and Paul puts his foot on the brake. We pull up on the shoulder.

"You sure?" He doesn't seem too impressed.

I don't know what he was expecting.

"I'm sure," I say, although there is this brief moment when I think I've got it wrong. Me and Mum didn't come here often. I have never actually been inside the farmhouse. When the family knew we were in town, we usually met at Auntie Despina's taverna in Horafakia. Neutral territory. This is an invasion.

We sit in the quiet of the car for a moment, squinting into the sunlight. Through a break in the tall wild canes that surround the farm, there is a stretch of chicken wire, and behind it fat beige hens are picking at the ground. A rooster swaggers up to the fence to blast out a *cock-a-doodle-do!*—a noise bigger than its body. Fighting talk. I wonder if Auntie Aphrodite has had it trained.

She lives here now, in the boxy white building with its blue-painted roof. It's just as Mum described it in The Story, but now modern stuff hangs off the house like cheap jewelry—a stainless-steel porch light, replacement windows with plastic frames, a satellite dish.

The rest of the property does not look as though it has been tarted up. A rough dirt track runs along the side of the house, just two gouges in the red earth. A large shed of corrugated iron sits, sorry for itself, behind the house. A couple of cars and a pickup truck are playing hide-and-seek in knee-high wildflowers. The only thing that looks tidy is the row upon row of melon vines that spread out as far as the eye can see, down into the dip in the earth, up high on the crest of the hill. The mountains sit behind, black and solemn. There is snow on those mountains in winter, Mum used to say, which always seems unbelievable when you look at them in the sweltering heat.

It's getting sticky in the car with the engine off and no air-conditioning. But still we both sit there, waiting for the other one to take the initiative. We watch an orange cat squeeze through a hole in the chicken wire, past the hens, who peck on, oblivious.

Paul speaks. "Shall we open the gate and pull into the driveway?" There is a wobble in his voice.

"No," I say. "Don't be crazy."

We get out of the car. In my hands I have the dove box. We approach the broad chain-link gate.

"She's not going to say yes," I say.

"Because she's cremated?" asks Paul. "Or because they don't do that here?"

"Because it's Mum," I say.

The gate blocking the driveway is a new thing too. An Auntie Aphrodite touch. Paul tries to open it, rattling the chain-link.

"It's bolted," he says, scanning the fence posts for a

doorbell. Red climbing flowers have wound themselves around the gate's hinges, making it look like it has never been opened.

On the other side of the chain-link, a small boy with thick black hair pedals toward us on a plastic bike. His long-sleeved top is covered in ducks, although they're hard to make out through the dust that covers him. An older boy, his brother maybe, runs barefoot behind, carrying a stick. The older boy's palms are red from playing in the soil. He gabbles something at the younger boy in Greek.

Paul waves. I wave. The older boy's face changes. Stranger danger! He hightails it back toward the house. The younger boy stays put, clutching his handlebars, eyeing us, curious.

"*Yia-Yia!*" yells the older boy. "*Yia-Yia!*"

That word makes her sound so soft, my great aunt Aphrodite.

And then a figure emerges on the terrace. We hear the rasping smack of a door on a spring. A short, solid woman steps down onto the driveway. She has a waddle, a roll to her hips.

"*Ela, ela,*" she calls to the boys, sending them back toward the house with the swish of one fleshy arm. The small boy struggles to begin with, pedaling up that slope of a driveway, but once the children have gone, the woman moves forward, creasing her eyes, peering at us. She is wearing a gray tunic, black trousers, and a thick, knitted tank top, as if the August heat wave is just a figment of our imagination.

When her face is right up to the fence, I say, "*Thea Aphrodite, kalimera.*"

Paul looks at me a little stunned, as if I've just recited

the Lord's Prayer in Greek rather than saying a simple word or two.

"Melon?" Aphrodite looks truly surprised. Maybe she didn't get Paul's letters. I remember Mum saying the postman only came once a month around here, if he ever bothered to come at all.

Auntie Aphrodite starts undoing the lock, still without a smile. The sides of her mouth couldn't do anything but turn down; the weight of those flabby cheeks is too much to fight against. She opens the gate, just a crack.

"*Pios ine aftos?*" She stares at Paul.

I speak back in English.

"This is Paul," I tell her. "Paul, this is Auntie Aphrodite." Paul nods. Aphrodite nods.

"Paul is, was, Mum's fiancé."

This is the first time I've ever called him this. He smiles at me, then at Aphrodite. He offers his hand to shake, but Aphrodite does not take it. She just nods again. She is respectful—iron-plated respectful.

"*Kalimera,*" she says, swallowing the word like a bad-tasting pill.

Flowers they are growing wherever she is walking; birds they are flocking wherever she is flying!

She eyes the box I'm carrying but doesn't ask.

"*Ela, ela.*" She gestures for us to follow. She speaks it sternly. We do not dare dawdle. She lollops up the driveway, and we walk behind, letting the red earth stain our toes and the edges of our flip-flops.

*   *   *

We sit around a table in the middle of a kitchen where ancient cupboards stand next to a modern gurgling fridge. The tiles are old and cracked, painted with fading blue flowers. The dark wooden dresser leans to one side on the uneven floor.

I place Mum on the table.

Auntie Aphrodite puts a cup in front of each of us, then asks us something in Greek. Paul looks to me, as if I've suddenly become fluent in the language. I've no idea what she's saying, so I nod and say, *"Né."* I decide that saying "yes" to whatever she offers is the safest plan.

Aphrodite pours sludgy black coffee into the tiny cups, her face still set in a bad-dog frown. Then she drops a plate of bread on the table—great hunks of the stuff. She leans over, her huge boobs near my face, and drizzles oil over the bread with her thumb hooked into the neck of the bottle. Then she pours honey on top from a little jug. She turns her back and Paul gives me a look that asks, *Is it ready?* I shrug.

What would Mum have done? She would have refused to eat it. She ate like a horse at all other times, only picking and fussing over what the family gave her. Why did she do that when she was trying to win them back? Could a little piece of her not resist the need to rebel?

I take a chunk of bread from the plate and bite. I get the flowery taste of oil first, then the sweetness of the honey that has stuck to my lips. Paul takes my lead, picks up some bread, starts chewing. Aphrodite stands over us, a thick "w" of skin pinched into her forehead.

She is looking at the box.

Paul gives me a pleading look. *Ask her*, it says. He has turned into a mouse. His phrase books and guidebooks can't help him here.

I put down my piece of bread, wipe my mouth.

"Inside this box," I say to Aphrodite, tapping the lid, "is Mum."

Aphrodite stares at me, giving no hint that she has understood. She has green eyes that would be really beautiful if only she would let them smile.

A shadow comes across the mesh flyscreen of the kitchen door. We all turn to see an old man in blue overalls. This is Aphrodite's husband—I remember him from our visits, always in the background, fingering his rosary. Another Manolis, like Granbabas.

The sun has carved itself deep into his face. He speaks to Aphrodite in words of just one syllable. His voice is low and bubbly like the sound a straw makes when you suck the last of a drink out of a glass. Aphrodite responds in a string of clanging sentences.

Uncle Manolis starts to push through the door.

"*Óhi! Óhi!*" goes Aphrodite, and then she throws more jangling words in his direction. Uncle Manolis eyes me and Paul for a moment, gives in to his wife and backs off.

"'*Daxi,*" he goes, lumbering away to be swallowed up by the sunlight. The door growls and snaps back into place.

Aphrodite's attention is back on me, back on the box.

Paul gives me a tight, encouraging smile.

"In here," I go again, "is Mum."

Aphrodite is still pretending to be confused. But I know

she understands me. This is the woman who used to tell Mum that if she turned to the side she would disappear. She knows her English.

"In here," I say, "is Maria."

"Óhi." Aphrodite jerks her neck back, steps away from the box, as if it is cursed, as if the curse is contagious. She splutters a mouthful of disgusted Greek.

"Né." I nod.

Paul nibbles at his honey bread.

"Mum wanted to be scattered here," I go on. "Her ashes." I make a throwing action with my hands.

"Etho?" she asks.

"Yes, here."

"Óhi," she replies with a firm shake of her head.

"Se parakaló," I say, I beg.

"Parakaló," says Paul, a word he understands.

"Never," says Aphrodite, strong, loud.

I knew it.

I knew Aphrodite could speak English if she really needed to.

I carry Mum back down the red path. Paul carries a watermelon as big as his chest. It is a gift. I can still feel Aphrodite's damp kisses on both of my cheeks.

She kissed me. She gave us fruit. This is more, so much more, than I expected.

When she kissed me, Aphrodite put a hand on the back of my neck, and for a moment her green eyes lost their metal edge. She silently wished me well.

"If I was you," I tell her, "I'd be angry too."

She nods. Her eyes tear up—I don't think I imagine it.

"I'll come back to see you next year," I say, and that makes her smile—sort of. But I'm not sure that I really mean it.

But Aphrodite is right. This isn't the place to be putting Mum to rest for all of eternity.

138 DAYS SINCE

The day hasn't even started and we're on the road. The beginnings of the hazy sun are making cardboard cutouts of the mountains. We drive the Akrotiri coastal route, then take a left where the road turns dusty and potholed. We follow the yellow line on the map.

We get to Tersanas Beach as the sun is rising. We park the car, take off our flip-flops, and sink our feet into sand that is cool from the night before. We walk past the wooden changing room on stilts, its door slung wide. We pass the volleyball net hanging loose and embarrassed in the quiet. Later, the beach will be filled with people and towels and squealing and action, but for now we have it all to ourselves. We pass the shack café with its chairs upside down on the tables, the palm leaf roof rippling in the morning breeze. We go down to the edge of the sea and stand with our toes in the water. A fishing boat lolls, drowsy, in the distance at the mouth of the cove.

There is just us and the sea, the water moving in and out, lazy, like it doesn't really have to. *Slurp, slurp*, it goes, licking the lips of the beach. It is clear in the shallows, then farther out it turns green, with a vibrant strip of turquoise dotted with a yellow buoy.

I have only ever seen this place busy, the beach heaving with oiled bodies, when Mum and me used to come here to sunbathe. Now it is still. This is the Tersanas Beach Mum would have known as a kid, when she came here with Christos. With Yiannis. With whoever. This is the beach from The Story—my story, and Paul's.

"Let's climb through the tide pools and get to the smaller bay," I say, and we start clambering over a tumble of pitted stone that divides the beach in two, stone that is so black that you expect soot to wipe off on your feet. Paul holds my elbow as I step from one salt-crusted mound to another, trying to keep hold of the dove box. Seawater glugs in and out of the pools, and when my foot goes into one of the small pockets of water I'm surprised how warm it is.

We step back down on sand again and look behind us. The road where our car is parked curves around to this bay too. We could have reached this piece of sand easier that way. We both realize this at the same time and smile, shrug. I should have known that. I should have remembered.

A woman pulls up in a black car and parks under the shade of one of the tired, knotty trees by the roadside.

"Could it get any more perfect?" she calls out to a tanned man with a large stomach who is fiddling around on one of the few sleek white boats moored at the jetty.

"It's a wonderful day," he calls back.

She locks her car and makes her way around to the jetty.

"Yes," says the woman. "Thanks for inviting me."

Then she boards the boat and their talk becomes too quiet for us to hear.

"Let's wait for them to go," says Paul.

So we stand and watch the sea wash over the rocks, furry with sea moss, watch the slippery seaweed waving and gesturing in the water. *Go away, come here, go away, come here.* Fish dance with their own shadows in the shallows. Flies find our feet interesting.

Eventually the man and the woman on the boat start puttering out to sea. Then the motor comes on full throttle, an angry lawn mower, and the boat moves out of the cove. There is no one to watch us now, just a squat orange house peering over the high rocks on one side of the bay.

I hold the dove box close to my chest, the wood warming in the sun. There is a light breeze in the air, and I worry about Mum going in the wrong direction. But then, what is the right direction? Paul has felt the breeze too. He picks up some driftwood and some sun-crisped leaves and tosses them into the sea. He's testing the current.

"We should say something," he says. "Some words."

I look down. Black dust from the rocks sways backward and forward in the waves.

"For I acknowledge my transgressions, and my sin is ever before me," I murmur. I can feel Paul watching me, listening. The words come easy. They are written across my mind. They will never be wiped away, even by time. "Behold, I was shapen in iniquity; and in sin did my mother conceive me."

I look up at Paul and he nods at the box.

"How do we do it?" I ask.

"With your hands. Take her in your hands."

I open the box and the container inside. I drive my fingers into the silvery remains of my mother. The sun slicks heat along my forearm. The ashes feel cool in my hands. I toss a handful into the sea and watch it slowly sink, dissolve. It becomes one with the black rock dust that is already there.

"Purge me with hyssop, and I shall be clean," I say. "Wash me, and I will be whiter than snow."

Paul has tears streaking his cheeks. He reaches across and takes some ashes from the box.

"I have this piece of thread," he says to the sea as he scatters.

I join in. "The piece of thread that connects my heart to yours."

We smile at each other for knowing the words.

"When something is tugging at your heart, I know, because I feel it too."

We toss the rest of the ashes into the water, handful by handful.

"Bye, Mum," I say.

And then I rinse my hands clean in the clear, cool water.

Epilogue

I take the bus. I climb the stairs to the top deck—to where I belong—and ride all the way alone. It's the middle of the day. No schoolkids, no commuters.

When I arrive, I go to the café across the road first and buy a can of lemonade. Really I'd prefer a coffee, but whenever I see an opportunity to have a small taste of the past, I grab it.

"You want a glass with that?" says the woman behind the counter. She has hammy arms and a mouthful of gravestone teeth.

"Actually, can I have a straw?" I ask.

The thin-strip-of-a-man making the sandwiches turns to see what kind of grown-up would ask for a straw. Because that is what I am now. A grown-up.

"If you want," says the woman with a shrug, plucking one from a box on the counter and popping its corrugated neck.

I take my can and my straw and sit at one of the plastic tables outside. It's almost warm enough for this now. Almost. Spring is rationing out a bit of sun. I scan the street for the Taj Mahal Tandoori House with the flat above it, the Mount Olympus Restaurant, where Mum might have waitressed. Silly, I know, because they don't exist. Kentish Town has always been a place for just passing through. But not anymore.

I cross the road to the Papadakis Washateria and stand outside for a while, smoothing down my hair. She dragged me along to this place seven years ago, so wrapped up in what she wanted to do that she didn't check once to see whose hand she had hold of. Now she's not here at all. But at the same time, she absolutely is. I try to make out the figure at the back of the shop, but the windows are steamed up. I can tell it's a woman, but I can't see her face. I will just have to go in, feel the instant mugginess of the tumble-dried air, hear those washing machines tutting and sighing.

She is younger than I was expecting, the woman. About thirty, I reckon. She is leafing through a receipt book, licking her thumb as she goes. She watches me walk in, suspicious, because I'm carrying no bags of laundry. She eyes me, ready for a contest.

"I'm looking for Eleni Papadaki," I say to the woman with hair just like mine bundled beneath her headscarf. She carries on flicking through the receipt book. She makes me wait.

"She's not here. Can I help?"

She looks me up and down then. My hands go to my head and give my curls another extra pressing down.

"I'm her niece," I say. "No, no, I'm not. I'm her great-niece. We haven't seen each other in a while and . . ."

The suspicion starts to evaporate. Or rather it is over-taken—by nosiness.

"Then that would make us . . . cousins?" She is squinting at the effort of figuring it out. "Or second cousins, wouldn't it be? Or once removed or something?"

She comes out from behind the counter, and I can see her baggy jeans now, with their trailing, frayed edges. On her big flat feet there is a pair of Birkenstocks. For a moment I think she might come over and hug me, but she stops.

"Funny we've not met before."

"I'm Melon," I say, "Chrysoula's granddaughter."

Well, that's it. The woman's face sort of explodes then. A huge, scandalous smile spreads across her lips.

"Maria's daughter!" She shouts it like she's hit the jackpot.

"Yes."

"Oh. My. God." She stands openmouthed. "The girl named Melon!" She shakes her head. "The girl named Melon!"

I can feel red sweeping up my neck and across my cheeks.

"Sorry, I'm Pitsa." She leaps forward, grabs my hand, and squeezes it hard. She shakes it up and down, up and down. "I'm Eleni's daughter. I'm sorry. I'm just gobsmacked. I never thought you actually really existed."

"Why's that?" I ask.

She puffs her lips and blows out some noisy air. "I just thought you were one of Mum's stories."

Pitsa shuts up the shop, leaving a sign saying, BACK IN 10. We walk together down Kentish Town Road, then onto a residential street.

"You know, I do have this vague memory of you," Pitsa goes. She swings the Laundromat keys around her finger like she's a cartoon jailer. The soles of her Birkenstocks rasp as she walks. "Really hazy, though."

"We've met before?"

"Not really. I remember this pregnant girl coming to stay with us when I was like twelve or something. She took my room. I had to sleep on Mum and Dad's floor. I think you were the bump."

"You've met my mum?"

"Like I say, not properly or anything. Not enough to, like, *judge*."

"Judge what?"

"You know, about the . . ." Pitsa checks my face quickly. Her fingertips fly up to her mouth.

"S'okay, I know all about it." I wave my hand through the air — it's nothing.

"She honest with you, is she, your mum?"

"*Was* she," I say.

Pitsa stops walking. She grabs my hand and yanks it close to her chest. "You're not saying she's, like . . ."

"Dead, yeah. Died about a year ago."

"How?" Pitsa all but wails.

"Hit by a bus."

Her mouth drops open. She is frozen.

"Sorry about that," I go, gently, trying to unfreeze her.

"Sorry for me! No, sorry for you! Mum never said. But, then, like I say, I hardly knew your mum, so. Oh, my God, are you okay?"

"Yeah, I'm fine."

"But how can you be? You're just a little girl!" I wonder how this must look to the strangers passing by — us standing there, Pitsa clutching my hand to her boobs.

"Actually, I'm sixteen now," I say.

Pitsa is stroking my head like I'm an animal that needs calming down.

"Your mum live near here, then?" I say brightly, trying to get us moving again.

Pitsa nods, turns, starts walking, although she won't let go of my hand.

"I'm so, so, so sorry," Pitsa mutters, shaking her head-scarfed head.

We walk past rows of terraced houses with low front garden walls. I think about Eleni telling Pitsa her stories about Mum and me.

"You were never in any of my mum's stories," I tell Pitsa.

She looks disappointed. "No?"

"I never knew Auntie Eleni even had children."

"Yeah, me and my older brother, Giorgos. Funny she didn't mention us."

We stop at a gate, and Pitsa clinks the latch. She pauses. "She might have been too out of it, though," she goes.

"Who?"

"Your mum. Too out of it to remember Giorg and me." She pushes the gate open and ushers me up the garden path. "No offense, like," she calls as I make my way to the front door.

I'm expecting the robust woman from The Story, the fat woman I met seven years ago. But in the kitchen I find a short, slim woman in a neat pantsuit putting mugs into a dishwasher. She has one of those haircuts that can be blow-dried solid, and on the ends of her fingers there are long plastic nails that make her touch things in a weird way. But the face I recognize. This is definitely Auntie Eleni.

"Mama, guess who's come to see us," bellows Pitsa, flip-flopping into the room. "The girl named Melon!"

"Melon?" Auntie Eleni turns to face me and her jaw drops. I realize now where Pitsa inherited her frozen mouth-open thing.

"Melon, no, you're, you're . . ." Eleni makes big, tall movements in the air with her fingernails.

"You're thin," I go, just to fill the silence. And to stop the arm waving. This immediately snaps Eleni out of her shock. Her hands go onto her hips and she twists her waist this way, then that.

"They make me Slimmer of the Year, four years ago now." She grins. "The weight-loss magazine give me makeover. I don't look back."

Pitsa tuts. "They took away my mother and they delivered this as a replacement." She is leaning on the kitchen counter, eating breakfast cereal out of the box.

"Panagiota!" Eleni snaps. "Shush."

Eleni turns back to me, nervous now after her initial astonishment. I feel like a ticking bomb. Her hands slide down off her hips. Pitsa watches, chomping. We are a movie for her entertainment.

"How do you do the laundry with those nails?" I go, again trying to fill the horrible silence.

"Mum doesn't do laundry anymore," chips in Pitsa. "She's above all that now."

Eleni rolls her eyes. "I manage all our stores—we have five now. And the hotel laundry side of the business, I am managing that too."

"No, Mama, I manage the hotels, thank you very much."

"Panagiota!" Eleni explodes, attacking Pitsa—and the air—with a splutter of Greek.

Pitsa fires back her own rat-a-tat of thorny foreign words before saying, "Mama, speak English in front of Melon. Don't be rude."

"Get back to the washateria," Eleni says, biting back. "People they will be waiting to get to the machines, and where are you?" She waves Pitsa away with her square-ended fingers. "Panagiota thinks standing behind the counter of a launderette is beneath her now. She is forgetting I do it for years."

Pitsa tosses the cereal box onto the counter with a sigh. "If Mama could find reliable managers who turned up at that washateria for a day's work," Pitsa spits, "then I wouldn't have to keep filling in for them, would I?" She gathers up her keys and *scuff-scuff-scuffs* out of the room.

"*Adio*, Mama," she drones. "See you later, Melon. You come back and we'll catch up, yeah?"

She *scuff-scuff-scuffs* down the tiled hallway.

"Bye," I say quietly to the sound of a slammed door.

"I'm sorry," Eleni says.

We're sitting in her tidy living room—me sinking into cushions on a huge boat of a sofa. I'm clutching a glass of milk that Eleni insists I drink. Eleni is perched next to me on the sofa's arm.

295

"I know about your mother and I don't come find you. I'm sorry," she says.

"It's okay." I feel bad for making her feel this way.

"No, is not okay. You are family and I held grudge. This is bad. But I was angry. All of what happened, none of it is your fault."

"I understand," I say. "Really, it's okay."

"Aphrodite, I was in touch with her and she tell me. I should have come. But I am not like Aphrodite. She is forgiving. I am hard. I am hard-nosed bitch—I know this."

"No, no, you're not, you're . . ." I don't know what to say. Does anyone really think of Aphrodite like that?

"And here you are . . ." Eleni throws out her arms, a game-show assistant showing off a set of silverware. Her smile fades. "With no one to look after you." She drops her head.

"I have Paul," I tell her. "He's Mum's fiancé—was Mum's fiancé. He's been looking after me. He's going to rent a house a few doors down so I don't feel so crowded, and so I don't feel on my own."

"A man?" Eleni's head bobs back up. She looks worried. "This is not right! No, no, no. You need a mother."

"Paul's kind of like a mother. Really like one, actually. Believe me."

Eleni tightens her mouth, raises her eyebrows. She's unconvinced.

"I did really good in my exams!" I pipe up. "Considering. Doing my A-levels now. English, social science, languages . . . I'll probably go to university."

"All this while living alone. This will be very hard."

"I have Paul."

"And now you have us." Eleni slips down beside me on the sofa. She puts an arm around my shoulder and squeezes. "It was right thing to come to us for help."

I sit there for a moment, enjoying the warmth of this half hug.

"That's not really why I came," I say eventually.

"Oh." She looks insulted, worried even, but still she says, "Go on."

"I'm writing this story, Mum's story, well, rewriting it actually. Putting my own twist on things, you know, and I wanted to hear your side of it."

"Something to tell *your* children?"

"Well, I'm not sure I'll be having . . .Well, yeah, yeah, if you like."

"Okay," Eleni says, "if you want to know the truth . . ."

"Oh, no!" I say. "I don't want that."

Eleni jerks her neck back at this, and it's a movement so abrupt, so ridiculous—so Greek!—that I burst out laughing.

"What so funny?" she asks, which only makes me laugh even more—proper laughing for the first time in so long. Eleni can't help but join in.

I recover my breath. Eleni pats my knee to show she's being serious again too and is ready to listen.

"The truth isn't what I'm after," I explain.

Eleni nods. "I just want to know the way you saw it," I say. "Have you got time to tell me?"

Acknowledgments

In researching this book, I owe thanks to Dr. Maria Kouroumali and Dr. Eleni Yannakakis for their expert knowledge of Cretan tradition and lifestyle—and for correcting my wonky Greek dialogue.

Mark Gurrey, who was at Barnet Children's Services at the time of writing the book, gave up his valuable time to explain Social Services procedure. Any bending of those rules is my doing, and is (sometimes) acknowledged by Poppy.

Some finer details of the effects of addiction were provided by Add Action (www.addaction.org.uk), and Shelley Gilbert of Grief Encounter was incredibly generous with her information and experience. If you have lost someone close to you, please do take a look at www.griefencounter.org.uk.

I'm grateful to Vassilis Gialamarakis and his family for their hospitality—and to everyone at the Mistral in Maleme, Crete. Thank you to Vassilis for the rootstock. Thank you to Thea for the bread drizzled with oil and honey. Thank you to Gail and Kavita for the road trip.

An Arvon retreat tutored by Chris Wakling, Mavis Cheek, and Jane Harris was instrumental in getting this book started, and a Spread the Word course led by Bernadine Evaristo put a rocket up its backside. I cannot recommend Arvon

(www.arvonfoundation.org) and Spread the Word (www
.spreadtheword.org.uk) enough.

I was also lucky to be a member of the tough-but-fair
Verulam Writers Circle in St. Albans while writing *Red Ink*.
Thank you for your feedback and general cheerleading,
especially Ian Cundell. Thanks also to Philippa and Thom
for reading early drafts.

Support and advice along the way came from Maria
McCann, Bea Corlett, Josephine Loukianos, Ann Thomas,
Rose Scarborough, Michael Price, Terry Sadler, Jenny
Thorburn, Sam Potter, Jenny Maksymetz, Donna Daley
Clarke, Julia Bell, Hannah Ferguson, Sheila Crowley, Sam
Baker, Sarra Manning, Simon Taylor, Literary Death Match,
the 2011 Arvon/Jerwood Mentoring posse, and Scott Williams
and his Impulse Company—and it was much appreciated.

An early version of the "15 Days Since" chapter previ-
ously appeared in Volume 10 (1) of *Stand* magazine.

Thank you to Emily Thomas, Georgia Murray, Kate
Manning, Jet Purdie, and the rest of the brilliant Hot Key
family. And thank you to Nicole Raymond and the folks at
Candlewick Press for welcoming me into a whole new
family in the U.S.

A high-five and a glass of melonita to Louise "Marvelously
Nitty Gritty" Lamont.

The churches and folklore museum of Hania, the
Monastery Agia Triada, with its rootstock, Kalathás Bay,
Tersanas Beach, and Haris's fortress (if you can find it) all
exist on an island far, far from here, where the sea is woven
from strings of sapphire blue and where the sunshine throbs
like a heartbeat. . . . Do go visit.